Susannah Waters was bor... next twenty years in America, and then moved back to England. She was an opera singer for ten years, singing in some of the most beautiful opera houses in the world. She has written for the theatre as well as for singers, dancers and instrumentalists. This is her first novel. She is married to an actor, and has two children.

For Kate
with love
Susannah

LONG GONE ANYBODY

Susannah Waters

BLACK SWAN

LONG GONE ANYBODY
A BLACK SWAN BOOK: 0 552 77221 6

First publication in Great Britain

PRINTING HISTORY
Black Swan edition published 2004

1 3 5 7 9 10 8 6 4 2

Set in 11/13pt Melior by
Falcon Oast Graphic Art Ltd.

Black Swan Books are published by Transworld Publishers,
61–63 Uxbridge Road, London W5 5SA,
a division of The Random House Group Ltd,
in Australia by Random House Australia (Pty) Ltd,
20 Alfred Street, Milsons Point, Sydney, NSW 2061, Australia,
in New Zealand by Random House New Zealand Ltd,
18 Poland Road, Glenfield, Auckland 10, New Zealand
and in South Africa by Random House (Pty) Ltd,
Endulini, 5a Jubilee Road, Parktown 2193, South Africa.

Printed and bound in Great Britain by
Cox & Wyman Ltd, Reading, Berkshire.

Papers used by Transworld Publishers are natural, recyclable
products made from wood grown in sustainable forests. The
manufacturing processes conform to the environmental
regulations of the country of origin.

For JAFW, with love

Acknowledgements

My thanks to Hannah Griffiths, number-one sleeve-tugger, ex-agent now friend, and I'm lucky to have her.

Thanks also to Camilla Hornby, for adopting me so willingly, and to Jane Lawson for having faith in the writer I'm to become.

Thanks to my first readers, Jonno and Kate, Kate Cottingham and Suzannah Dunn. Thanks to Karl Daymond, Kimberly Barber and Markus Phillips for writing space. And special thanks to Kim for being so encouraging and inspiring to me on so many levels, and for the spot on the wall.

The most thanks of all to Jonathan Cullen, for making everything that I value most in my life entirely possible and joyful.

Darling, remember,
when you come to me.
I'm the pretender,
and not who I'm supposed to be.
But who could say if I'm a traitor?
Time's a revelator.

Gillian Welch

There's a saint called Kevin. An unlikely saint name, I know, but it's true.

Kevin was kind of like a B-list Saint Francis. A nature saint, a tree lover, a saint for the flowers, the animals, the birds. One day he decided to go on a retreat; he decided he was going to live in a little three-walled hut for a month or two, in the middle of a forest, far away from people, far away from the speed and the clatter of their things. Every day he sat in front of his hut, on the dirt and the pine needles, and he meditated. All day long. And all the animals in the forest got so used to him just sitting there, eventually they weren't scared of him at all.

So one day this brown bird flies down and lands on Saint Kevin's open hand – Kevin liked to meditate with his palms lying open to sky. The bird perches on Kevin's hand for quite some time, while Kevin keeps on doing his thing, and because Kevin was so still and peaceful, so in tune with the quiet rhythms of God's creation, the bird was undisturbed. When at last it did fly away, Kevin saw that it had laid an egg on his hand, a small blue egg sitting warm in his palm, and to cut a long story short, Kevin, Kevin the merciful, Kevin the gentle, proceeded to sit in that spot without moving for twenty days and twenty nights until the egg was hatched and the little birdie emerged and flew away to find its mother.

There aren't a lot of people willing to sit still these days.

New York City

And now I can begin.

I left home on 1 October 1982, a week before my nineteenth birthday. I left in the evening and drove through the night, in the car I'd been saving up for all summer, working double-shifts with my best friend Barbara, at the beer stand in the ballpark.

'Where are you planning on going?' she'd asked one night, towards the end of the summer. I was wiping up the counter, which didn't really need it, but just so I'd look busy if the boss came out and thought about telling me to do something else. Barbara was finished for the night.

'What do you mean?'

'In this car of yours when you get it – where are you gonna go?'

'I dunno. I've been thinking about New York City, actually. I could scout it out for you.'

Barbara had been accepted at a music college in New York – she played drums – but she was deferring for a year. I wasn't sure why.

'What are you going to do in New York? How are you going to live?'

I shrugged my shoulders. 'Get a job? There must be beer tents in New York. I'm experienced!'

Barbara didn't laugh.

I drove through the night, that first night, and I must have been nervous, because at about 4 a.m. when an ambulance passed going the other way on the Interstate, and its flashing lights were picked up a second later in my rearview mirror, I jumped, and a huge dose of adrenalin flooded through my veins, making my accelerator foot shake. At dawn, just after the New York state border, I stopped at one of those highway eateries, hoping they sold donuts. Donuts and coffee – all I wanted for my first on-the-road, on-my-own breakfast. I was feeling like I was in a movie, a runaway movie, an NBC after-school movie. This was sort of like the game James and I had played down in the basement when we were little. Lost Children. Isn't it strange that you never really feel as old as you actually are? Or you get to certain milestones, finishing high school, leaving home, experiences that you've imagined, fantasized about for years, and then they don't feel like they're actually happening to you? You can't feel them, or it's never as shining a moment as you imagined. But then again, the other little things that happen, the things you never expected or thought about, sometimes these things make up for it, and there's where you find your real life, the one you can feel.

I pulled into a parking space next to this big old Ford, with half of its faded brown paint rusting away and a crack starting along the back window. Inside the car sat a little guy with raw skin and black hair – he looked too small for the car. He was trying to start the engine, without much luck, but he wasn't cursing or hitting the steering wheel or anything. He was acting very calm, as if he knew that finally it would start. He tried it again and the engine made a sort of whiney noise and then cut out completely. The guy looked at his watch and then glanced at me as I got out of my car. I locked the doors.

Inside the restaurant, I bought a chocolate-covered donut and the biggest coffee they served, and then I couldn't decide whether to sit down for a while or just take the stuff to my car and keep on going. In the end, I decided I needed a rest from driving, so I bought a *New York Times* and found a table. There weren't a lot of people about the place at this time in the morning, mostly just drivers on their own, looking distracted, bug-eyed, still trying to get somewhere, not there yet. I thought about taking my photo in one of those little booths, documenting the beginning of it all, of my new life, but I didn't want to attract attention. Glancing up from my paper, I saw the little man from the broken-down Ford walk by, heading to the Gents. He was wearing a pretty snappy suit and dressy shoes, and in general his appearance didn't really go with the vehicle he was driving, or not driving. I like it when people surprise me this way. I love how everyone chooses what they wear each day. I love it when I see a woman walking along the street and she's wearing tight zebra-patterned pants with matching zebra-patterned shoes. That's great. It makes me happy. I also like, when I'm on the subway or something, sitting opposite a row of people and staring at the row of shoes they're all wearing, then trying to guess, without looking up, what sort of head and shoulders will go with each pair of shoes. It's best when I'm wrong.

When I went out to the car again, it was sunny outside and I was armed with a good supply of junk food and other stuff I'd got from the store. The Ford was still there, with its guy sitting inside it. It seemed like he'd got his hair wet while he was in the bathroom – it was slicked back over his head, gangster-style. He looked up at me as I approached and before I thought about what I was doing, sort of on auto-pilot, I smiled. He smiled back, and lifted a hand in greeting. He looked really happy to see me.

I got into my car, cracked a soda and turned on the radio, because it was important to find a good song before I set off again. When I'd found a good one – 'Landslide' by Fleetwood Mac, not a group I like, but a great song – I sat there for a while with my hand on the key in the ignition, listening to the music. My throat started to ache at the same part of the song it always does. When I got the feeling someone was watching me, I looked over at the Ford, and the man had rolled down his window and was saying something to me which I couldn't hear. For a second, I wondered what to do, then I stretched over and rolled down my passenger window.

'How ya doing?' he said.

'I'm fine. How are you?'

'Yeah, I'm OK. My car won't start though.'

'I noticed.' We nodded at each other, and I took a couple more swigs of 7-Up. It seemed rude to just roll up the window again.

'Too bad about your car,' I said.

'What are you listening to?' he asked. 'I saw you singing along.'

'You did?'

'Well, not really loudly. I mean you weren't waving your head around like Stevie Wonder or anything, but your mouth was moving.'

'It's just the radio.'

'Oh. Right. So where are you heading?'

'New York.'

'Oh yeah? Me too, if I can get my car to go.'

'What's wrong with it?'

'If I knew that . . .'

Another man, about my dad's age I guess except he looked like a stockbroker, got into the car parked in front of mine. I saw him sneaking a good look at the two of us, over his steering wheel as he backed out, and it flashed through my thoughts that he would be the one to identify us both to the police later on. 'Yeah, sure I saw her, officer. Young girl, fresh-faced, talking to that little man with the slicked-back hair. The man in the beat-up Ford.'

'Do you live in the City?' he asked.

'No.'

'Going to visit somebody?'

'Yeah.'

A song I hated came on the radio, 'Covergirl', the J. Geils Band, so I turned it down.

'You know', the man continued, 'if you've got nowhere to stay in New York, my mom has this big house in Brooklyn, and she's always taking people in, you know, as lodgers. I'm sure she wouldn't mind, if she's got a room. I think there's a room right next to mine, in fact. Free, I mean.'

His mom? How old was this guy? He had to be over thirty. Maybe people in cities stayed at home longer. Because there was less space.

'Wow. That's really nice of you. But I'm OK. I've got some contacts.'

'Oh sure. Sorry, that must have seemed really freaky. Just coming out with an invitation like that. I mean, I'm not a creep or anything. I'm not trying to pick you up. I'm a homosexual.'

He said it like he'd just told me he was good at spelling.

'No, that's fine – I'm sure I'll find some place.'

Maybe there was something a little developmentally backward going on here, I thought – or was it just sad, that I automatically assumed someone friendly, someone sweet and open, must be a little retarded? Whatever it was, I felt like between the two of us, I was the grown-up.

'Well. I should get going, I guess.'

'Me too,' he said. 'I'll try her again.' This time, the engine didn't even whine. Not a sound. I have no idea why, but I decided right then, if I liked the next song that came on the radio I would offer this poor guy a lift and maybe see about the offer of his mom's place. What did I have to lose, really? It seemed like the thing to do, the adventurous choice, the decision my viewing audience would want me to make. Also, I was always saying that I liked people to surprise me, but then I never let them close enough to get a chance. People walk around today wishing the world were more like a Jimmy Stewart film, but when they actually come face to face with a comparable situation, when they meet a friendly stranger, or encounter an opportunity to be neighbourly themselves, what do they do? Look the other way. Every time. If this was the first day of the rest of my life and all that, I wanted to at least start out trusting someone.

The first song that came on the radio was OK, but not that great, right in the middle on the audience clap-o-meter. So I decided if his name began with a letter at the end of the alphabet, last ten letters or so, I'd go with that.

I slid over to that side of the car and leaned out of the window.

'What's your name?'

'Huh?'

'What's your name?'

'Louie.'

Shit.

'Louie. Nice to meet you. I'm Queen.' 'We Will Rock You' was playing low on the radio; I wondered if he could hear it. 'Queenie.'

'Queenie? That's a cool name.'

'Do you like it?'

'Yeah, it's different.'

'Thanks. Look, Louie, do you need a lift?'

'A lift?' He spluttered, as if he'd never, ever thought of that possibility. '*Really?* That would be *great*. I mean, I'll pay for gas and everything, and like I said, my mom's place is an option. You could stay for just a few nights, even.'

'What are you going to do with your car?'

Louie looked around the car's interior, as if he'd forgotten he was in a car.

'Hell, I'll just leave it. It sucks, anyway. Used to be my dad's. I'll leave the keys, and if anyone wants to spend some money on it, they can haul it away themselves.'

'What if they give you a fine? Won't the police be able to track you down, through the plates?'

'They can try. But it still belongs to my dad, and he's dead, so they won't get far. I don't know how they'd be able to track it to me.'

It turned out that Louie was coming back from Detroit where he'd been attending his dad's funeral. That was why he was all dressed up.

'Are you sure your mom will be up for a visitor right now?'

'Oh sure – you mean 'cause of my dad? They split up years ago. No big deal.'

Louie only had one piece of luggage, a little cylindrical sports bag, and it looked half empty. We drove for about an hour without saying much, just eating some potato chips I'd bought and listening to the radio. Occasionally I'd think he'd fallen asleep until he'd suddenly start singing along to a song, or make a rude comment about something the disc jockey had said.

'I'm sorry about your dad.'

He turned and smiled at me. He had this air of bovine unflappability, which is what made him seem sort of backward. 'Yeah, well, one of those things. But I thought I should go, you know. To the funeral.'

'Sure. Is it just you? I mean, no brothers or sisters?'

'Yeah, I got a brother. But he didn't go. What about you?'

'What *about* me?'

'Do you have any family?'

'I have a brother. James – he's fifteen.'

'Oh yeah? That's great. A little brother. That's great. I wish I had a little brother.'

We didn't talk much after that, which suited me fine and wasn't strange in the circumstances. About eight hours later, sun starting to draw parallel to the car, making everything glow and look beautiful, we reached the outskirts of New York City.

'You know what?' said Louie, as we passed through a tollbooth on the New Jersey Turnpike. 'Why don't we drive on into Manhattan? I just had an idea – tell me if

20

you think it's too weird – but my brother has this apartment on the Lower East Side. It's just sitting there empty at the moment, and you know, you could stay there for a while. It's much more convenient than Brooklyn, if you want to get a job on the island, which I figure you'd wanna do.'

'What about your brother?'

'He's out of town – he'll be away for a while. It's not a problem.'

'Won't he mind? Somebody staying in his place he doesn't know?'

'Nah, he's not like that.'

'And what about the rent? It's probably too expensive for me.' The Lower East Side – I had no idea what kind of neighbourhood we were talking. 'I'd have to pay him rent.'

'Don't worry about the rent. I mean just a few days, to get you settled, while you look for somewhere permanent. To pay you back for the lift.'

'Wouldn't you like to stay there yourself, while he's away?'

'No way – Manhattan gives me the jitters. Besides, I like it at my mom's. I got all my things there. She does my laundry and stuff.' He drummed his fingers against the dashboard. 'So, what do you think? This is the exit coming up, the one you want to take – this is it just here, for Manhattan.'

My foot came off the accelerator, hovered over the brake. 'I don't know.' Hand pulled down on the indicator and I cut off a white Toyota, changing lanes so I could make the exit.

'Look, it'll be a lot cheaper than a hotel. I don't know how much money you have with you, but you could end up blowing your life savings on a few nights in a hotel. Let me do you this favour. You saved me from a parking lot in the middle of fucking Ohio. God, I would have had to take a *bus* or something.'

And that's how I became a female escort.

Louie set me up in his brother's apartment, and in his brother's business. His brother never actually turned up, but after a while, I began to suspect he must be in prison. That made the most sense, anyway. I figured this apartment had been the usual place of business – it didn't feel very lived in – and the rent in advance with a little extra cash in the envelope meant no questions from the superintendent. The first week or so, before I knew about all this, I couldn't believe my good luck and I didn't understand why Louie was being so nice, except maybe he was built that way. From all I'd read about New Yorkers though, even non-predatory homosexuals didn't go around just letting people stay in their apartments for free. It was weird.

One night, about ten days after I arrived, Louie got to the point.

'Queenie. Could I ask you a big favour this weekend?'

'Sure. Do you want me to leave?'

'Nah, nah – stay as long as you like. No problem. It's just, I've got this friend, an old friend from back in Detroit – I saw him again at the funeral – and his dad is coming into town on business this weekend. His parents, they just split up about a month ago, and his dad is sort of lonely, wants to go to a show or something, but he's embarrassed to go alone. He's not used to it.'

'Uh-huh,' I said. The television was on. Louie had come round to pick up his brother's mail, and then he stayed to talk about the heat and electricity bills. I'd already offered to pay the bills for this week; it seemed the least I could do. We were eating a pizza he'd brought with him.

'So,' Louie continued, 'I was wondering, would you mind going out with this guy? With my friend's dad?'

'Me?'

'Yeah. *I* would, but I have to go out of town this weekend. With my mom. One of my cousins is getting married.'

'How old is he? This friend's dad.'

'How old? He's not that old – well, he's old, sure, but he looks good.'

'Are you sure he had someone like me in mind? Aren't I a little young for him?'

'I'm sure he'll love you.'

I switched off the television then and stared at Louie.

'Are you asking me to have sex with this guy?'

'Only if you want to!' He laughed so hard that some of the cheese on the pizza slice he was holding spilled onto his shirt. 'Just kidding! God, no! Honestly. You're awful. He just wants to go to a Broadway show and he'd like it better if he could go *with* someone, that's all. Frankly, I don't think he's really up to sex much these days.'

'I thought you said he wasn't old.'

'He's not, but, you know, he's depressed about his wife and everything.'

'So he'd like to just hang out with a nineteen-year-old?'

'Sure. What guy wouldn't? I mean, straight guy.'

'Yeah, I don't think straight guys have the monopoly on that sort of thing, Louie.'

23

He didn't respond to that. 'I'm really sorry about this. I would never ask you if I didn't know the man. But he's a total – it's totally safe.'

'And you don't know anybody else who could do this? You don't have any sisters? Or cousins?'

'Nope, no sisters. No cousins. Except the one who's getting married.'

I put the remote down on the coffee table and picked up another slice of pizza.

'Well, firstly, I don't have anything to wear. Anything appropriate for a female escort, that is.'

'So how about I take you shopping?' said Louie. I noticed he hadn't contradicted the female escort reference.

'Why would you do this?'

'It's the least I can do.'

'Since I'm staying in your brother's apartment rent-free? I don't think so. Look, OK. I mean I don't know you very well. You seem like a nice guy. And I only met you a short while ago, so maybe I'm being unfair, but if you want this to be the deal in exchange for me living here, I mean, if this is a job you're offering me, then just say so.'

'No, no . . .'

'It's OK. I'm not stupid. I could do worse things, I guess.'

'What are you talking about? I would never ask—'

'But I don't want my phone number up in phone booths or anything – no way – and if I do have sex with these friends' fathers, that is totally up to me, and not necessarily part of the deal. And that will be my money, that extra money, with no percentage going to you, OK? And only men you know something about, not some horny guy you met in a bar, and I don't want to meet them here – they'll have to take me out. I've never been to a Broadway show. Then if I feel like it, if the guy's lucky, we'll go back to his nice hotel room, where there are lots of other people around. How much will you charge, anyway? And how much will I get? I'll need to live on something, if you want me available whenever, that is, which means I couldn't really get a second job.'

Louie was sitting there, just staring, his mouth hanging open.

'What's the going rate?'

Very slowly, Louie's face relaxed, almost imperceptibly. He closed his mouth, looked at the floor, smiled a little half-smile and coughed into his hand. 'A – a hundred dollars an hour?'

'Fine. I'll take twenty-five an hour for day-to-day expenses, food and that, plus the extra money I get for sex, which I'll negotiate myself, directly.'

Louie just nodded, and after a pause I turned on the television again and we started watching whatever was on.

A few minutes later, Louie chuckled.

'What?' I asked.

'You do have a pretty good name for it.'

'What?'

'You know. Queenie.' He glanced sideways at me and ducked as if I might hit him.

'I'll have to get an appointment diary,' I said. And the funny thing was, it turned out to be not such a bad job.

Maybe this was because Louie was just too soft-centred and disorganized to be an effective pimp. For the first two weeks after my initial date, for instance, we just sat around waiting for the phone to ring, until

25

we figured out it had been disconnected because no-one had paid the bill last month. And the guys he did hook me up with were mostly sort of sweet, and a little sad, like him. Men who probably still lived with their mothers too, or with wives that might as well have been their mothers. I did have sex with some of them, I did, and I'd like to say it was because they were attractive to me, but it wasn't, it was for the money. Money's the thing when you don't have much, and you don't have a safety net either. I wanted to make this work, financially. I was living in this great apartment, tiny and square, but all my own, and pretty amazingly convenient. The sex was OK – I'd had sex before, of course, with a few guys in high school, but I'd never been in love so I didn't know what I was missing, and if the truth be told, the part of my psyche that dealt with that whole area was pretty cold. The sex was a tiny part of the job, anyway. It was really the art of conversation I learned about on these dates. How to smooth over those awkward pauses, how to make another person feel comfortable, how to appear fascinated by every little thing the man tried to say. I prided myself on this, and I learned more than I'll ever need about the preoccupations of men in middle management. I think some of the men were surprised to be with a girl who could think, and they didn't like it. It put them off their food. They had hired a bimbo to possibly have sex with – and they didn't want a high school graduate who had always finished her homework before she did any drugs, and ended up top of her class. These were the men who occasionally got nasty, in their pathetic, soft-shoe way. But I always carried a can of mace with me, and one of those rape whistles, and I made sure we were only in public places, the theatre, the restaurant, a taxi, so it would have been pretty hard for any of them to force themselves on me. I suppose the ones I did have sex with, in their hotel rooms, could have suddenly revealed another side to their personalities. Scary to think of, the risks you take when you're young. Praise be to Saint Hallvard, patron saint of innocence.

I don't know what kids thought of me in high school. I was very quiet, I guess, and weirdly smart. People knew about what my mom did – there's always somebody who knows somebody who knows all about you, and the grown-ups gossiped more than the kids. So for a while afterwards, people kinda avoided me, or maybe that was my imagination. I went to a private school, on scholarship, and most of the students there had been together since they were six. They spent their vacations together too, on Sanibel Island, or in Puerto Vallarta, Mexico. They lived in gigantic houses, Gothic stone mansions on the lakefront, or new-built palaces of glass and wood, with four-car garages and surrounded by seven acres of woodland, which they owned as well.

I did make one really good friend in high school: Barbara Walters. Obviously not *the* Barbara Walters – I wasn't talking to the television or anything. And Barbara always hated her name because people called her Baba Wawa all the time, and mispronounced their 'r's and all that. But her parents had named her that in 1964, long before the famous one had become known, so it wasn't their fault.

We met at a school dance, the end of sophomore year. I was there with a boy, I guess, but I must have been hanging out on my own when I saw this girl, wearing green army pants, a hooded navy-blue sweat-shirt and dirty Hi-top sneakers, dancing around one of the green trash receptacles full of people's used plastic cups. She must have pulled the bin out onto the floor. She had short brown hair and was wearing a red knotted bandanna round her head, Rambo-style. I remember thinking how brave she was, dancing by herself, and dancing really hard, if you know what I mean, to a Stray Cats song, without seeming to care what anyone thought of her. The Stray Cats were a little diesel for most of the kids at our school, and I found out that Barbara had brought a home-made tape of New Wave stuff, the Beat, B-52's, Gang of Four, Pretenders, Blondie, and slipped it to her friend Billy, who was DJ-ing. I really liked this music, and by the end of the night, my date must have given up on me, and Barbara and I were dancing away, alone on the dance floor, acting crazy, twirling the trash bin around like it was Fred Astaire, even after the Student Council kids had turned the lights on and were trying to clean up. I got a ride home with Barbara and Billy that night, in Billy's Toyota Corolla.

Billy was different, too. He looked sort of nerdy, and the most embarrassing fact about him was that every single weekend he listened to K.C. Casey's Top 40 on the radio and religiously wrote down the names of each song, week to week, in these tiny red spiral note-books. Why? But he was great. If high school taught me anything, it was not to judge any book by its cover: nerd, pothead, jock, or even preppie. There was one guy in my American history class, for instance: Malcolm, with long frizzy hair, bad skin popping, always wore a leather jacket and a chain for a belt. He never said a word in class, never raised his hand, kept

his head down. But he and I were the on̲l̲y̲ ones to earn
fives on the AP exam. I bet he's doing some̲t̲h̲i̲n̲g̲ really
genius now, something I wouldn't be able ̲t̲o̲ ̲u̲n̲d̲er-
stand even.

Barbara and I lived far away from each other, ̲w̲h̲ich
was a pain until we got our driving licences. She was
in the city, and I was in the boonies, Rural Route 54, a
few miles from the Saint Boniface church, that
Episcopalian den of iniquity which featured largely
in the events of my childhood. Our school lay in
between, in the sprinkler-soaked, country-clubbed
suburbs. Barbara's parents were still together, but they
were pretty kooky. Her dad was a musician, a wind
player in the city orchestra, but it seemed like he was
sick most of the time, so her mom worked a lot, in
social services or something. I had this real blank
about her mom – grey, that's all I ever got when I was
around her, or thought about her. A talking grey, like
an alien on *Star Trek*, maybe. I was kind of scared
of her, not scared like in a horror film, just uncomfortable.

All through high school, Barbara and I were always
doing crazy things, breaking into the school snack
shop after hours, smoking pot in the loft we found
behind the auditorium stage, taking out her mom's car
for a spin before either of us had our licence, dropping
acid and then taking the bus downtown to go to the
museum. No-one ever suspected me because I was a
good student, or Barbara because she was so charming,
and funny. She was very funny. She had this way of
turning things upside down, normal things that you
see every day, and it wasn't just when we were on
drugs. Like we'd be in a drugstore waiting to pay for
our soda and stuff and suddenly behind us in the line

would be this incredibly tall man. Incredibly tall, out of the *Guinness Book of Records*. And Barbara would turn and see this guy and just slowly look up at him with this poker-straight expression on her face. I'd have to leave the store. One night, a few weeks before I left home, we were smoking pot in my room, just hanging out, and we decided to tape ourselves. When I listened to it the next day, there were all these long silences punctuated by little gasps of air, places where we'd been laughing so hard we couldn't breathe.

And Barbara was the first person I ever talked to, about everything. At the very end of our sophomore year, a few months after we'd met, our whole class was forced to go on this Outward Bound camping experience thing, over a weekend. It took place every year, on an old Indian reservation, now public land, and we were expected to hike and swim and have campfires and do fun 'activities' – the teachers probably hated it as much as we did. Most kids looked upon it as an opportunity to drink and smoke and get off with each other, but as I preferred any experimentation of that sort to be done in groups of one, possibly two, I'd been dreading this weekend since Easter. Even with Barbara going along, I still anticipated a truly horrible time.

When we got to the camp, it transpired one of the girls' cabins was unusable, due to a skunk having done its business the week before, on the last day of a transcendental meditation retreat. When two girls were asked to volunteer to sleep outside in a tent, everyone raised their hands, including me and Barbara. I think because we two were the least-known evil, or just the least known, Ms Reilly the gym teacher chose us. She provided us with one tent, two sleeping bags, a groundsheet, a flashlight, some insect repellent and some toilet paper, in case we didn't want to walk all the way to the bathrooms in the middle of the night.

'In fact, I'd prefer it if you stay put, girls,' she said, poking her head through the tent flap when she came to check on us before she went to bed. 'Is there anything else you need?' She looked slowly back and forth, from Barbara to me and back again. 'Nothing? You're sure?'

It flashed through my mind she meant tampons or something.

'No thanks,' said Barbara.

'We're fine,' I agreed.

Ms Reilly sighed. 'OK. Have a good night. If you get scared during the night, I'm in Haystacks and Mrs Sieckman is in Long Meadow.'

'OK. Thanks, Ms Reilly.'

'Yeah, thanks, Ms Reilly.'

'What was *her* problem?' said Barbara, after Ms Reilly had finally left.

'I dunno.'

'Obviously a lesbian.'

'What do you mean?'

'All female gym teachers are big lezzies, everybody knows that.' I couldn't tell if she was kidding. 'And she's totally in love with you, obviously.'

'Yeah, right. More like you.'

'I don't think I'm her type. She likes them brainy.'

'Shut up.'

It was a humid night, so we covered ourselves with bug spray and lay on our backs on top of the sleeping bags, our heads sticking out of the tent. There weren't a lot of stars, but more than in the city, and the air smelt like pine trees and lake water.

'OK,' said Barbara, 'let's play a game.'

'What game?'

'Twenty Questions.'

'What, like animal, vegetable, mineral?'

'No. I get to ask you twenty questions, like "do you like school?", or "what's your favourite brand of cereal?", and so on, and you can't ask any questions back until I'm finished and then you get to ask me twenty questions.'

'What's the point? How do you win?'

'You don't win. It's just to find out about each other, like Truth or Dare, the things you never knew about Barbara Walters—'

'But the whole world knows about Barbara Walters.'

'I'll pretend I didn't hear that.'

'You do realize this is a really girlie game. I can't exactly imagine two guys playing it, can you?'

'Their loss. OK? Ready? I'll ask first.'

'Wait. Are you allowed *not* to answer questions if you don't want to?'

'Of course. Just say something – we'll have a code word.'

'Aspen.'

'Aspen? OK. What made you think of that?'

'Isn't it obvious? Look around. Was that your first question?'

'No way! We haven't started yet. So . . . my first question is . . . what was your first pet called, if you had one, and what happened to it?'

'Mimi – it's a cat, and we still have it.'

'You mean that black and white one? Wow, she must be old. Why is she called Mimi?'

'Is this another question? Or a subordinate question?'

32

'That's a good idea. We'll have subordinate questions. And you're allowed three subordinate questions for each main one, but they have to stay on the theme.'

'Jesus. This is going to take all night.'

'So what? Why is your cat called Mimi?'

'Because that's how my little brother used to say "meow".'

'Do you like your brother?'

'Is this a new question?'

'Yes. Come on, you're not allowed to think too much before you answer.'

'Yes, sir. God, this is like an oral exam or something.'

'Well, you're good at tests. Do you like your brother?'

'Sure I like him. He's my brother. He's a kid – I feel sorry for him. But I don't know him that well, really.'

'You don't know your brother?' Barbara was an only child.

'Well, we don't really talk to each other that much. I mean I don't know what he thinks about all day. He watches TV when he gets home from school, and then he goes to bed. We used to have fun together when I was little, I guess. And he knows stuff nobody else does, little family jokes and things.'

And our mom, I thought. He knows our mom; he remembers things about Mom. At least I presumed he did.

'What would you rather have to eat in thirty minutes, ten bags of potato chips, or ten ice-cream sundaes?'

The questions continued. What did I want to be? I didn't know. My favourite song? Too many to choose from. Did I believe in God? Not sure – though I was, but I said that because I thought she might think it was weird that I did.

'Do you miss your mom?'

The twentieth question.

'Do you miss your mom? You can call Aspen if you want.'

I rolled over on my side and looked at her. 'You know, you are the first person, the *only* person who has ever asked me anything about her, in like a year. Including my own family.'

Barbara nodded up at the stars. 'People are embarrassed.'

'It's just so weird,' I said, and lay back down again. Neither one of us spoke for a little while. Maybe Barbara was waiting for me to say something more; I wasn't sure.

'She must have been desperate,' said Barbara.

'About what?'

Barbara kept quiet.

'That wasn't a question,' I said.

A few months after I moved into Louie's brother's apartment, I received the first postcard.

'You got mail,' said Louie, handing it over.

'I did?'

'Uh-huh. Queenie. That's you, right?'

On the front of postcard number 1, there was a picture of a saint. A picture-postcard saint, perched on a little wooden shelf protruding from a grey background with the plaster flaking off it like wall dandruff. Underneath the picture, in the surrounding white border, the saint was identified as Saint Avertin, 'qui guérit les maux de tête'.

'What does that say, Louie?' I knew it was French, but

I'd never taken Mrs Regan's French classes, and Louie was Spanish so I thought maybe he could decipher it.

He frowned at the card. 'It means he's good for headaches. He's who you pray to if you have a headache. I guess.'

On the back of the card there were four words, hand-written, with no signature. *Did you forget something?*, they said.

'Who's it from?' Louie asked, trying to sound uninterested.

'I dunno.'

'You don't know?'

I shook my head, put the card, writing-down, on the kitchen counter.

'Well, who knows you're staying here?'

'No-one.'

'Maybe it's from a client.'

'I never bring them here.'

'Or a friend? Maybe it's from someone you met since you got here. Where's it been sent from – can you read the stamp?'

I grabbed the postcard before he got hold of it.

'I haven't met anyone here, Louie. Forget about it.'

'What about your family? Did you forget something at home, maybe?'

'Guess you read the card, huh, Louie? It's not from my family.' I hadn't forgotten them.

My mother's name was Lydia, after Saint Lydia, the patron saint of fabric dye, the patron saint of cochineal, and indigo. The last time I saw her she was wearing a bright red sweater. I didn't know then it was the last time, but then I hardly ever recognize last times. Even if someone were lying in ICU beginning to

35

rattle, doctors glancing at the clock on the wall trying to decide whether to go home before or just after, family members edging together like clumps of fridge magnets attracted to the iron hospital bed, even with all that, I'd still figure on seeing this person again. I've been proved wrong.

There's another saint, Saint Sinthim, who publicly stated he would rather be the patron of mad dogs than of anyone female. I guess that's pretty how much my father felt after my mother was gone. My dad's a nice enough man, but he has a sort of blind spot around women – not a blind spot actually, a grey spot, like the blurs you get in your vision after you've looked straight into the sun. He spent most of my adolescence warning me off them. I used to wonder if he'd forgotten who I was.

'That one's tricky,' he'd say, referring to the very occasional friend I brought home from school. 'Want to keep your eye on her.'

Was he kidding? According to Dad, the situation was helpless; all women were beyond help. Maybe he was the one beyond help, I figured. Or maybe he just didn't want to see me get hurt again.

He never talked about my mother though. Except one time I came into the house from the back yard and he was talking on the phone and I heard him finish the following sentence: '... as if she swallowed a wolverine or something and the thing was gnawing its way out from the inside, barking and snarling ...' I wondered if he meant my mother, but he wound down pretty quick when he saw me walk in. It was strange. To me, she always seemed sweet. A little spacey maybe, a little removed from reality, but never wild, never fierce. Dad was the one with a temper, in a back-handed, tight-waisted, Midwestern sorta way. He worked as the manager of a large shopping mall and when I was little, I used to think he could have anything in any store, if he wanted.

Then there was my brother James, four years younger than me, only fifteen when I left, the age I was when Mom left and don't think I wasn't aware of the parallel. James was the one I spent good time feeling guilty about, the only one I felt sorry for. I knew he was a complicated kid already. I had tried to call him about a month after I got to New York, but there was no answer and I hung up after the fourteenth ring. Probably for the best – what good would it have done him, just knowing where I was? He knew I wasn't there.

The only person I got to know, the whole time I spent in New York, was Michael.

It was about two months after I moved into Louie's brother's apartment that I first had a real conversation with him. I'd actually met him on the day I arrived, but I'm not sure he remembered that. When the elevator doors opened on the seventh floor for the first time, revealing me and my strongbox, plus the two ridiculously large and impractical suitcases I'd bought at the Goodwill back home, there was Michael in his wheelchair, stuck in the steel gates of the elevator door opposite. The gate was making a whining sound, clamped around the wheelchair; Michael was trying to wheel himself backward; and an old lady in a hat was standing there staring. I asked Michael if he could tell me which way to Apartment 7E, and he replied very suavely, as if nothing at all was wrong, 'Down the hall to the right, miss.' 'Miss'! If he'd been wearing a hat, I think he would have tipped it at me. But I could sense he'd rather I didn't mention his predicament, so I just thanked him and moved on.

It was in December I knocked on his door and asked if I could use the phone; this was just after Louie and I had figured out ours had been disconnected. Michael answered the door in a T-shirt and shorts, looking as if he hadn't seen the outside of his apartment for a very long time. His skin was pasty and he was squinting, even at the muted light of the hallway interior. His bare legs were showing in the chair, thin and flabby.

'Hi,' I said.

'Hi.'

'I met you a few weeks ago, when you were stuck in the elevator.'

'Oh. Yes. I remember you.'

I nodded. 'Well, I live down the hall now.'

'How did you know which apartment was mine?'

'I didn't. This is the third door I've tried. Everyone's out, I guess, or not answering.'

He was staring at me with the volume turned up, if you know what I mean. That way of looking at someone so that the air between you gets a little thicker, or slower, like you're under water together.

All of a sudden, he said, 'Do you want to come in?' in this smoothy-smoothy voice, as if I had looked away for a second and some ladies' man had switched places with the guy in the wheelchair. I almost laughed, except that right away he looked worried again, so I didn't want to embarrass him.

'I was wondering, actually, if I could use your phone. Something's wrong with mine, and it's kind of urgent.'

'Of course.'

He reversed the chair into the room and let me in. The apartment was tiny; a shoebox could have held more shoes. But it wasn't as messy as I had expected. It was just dark. The curtains were drawn tight and the only light came from a small desk lamp next to a typewriter on the drop-down kitchen table. When I turned around, I caught Michael throwing a towel over his exposed legs.

'The phone?'

'It's over there, by the bed.'

'Thanks.'

'My name's Michael, by the way.'

'Hi, Michael. I'm Queenie.' I was getting used to it now.

'Queenie?'

'Uh-uh.'

'Like Her Majesty?'

'That's right.'

'Or the rock band.'

'Them too.'

Michael probably realized right away Queenie wasn't my real name; he was too much an observer of human nature not to. But unlike Barbara, or even Louie, Michael didn't ask questions. I always appreciated his discretion.

'Louie, hi, it's me. No, I'm not there – have you been trying to phone me? Yeah, well, you were right, something's wrong with it, because it never rang. No, he didn't call – how could he have called? – that's why I'm ringing you. I'm in a neighbour's apartment. No, it's fine. Really. So where am I meeting – what's his name? – Robert Miller, OK . . . Which one? Oh, too bad, I've seen that already. That's all right. OK, I've got it. You coming round tomorrow? Check out the phone – has a bill even come since your brother left? OK, bye. Bye.'

Throughout the phone call, Michael was sitting at his desk, typing. He acted like he hadn't heard anything, like he'd been concentrating really hard on his work, but it was a tiny apartment.

'I'm a female escort.'

'Oh.'

'It's really not a bad job, so far. But my phone's broken, which makes it kinda hard.'

'I see.'

'What do *you* do?'

'I'm a writer.'

'What do you write?'

'I write for magazines – for newspapers.'

'So you're a journalist.'

Michael laughed. 'To be more precise. Yes.' Then he did a funny, frantic typing dance with his fingers over the keyboard, and made a goofy face at me. I had no idea what he was doing, but it was sweet.

'What are you working on?'

He looked at the typewriter and frowned. 'I'm not sure. It's about birds. And famous people. About being famous and how it can sometimes make one bird-like.'

'Are you famous?'

He laughed again. 'Me? No.'

I felt like asking him what had happened to his legs, why he couldn't walk, but I didn't. He was pretty attractive, I was beginning to notice, in a quirky, old-fashioned way. He wore his hair longish in front and it swept sideways and back. He looked a mess.

'Well, thanks for letting me use the phone. I should go.' Michael rolled himself back from the table.

'Don't bother, it's OK. I can show myself out. Really.'

Six days later, Michael knocked at my door to tell me some woman had phoned for me at three in the morning. I think he'd come around pretty pissed off, to complain, but then didn't have the heart. I had used his phone several times again that week, but I'd never given out his number – I didn't even know it – and now Louie's phone was working anyway.

'A woman? Really? Did she ask for Queenie?'

This freaked me out a little. I didn't see how anyone could have traced me. Unless Louie had made some calls home, checking up on me. That seemed way too grown-up a thing for him to do.

'Well, actually she used another name, until I described you, and we agreed it was you she wanted to talk to in the middle of the night.'

'God, I have no idea who it was – must have been a wrong number. I swear I haven't given your number to anyone. Like I said, I don't even know it.'

There was one other possibility. What I hadn't told Michael, or anybody, was that one of the numbers I'd dialled on his phone the other day, just once, was my home phone. I was still trying to get a message to James, that's all. But nobody had answered, so I'd hung up. Now I was wondering if Janine had just missed the call and then done something tricky to trace it.

Janine was my dad's second wife. I'd only lived at home for a year after she moved in, but that was enough. In that one year, I saw our average suburban ranch house transformed into an emporium of country corner furnishings. This woman had been waiting all her life for a house to decorate. She'd been saving up clippings, collecting swatches. And she liked a

41

hygienic house too, every surface brushed, wiped, scrubbed cleaner than a surgeon's fingernails. The rooms had to 'smell' nice – made me want to open all the windows and stick my head out screaming for justice. She used to make these little handmade sachets out of white muslin and lace, fill them with dried lavender and then slip these stink bombs everywhere, in every drawer, under my pillow, between the layers of clean laundry. I was still trying to get the smell out of my clothes. Maybe Dad had felt he couldn't mistrust a woman who was so clean. What time would she have for extramarital affairs, between the ceaseless ironing and the cleaning of the bathrooms? Dishes were washed up before we'd finished eating off them; I think she changed the beds twice a week. She had a real problem.

And it would have been just like Janine to trace a missed call – but not like her to phone someone at three in the morning. Was something up? Was James all right?

Michael was still there in the doorway. 'I'm really sorry you were bothered. Can I make you some breakfast?' I asked.

I made him French toast, cooking in my pyjamas. He was such a funny guy – I'd never met anyone like him before. He seemed fascinated by the things I said, the words I used, which maybe all writers are, but the words that stopped Michael in his tracks weren't fancy words, or strange ones, just ordinary words that most people use all the time. Maybe it was just that he didn't talk to many people. I never saw him with another person, except Louie one time, and he never went out to work. He did all his necessary journalist communication on the phone, and even that seemed painful. He was a real-live hermit.

But he liked talking with *me*. For instance, if I said, 'I'll just rustle up some eggs', Michael would get this faraway look in his eyes and I'd know he was thinking about the words 'rustle up'. Why had I said 'rustle'? It didn't sound like a rustling, the breaking of eggs. And why up? Why not down? He also liked how I made up words — Barbara and I used to do it all the time — and he'd write some of these words down. He said he collected words and once showed me a little book in which page after page was filled with words that nobody uses any more, great words like bosom-serpent, fribbler, godzip, blash. They were old words, I guess, from two hundred, three hundred years ago, but the words I made up he put down in a different book, a new book. Since he only ever talked to me, I thought it was going to take a long time to fill.

'You should make up some words yourself — it's easy.'

'I'll think about that,' he said.

Once, for a whole week, he got on to this kick about emigration, immigration, and migration. Why is it, he asked me, only animals are allowed to migrate? Whereas human beings always emigrate, or immigrate, must always be leaving somewhere or coming some-where. He saw it as a sad statement about mankind's lack of spiritual freedom, people's inability to trans-form themselves and truly escape the past. I sort of understood what he meant. I liked to think that I myself was capable of simply migrating. I hoped I was, but I wasn't sure.

Most of all, he made me laugh, like Barbara had done. He was a great mimic, not just of people on TV and such, but people we saw in the building as well.

Even more, he was funny in everyday life, without meaning to be. I loved his awkwardness, the way he didn't know how to do simple things, like where to buy a new glass coffee pot when his got smashed one day, or what to do with his toothbrush when it got old. 'You throw it out, Michael,' I said. The way he was always getting his wheelchair stuck in doorways and elevators. He didn't know how to cook anything; all he ever ate was cereal and Pop-Tarts, or sandwiches and take-outs, pizza, Chinese food. Even though he had lived in New York for at least ten years, as far as I could tell I taught him more about the practicalities of everyday city living than he taught me. We learned about it together, where the grocery store was, and the drugstore. He did know about the stationery store, because of needing typewriter ribbons.

I didn't see him a lot, actually. He wrote most of the time, and that meant he was alone and wouldn't answer the phone or even the door. He'd turn the ringer off and he'd swear up and down he'd never heard me knocking, as if, if he had heard, he would have thrown down everything and invited me in for tea. I soon found out that I needed to wait for him to come to me, which made me lonely at times because he was the only person I felt close to in New York, and I had a lot of time to kill. I think it was the nature of this waiting game that made me start to think about sleeping with him.

'Did you know that you are the patron saint of produce merchants?'

Michael looked up.

'I had a feeling.'

One of my most precious possessions, and the first

thing I hid away when Janine moved in, was a book that had always been on my mother's bedside table. At first I just wanted it because it had my mother's maiden name, Lydia Harding, written in it on the first page. Up to now, I had never looked to see what the book was about. But when I unpacked it in New York, maybe because I had the time, I started to read it. It was called *Saint Days*, by Sister Joanna Reid, and it was simply a list of all the saints in existence, their stories, their ups and downs on the road to sainthood, their little quirks, and for which ailment they could be invoked, everything from fainting to free-thinking. Too much free-thinking, that is, it being a bad thing. There was a saint for everything and everyone: Saint Apollonia for dentists but also to be invoked against dental pain and tooth decay, Saint Quiteria, invoked to prevent dog bites, Saint Blaise, patron saint of wool-combers, once himself tortured with wool combs, and Saint Dominic Savio, a favourite of mine, patron saint of choirboys and juvenile delinquents. In New York, the book became a sort of touchstone for me, an almanac to which I daily referred for random guidance. I looked up people: Saint Barbara, the patron saint of firemen, Saint James, who can help you if you're suffering from arthritis, rheumatism or other bodily aches.

'And for what protection may we invoke you, O Queen?' asked Michael.

'I don't have a name-saint.' Which wasn't true, but of course Michael didn't know my real name.

'You're a queen. You don't need a saint. You have a direct line.'

'I guess that's right.'

'But which queen are you? Queen Elizabeth? Queen

Nefertiti? Or what about Queen Mab? That's a good one.'

'Of those queens, two are dead, unless you mean Elizabeth II who's not someone I really wanna be, and the other is a fairy who only comes out at night, and then ruins people's fun. It doesn't really attract me, that line of work.'

'Not like being a female escort?'

'Well, at least I'm not ruining anyone's fun.'

'Quite the contrary.'

'You know, I don't sleep with the majority of them.'

'It's none of my business,' he said, and went back to his book, sort of abruptly. That's when I realized he'd been thinking about sleeping with me as well.

We were in my apartment at the time, reading and eating. These were my two favourite simultaneous activities, and after trying it out, Michael now agreed with me as to their symbiotic charms. He seemed to be in a hiatus at the moment, between article deadlines, which happened occasionally but not very often. Michael was reading a biography of some count who tried to assassinate Hitler during the Second World War, but didn't manage it, obviously. I was reading a wild book Michael had lent me, about a lady who wakes up one morning to find everyone in the world's disappeared and there's an invisible wall around her house in the woods, which she can't break through. Where do they come up with these things?

'Enjoying your book?' I asked.

'Delightful. Pithy.'

'Are you nearly finished with a chapter?'

'No. Why?' he said, carrying on reading.

'I thought we could do something else.'

'Like what?' he said, carrying on reading.

'I dunno – kiss?' I laughed as if I hadn't meant it, as if this was just a lark, a jape, a jest.

Michael looked up, holding one finger at his place on the page. 'Did you say "kiss"?'

'I did. Familiar with the word?'

'Vaguely,' he mumbled, looking down again at his book.

Neither of us said anything for a few moments, and I began to wonder if I had read the situation totally wrong.

'Queen?' He always called me Queen, not Queenie.

'Yes?' Shit. Was he going to ask me what my real name was?

'How old are you?'

'Nineteen.' I smiled. 'And a half.'

'Nineteen.' He sighed. 'That's what I thought.'

'And I'm guessing you're in your late thirties?'

He laughed. 'No. I'm twenty-eight.'

Wow. I really had thought he was much older.

He stared at me and I stared back at him, for what seemed like five hours. We didn't say anything – it was great.

Finally Michael said, 'I do want to.' And then he rolled his chair over to the sofa where I was laid out. I suddenly felt very shy and a little worried, things I hadn't felt in a while. I sat up, wondering how we were going to do this with the wheelchair between us like the biggest nose on anybody's face. Michael picked up my hand and put it to his mouth, kissed it. When he had finished doing that, I leaned over the arm of the sofa, and taking his face in my hands, kissed him on the mouth. When that was finished, he turned his head a little and kissed me on the neck a few times, all in the same little area. When that was done, I kissed him on the ear. His hair smelt of baby shampoo. He kissed me on the mouth then, and we kept on kissing.

Later, when I asked him what I could do where, and with what effect, Michael looked embarrassed, and mumbled that he was sure he'd enjoy anything I had to offer. By this time, it was the middle of the night and, after stopping to open a bottle of Scotch and eat some crackers and cheese, we continued our kissing, this time on the bed. Michael lifted himself out of the chair and dragged his legs over. I remember being conscious that it was a virgin bed – at least for me – and I was glad I had never brought any client back to the apartment. It was April Fool's Day.

But Michael seemed hesitant to go all the way. Maybe men just took their time more when they weren't paying by the hour – I didn't know. There were logistical problems, of course. Michael couldn't just roll me over and get on top – the good old missionary position was not an option. Still, it seemed like there was something else wrong. Just as I was hotting up, Michael appeared to be cooling down. I wondered if it was the age thing bothering him.

I stopped sucking and looked up. 'Should I get on top?'

There was a silence.

'Michael?'

'Yes?'

'Are you OK?'

'I need to tell you something.'

'OK.' I came up and laid my head on the pillow next to his. 'Am I being too slutty?'

'No, no – are you kidding?' He kissed me. 'My God. You're amazing. But I should be truthful with you before we go any further. So that we can go further. I'm just not sure how.'

Was this the part of the movie where he, the older man, told me he had a wife and four kids living in Peoria, Illinois? It would have definitely surprised me to hear that about Michael, but I don't think it would have upset me. Not in a jealous way. Did that mean I wasn't really in love? I lay there, waiting, but he didn't say anything more, and I needed to pee.

'Michael?'

'Yes?'

'I really have to go to the bathroom. Can you hold that thought?'

When I came back, the bedside light had been turned on and Michael was standing by the window.

'What are you doing?'

He turned. 'I don't really need the wheelchair any more.'

'What do you mean you don't need the wheelchair? Since when?'

'Well . . .'

'It was the sex, right? I *am* amazing.'

He smiled.

'No, really, have you been to the doctor lately? Have you told them about this?'

'They already know.'

I climbed back into bed and pulled up the covers because I was cold.

'Know what, exactly?'

'Well, you see, I haven't really needed the chair for a few weeks now. For a few months, I mean. I – I had a traffic accident last summer, four or five months before you came. It was raining and I was thinking about something else—'

49

'Birds, right?'

He smiled again. 'No. And a taxi drove into me – it couldn't stop in time – and broke both my legs. That's why I had the chair.' He laughed a little weak laugh. 'But then my legs got better.'

'Like they do.'

'Yes.' He nodded. 'Even when I met you, that first day I saw you in the hallway, I didn't really need the chair any more.'

'You just liked getting it stuck in elevator doors?'

He didn't smile this time but came and sat down on the side of the bed, put his head in his hands, and said in a little sad voice: 'I just like it. It's done something to me, being in the chair. I became a different person, easier with people. I felt like Cary Grant, just so *darn* winning. And my writing! It got clearer, more acerbic, more to the point – unlike this sentence. Just better, really. I've been getting so much work . . .'

He trailed off, looking at the carpet. As if this was such an awful thing to admit, as if he was a big fat cheat who'd swallowed a magic potion that was affording him his success, like Sparky and the magic piano who got all the way to Carnegie Hall and then the magic piano wouldn't play for Sparky any more.

I laughed. 'It's still you who's writing the stuff, isn't it?' I wrestled him back onto the bed and climbed on top of him, started to pull off his pants. Have I said that he always wore the same clothes every day? Not the actual same clothes, but the same sort. He must have had at least ten pairs of identical white chinos, and a few dozen pale blue shirts. I never saw him in anything else. He may have owned a sweater.

Weeks later, after we'd had lots of stick-it-in-there, full-blown, juicy intercourse, Michael asked me if I had wanted to sleep with him initially out of pity, or even curiosity.

'What, some weird yen for disabled men? Well, if that was the case, would I still be sleeping with you?'

He seemed to accept this answer.

Michael and Louie only met once; they were my two desert islanders, Robinson Crusoe and Tattoo. Tattoo turned up one afternoon in the summer, unannounced, and since he had his own key, he just rang the doorbell and walked in.

'Hello?'

Michael and I were in the bedroom, just about to finish.

'Shit,' I whispered.

'Who is it?'

'It's my boss. So to speak.'

'What – your pimp?' The combination of the way Michael said that word and the terrified look on his face was too much for me. I started to laugh.

'Sshhh, shut up,' said Michael, stuffing a pillow in my mouth.

I spat out the pillow. 'He's not going to shoot you, or anything.'

Louie was standing in the bedroom doorway.

'Hi, Louie,' I said. Michael was lying on his stomach now, with his face in the pillow, pretending to be asleep. 'Give me a minute.'

Louie nodded, and went back into the kitchen.

When I joined him, after throwing on some clothes, Louie was leaning against the kitchen counter, with his arms crossed. An uncharacteristically butch position.

'Hi, Louie.'

'Hi.'

'Do you want some coffee?'

He shook his head. 'No thanks.'

'Is something wrong?'

'Could I speak to you out in the hall, please?'

'Out in the hall?'

'Well, is your—' he stammered on the word — '*friend* really asleep?'

'Probably not, no.'

'I'd like this to be private.'

'OK.'

We went out into the hall.

'What's up?'

'I could ask the same question. Are you running your own business on the side or something? 'Cause it's actually been pretty hard to cover the rent on this place lately — I had to borrow the money from Mom last month — and if you're earning your own money that I don't know about, then I think you should at least be contributing to the rent, because you sure as hell haven't been earning anything for me!'

'Woah. Calm down there. He's just a friend. He's not paying.'

'A friend?' Louie lowered his voice as the singing teacher from 7B passed, carrying her little dog in its doggie coat. 'I didn't think you guys had those sort of friends.'

'Us guys?'

Michael opened the door and stepped out into the hallway. 'I'm extremely sorry,' he said to Louie, and walked down to his apartment, let himself in, closed the door behind him.

I laughed. 'He is a friend. He's the one whose phone I used to use.'

'Oh. So he knows about what you do?'

'Uh-huh.'

'And he's not going to call the police? Or the super?'

'I don't think so. I don't think he wants me to get thrown out. Do you?'

'No, I guess not.' Louie was still staring down the hall towards Michael's door. 'Maybe I should go talk to him. What's he do again?'

'He's a writer. For the *Times*. I wouldn't go talk to him.'

'For the *Times*? My God, he's probably writing some sort of sleaze report on us—'

'Oh, come on, be serious. We're not that big time now, are we, Louie? I think the last time I even went out with anyone, let alone had sex, was about five weeks ago.'

Louie looked down at the floor. 'Yeah. I've been meaning to talk to you about that.'

'Do you think we can go inside now?'

'Sure. Sorry.'

Louie had come to tell me he'd run out of steam. He'd managed to pay next month's rent two days ago, but he'd told the super that he'd be vacating the apartment at the end of the month. Which meant me.

'What about your brother?'

'He told me to let the place go – he won't be coming back any time soon. I'm sorry, Queenie. I'm just not very good at this business, I guess. I think I'm going to try something else. You're welcome to move in, if you can afford it yourself.'

Fuck. I was all out of cash as well; the beer-tent savings I had brought with me long gone. In fact, lately Michael had started paying for things, without saying anything about it. He'd bring me groceries, and rent videos. Maybe he'd been happy I wasn't getting any customers. And at first it was nice, feeling like he wanted to spoil me. But as it went on, sometimes I felt like I'd just replaced a group of clients with one.

So as soon as Louie broke the news, I figured it was a sign. I figured it was time to go. I mean, I was surprised I'd stayed this long, if you want the truth. I come from a family of runners, after all.

When my dad was eighteen, he'd run off to Canada to avoid being drafted. He lived on a sort of commune for draft dodgers run by a woman called Besse. He used to get a Christmas card from her every year, Saint Besse, and every year, as soon as my mom saw who the card was from, she'd make this snorting sound and walk out of the room. Dad was embarrassed about this episode in his life, because it's not like he's a hippie. If anything, he swings right of centre and his family always voted Republican, that's for sure. I figured at least my dad had faced up to his own limitations – it would have been worse if he'd pretended he was brave enough to be a soldier and then sat there shitting himself when people's lives depended on him. At least he hadn't got married, had two kids, and then decided he wasn't up to it.

So when Louie decided to choose another career, I thought I'd better not outstay my welcome. It was coming up ten months I'd been in New York and I'd started this weird thing lately, whenever I was alone, of putting pillows all over the floor and using them to walk from place to place. The bed pillows, I mean, and the pillows from the sofa. It began as a sort of game when I was bored one afternoon – try to travel across the apartment without ever touching the carpet – but now it was becoming more like a need. I even thought about it when other people were around. I needed my feet not to touch anything harder than polyester foam. I would walk everywhere with two pillows, one to fling ahead and step onto, so that I could turn back and pick up the one I'd just come off, fling that one ahead, step on it. Plus, I'd been sleeping more and more, only surfacing for a few hours in each day, in the summer heat. Michael liked to write all through the night, so on the days he did come over, about four days a week, he'd usually arrive about one, hang around until about nine o'clock, and then after he left, I'd just stay in bed for the rest of the evening, having never really got up in the morning. Weeks had been flying by, nothing more than this.

Of course, as these things often go, Louie suddenly found this new cache of clients in August and I dutifully went out on the dates, trying to save up money again. But I'd lost my knack for conversation, as well as the talent for concealing my tedium, and the clients complained. In fact, the very last date I had was a repeat date with my very first client, Louie's friend's father, whose wife had left him. On our first date, he'd told me I reminded him of his daughter, who lived in Texas and was about to have a baby. This time, halfway through dinner, he looked at me in a worried way, but also a little irritated though he was nice enough to try and hide his irritation, and said that I seemed different.

'You should stop doing this,' he said. 'I don't think it suits you.'

I agreed.

The very next day Louie handed me postcard number 2. Saint Gabriel – patron saint of childbirth.

'Who sends you these things?' asked Louie. 'Your grandma?'

Once again, the message was to the point.

What are you doing?, it said.

I didn't know what I was doing. And I didn't want anyone asking me either, especially not some phantom postcard-sender who didn't even have the courage to sign their own name. I figured the best thing, the thing that would really make them mad, was to ignore them. To just not care about the postcards, to pretend I wasn't listening, like not listening to someone teasing you in a playground. How the fuck could *they* know what I was doing, anyway? I guess if they knew where I was, they knew what I was doing. Maybe it was Michael sending them, but then I remembered the first one had come before I'd ever knocked on his door. I had to get out of here.

There was one other thing made me want to go. One morning in early September, I couldn't sleep and I went out at about 7 a.m. to get some milk. I was walking down the street and I passed by an alley between two buildings, where people liked to park their cars illegally, especially on the weekends. There were two cars there today, and some kind of municipal truck was driving down from the other end, even though it was going to have a hard time getting past the parked cars. Also wandering down the alley was a woman. It was a cold morning; she was dressed in a denim skirt and black sweatshirt top, bare legs and beat-up shoes, a woollen hat pulled down low on her forehead. A man in a puffy body-warmer and a nice, clean shirt walked past me and towards one of the cars parked in the alley; you could tell he felt sort of nervous he'd parked there and wanted to get it out of the way of the truck before there was any trouble. Anyway, he let himself in and got into the driver's seat just as the woman came weaving past, sort of smiling and singing to herself. She saw him and then she went and stood right in front of his side of the car and lifted her skirt, spread her legs, doing something with her hands down there. I couldn't really see, but it was clear she didn't have anything on under her skirt. She said something to the man and he ducked his head, shaking it and smiling, as he started up his car. The woman started wandering back up the alley then and I stopped, half hiding myself behind the next building to watch what she'd do next. She did the same skirt-lifting thing for the guy in the truck.

I don't know why this had such an effect on me. It was like seeing myself, somehow. It scared me. I was gone by the end of the week.

Louie was sad to see me go, but he blamed himself, and he returned my car in spotless condition. He'd been keeping it at his mom's and I don't think he even drove it that much. His mom, whom I'd never met, had packed me up a bag of food for the journey.

'You sure you don't want to come stay with me and Mom for a while? Until you find another job? I feel responsible.'

'Thanks, Louie, but really, I'm OK. I want to go.'

'I'm going to try hairdressing,' he said. 'What d'ya think?'

'I could see you doing that.'

'Because I'm queer?'

'Yeah, that's it. No, I'm kidding. I could just see it.'

'Anyway, I guess we both weren't really cut out for this line of work. It made me so *nervous*, breaking the law. Are you gonna go home?'

It had never even crossed my mind. 'I was thinking of driving to Canada.'

'Nah, you should go south. It's supposed to be nice. Much warmer than Canada. What about your friend though? Couldn't you stay with him? Doesn't he want you to stay?'

'His apartment's a little small for two.'

I didn't tell Michael I was leaving, not even the littlest hint. This might seem harsh, and it was, but it was the only way I knew how to leave. He'd be OK; he wasn't the sort to expect consistency, I didn't think.

And, even now, he's one of the few people I still think I will see again. Some day, I'll be stuck in traffic somewhere and I'll look over, idly, to the car in the lane next to me and there will be Michael, sitting behind the driving wheel. Except that I don't think he knows how to drive. Or maybe I'll be on a train, sitting in a station waiting to leave, waiting for another train to leave first or something, and meanwhile a train going the other direction will come into the station and it will sit there as well, so that the windows are right there, lined up with our windows. And I'll be looking at all the people in that other train, wondering what their lives are like, trying to guess their names and occupations, wondering about their footwear, or what they're reading, when I'll suddenly realize it's Michael sitting there. Just sitting on his own, reading a book and eating a sandwich, reading and eating.

North Carolina

I have this dislocated memory of sitting on a high-backed chair, a chair with a green leather seat, waiting for my mother to pick me up from kindergarten. My mother must have been late, because there were no other children and my teacher, Miss Apple, was sitting down too, something she never did usually. Rising up to the left of me, a full-sized statue of Abe Lincoln in white marble. He looked like a friendly man to me, with his very very tall hat. Sometimes in the mornings, on the way to my classroom, I liked to reach up and stroke the cool fingers of his left hand as I passed. As per usual with most of what I call my mom memories, I remember more about the things around us than I do about her.

I looked through a large square window on my left and I saw my mother approaching, stopping to wait for traffic before pushing the baby carriage across the street.

'Here she is!' said Miss Apple, rising from her seat opposite – we must have been waiting a little while. I climbed down from my chair, clutching today's art-work. As my teacher opened the heavy front door of our school, we both heard it, the sound of my mother laughing. She was cackling; she was hooting – she was laughing so hard she had to stop and bend over, wipe away the tears.

'Mom!' I rushed towards the red rectangle of her skirt and tried to put my arms around her, but she told me to hang on a second, while she got some Kleenex out of her purse. She was still giggling as she asked, 'Are you ready?' and took my paintings without looking at them. I saw the white door of a house across the street open and a lady came out wearing a headscarf and a baby blue dress which reached to just below her knees. She took the hands of her two children, a girl and a boy, on either side of her, and together they walked carefully down their narrow front path to the pavement.

I looked up at my mother again. She was still chuckling as she turned the baby carriage around. I was proud of her beautiful skin and her long blond braid. I looked back at the school one more time, for Miss Apple's benefit, to let her know everything was fine now. But she was frowning at my mother, so I didn't wave.

Who decides how mothers are meant to be, anyway? There's a film with Doris Day, the Hitchcock one where her cutesy American son, Hank, gets abducted by some weirdy English couple, and she ends up singing 'Que sera, sera' during a climactic scene in the Peruvian Embassy. Not Peruvian really, I'm making it up. Anyway, 'Que sera, sera' is a very fucked-up song. As far as I can remember, in the song this mother keeps telling her child to just let things slide, that what will be, will be, anyway, and there's nothing you can do about it, and no way to predict, so forget about it and stop worrying. This just doesn't feel like great mother love to me. You know, you want your mom to be concerned about your future, to obsess alongside you about your decisions, your successes and failures, and to give you positive, constructive advice. You don't want to hear fatalism – you don't want her reaction to you not getting into an Ivy Leaguer, or you not getting asked out on one date your entire freshman year, to be 'What the hell, honey! Whatever will be, will be.'

What my mother was great at was holidays – she loved rituals of any kind. I think that's why she liked going to church, just the ritual of it, the way it organized the week. I think it was that more than the religion stuff, but maybe I'm wrong. Whatever the reason, she loved to mark the passing seasons of a year, and she spent a lot of time doing it. Any holiday, no matter how slight, was acknowledged in our household: President's Day, Fourth of July, Father's Day, even Labor Day and Memorial Day. And she didn't just go down to the local Hallmark shop and get tacky crêpe paper turkeys or something like that. She had a whole collection of objects she'd collected through the years, from all over, I guess, which she would bring out in strict rotation.

So, for instance, on President's Day there were two little reproduction paintings in gold frames, one of Washington crossing the Delaware, and one of Lincoln in his top hat, standing on a podium, giving a speech, and there was also a copy of the Declaration of Independence printed in old-timey handwriting on a piece of stiff yellow paper meant to look like parchment. She would hang the paintings up in the front hall, taking down the calendar and family photo that usually hung there, and the Declaration of

61

Independence she'd unfurl and attach to the fridge with magnets, at kid level, so we could read it as we passed, and realize 'people weren't always as free as we are now'. That was President's Day.

On Labor Day, no-one was allowed to do a stitch of work. Ever. She'd cook breakfast the night before, muffins or something, cold cereal, and we'd leave the dishes, then lunch and dinner we'd eat out, although Mom always felt guilty that we were being served in those restaurants by people who should be having the day off. The Labor Day display consisted of a photograph of her grandfather with some other men gathered outside the paper mill where they had worked, in Pennsylvania. I couldn't tell it was a paper mill, but that's what Mom told us. And when I was smaller, I used to love this colouring book she brought out on Labor Day. It had pictures of all the different jobs – nurse, cowboy, fireman, poker player – no, I'm making that one up. I coloured in every one of those pictures before James even got a chance to look at them. I think she got a new colouring book for James, but I don't think it was as good. Because she couldn't find the same one again.

Saint Valentine's Day – a heart-shaped white cake with red icing, and a silver heart on a delicate chain which she would get out and wear around her neck that day of the year and no other.

Flag Day – a long string of the flags of every nation which she would hang up on little nails so the flags flew across the length of the kitchen, also a large American flag hung across the front porch window, and a red, white and blue scarf woven into her long tight braid. Her mother's family had moved to the US from Sweden, when her mother was eight years old, and they'd all been brought up pretty patriotic about their new country. I never met my Swedish grandmother, though. I think she died before my dad and mom met.

Another good thing about my mother: she never made us do anything we didn't want to. I don't mean things like going to bed, or having baths, or not putting marbles up our noses. She was pretty tense about those things. But I mean with things like these holiday observances of hers. She didn't mind if we didn't play along. She'd just offer up these items and we could take advantage of them or not. It was the same with our birthdays.

Our birthdays were our day – we could do whatever we wanted. That included doing nothing. Not going to school, if we didn't want to, spending the whole day with Mom, if we wanted, or with our friends, or even spending the whole day alone, going to a late movie, going to anything, anything we could think up that wouldn't kill us. Mom's contribution on our birthdays was a book of our baby photographs, with a lock of hair and birth certificate, and the story of our birth related as many times and in as great detail as we wanted. Each meal that day was our call, and it was the one day of the year when you didn't have to share with anybody, if you didn't want to. So I don't know what James did with Mom on his birthdays; it was his business. I went to a shopping mall once, when I was nine or ten, and spent the whole day there, just wandering from shop to shop. Mom set a budget of what we could spend, and the rest of the time we just looked, had lunch, got our hair done in a hairdresser's because I wanted to get a Dorothy Hamill cut. It looked awful. Another birthday we drove to a wood, and took a long walk. My birthday's in October, so it was still warmish, but the leaves were just beginning to turn. I remember I was sad because some girls were teasing me at school. And one birthday, when I was thirteen, I stayed in bed the whole day, and Mom got in with me for a lot of it. We read, and played board games and wrote letters, me to a pen pal in Switzerland, and her to an old friend I'd never met. Dad had taken James to school, I think, so Mom was still in her flowery cotton nightgown and robe, and until she had to go pick up James from school, she only got out of bed whenever we wanted to eat something. She would go and make it and bring it back on a tray.

I've often considered the possibility that maybe my mother gave too much to us, as a mother. That all that special, focused attention just wore her out and suddenly, quite suddenly, she had nothing, absolutely nothing maternal left to offer. That's why I'm careful with how much I give myself away to people. You never know when it might backfire and you end up making your getaway in the middle of the night, without warning, because you just can't do it any more.

I ignored Louie's advice and drove North. It was September and I'd heard that New England was pretty in the autumn. I drove all the way up the Taconic Parkway, then turned right at Vermont, took about two and a half hours to cross the whole state, turned north again in New Hampshire. Halfway up the state, I stopped for something to eat in a small town. In the free local paper I picked up at the door of the diner, so that I had something to read while I was eating, there was an ad about fruit pickers needed for the apple harvest, starting this week at a farm I presumed was nearby. After lunch, I found out where the farm was and drove out there, and that's how I ended up picking apples for a living.

I told them my name was Meg – seemed a good apple-picking name.

The whole crew lived in a dilapidated old farmhouse that had been converted into a sort of dormitory. I managed to get my own tiny room, because out of the five women picking, I was the only one who hadn't arrived with a friend. There were fifteen of us in all, and I wasn't used to being so sociable, but everyone got on pretty well. People worked together and then ate together and sat around at night playing cards and board games, huddling by the wood stove, mostly so physically exhausted they were ready to go to bed as soon as the sun had set. The bedrooms were freezing at night. I slept alone the first week, but as soon as Jonas arrived, I hoped it wouldn't be for long.

Jonas came from North Carolina and he was the first guy I ever really desired. I can still call it up, the smell of Jonas's skin, his forearms, his waxy shoulders, his fingertips, a combination of hand-rolled cigarettes and something musky like sandalwood, though I never saw him put on any kind of oil. There was a sweetness too, like, I don't know what it was, sap, or the resin that gets put on a violin's bow. The hair all over his body was soft and fine, like a baby's, and on his head it never settled. He had crooked teeth and full lips, and blue blue eyes which were always half closed. And he was just incredibly sexy, without knowing it. I think he didn't know. A lot of people were friends with Jonas already because he'd been coming up to this same farm every harvest for five or six years. This was the first time in a few years he hadn't come with his girlfriend, Elizabeth. I tried not to be obvious when I listened in on conversations about what was going on with them, how Elizabeth had decided she needed some time on her own this year. Jonas was very friendly to me – but he was friendly to everyone. He was very tall and wiry and he liked to bake bread.

It was like another planet for me in that community, and one big thing was the food. Everyone was a vegetarian, and all the food was 'health food', something I'd vaguely heard of back home but never come across. Mom had cooked us recipes out of magazines; she was always trying new things, but they usually went wrong and they were the kind of recipes that used things already made, a cup of Philly cream cheese, a crust made of mashed-up graham crackers, that sort of thing. She fed us well, don't get me wrong, but it wasn't aesthetic. In New York, I'd eaten the usual away-from-home, can't-cook things, mostly convenience food from the supermarket, or I'd make eggs and pancakes from a mix, or I'd go and get some take-out. I'd certainly never made bread, never even thought about it, or about putting together a meal for sixteen people. There was a rotation of duties in the farmhouse, and though at first I begged off cooking, saying I didn't know how and would do an extra dishes rotation instead, that got boring quick and meant I always had to work after dinner, when you just wanted to kick-back.

Back home in North Carolina, Jonas worked as a cook in a health food supermarket, so he knew how to do it all. He did the baking once a week, all through the night on Saturday night, after most people were in bed. One Saturday, I stayed up with him; it was my twentieth birthday.

'So, Meg, how long have you lived in New York?'

He was at the big kitchen table, measuring out flour by the bucket. I was curled up in an old chair by the wood stove, reading a novel someone had left behind in a previous season, and eating toast. It was the middle of the night.

'About a year.'

'Do you like it?'

'Some of the time.'

'I've got a friend who's just moved to New York. He used to come here every year, to pick. I think he's enjoying the whole buzz of it, the night-life – that's what he says.'

'Uh-huh.'

I was thinking of the pillow trails all over the floor. I was thinking of the woman in that alley. Not to mention my former occupation, which I had already kind of blanked out, and which seemed a million miles away from where I was now, who I was trying to be now. I was a chameleon that way – I always morphed into the kind of people I was with, and the people I was with now weren't the sort of people who would give some stranger a lift and then start working for him as an escort in his absent brother's apartment. What would they have thought?

'I should give you Jeff's number,' said Jonas. 'He doesn't know that many people and I think you'd like him.'

'I actually don't think I'll be going back to New York.'

'Really? Where are you heading?'

'I don't know. I mean, I'm not sure yet.'

'That's exciting. Isn't it? Sounds good to me.'

'I guess it is.'

I went into this little fantasy about Jonas and me driving around in my car, working on farms, living off the land, maybe we'd even head over to Europe, work the lavender fields, in the vineyards – then I remembered Elizabeth.

'Does your girlfriend like to travel?'

I don't know if it was my imagination, but Jonas looked sort of guilty for a second, as if he'd been caught out in a lie. Maybe he was just surprised I knew about Elizabeth. We'd been picking on the same trees for the last couple of days, working down the same row, but we hadn't talked much yet. You didn't when you were up a ladder, picking; the work was hard and solitary. People brought tape players, propped them up in the fork of branches, so there was always music blaring, different music in different corners of the orchard, depending on who brought the tapes that day. People sang along to tunes more than they talked, and if you both liked the same music, that was one way you found your friends.

'I could live on this bread,' I said, getting up to cut myself another slice.

'It's easy to make – do you wanna learn?'

'Me? Sure.'

I sort of skipped over to the table, which is pretty uncharacteristic behaviour on my part, and this made Jonas laugh and when I came around the table he was still laughing, and he reached his hand out for mine, which I gave him, and he said, 'You're so priddy, girl,' in this goofy voice. It was the sort of upfront, unguarded gesture characteristic of him, which would set my teeth on edge, given time. But for now, it was just what I needed. These people were very different from any people I'd met before. They were great, really loving and kind, and ethical, and interesting, and they thought hard about their lives and their relationships with other human beings, and took things seriously, and loved life. I didn't think I loved life – I just lived it, because I had to. Was something wrong with me?

Sex with Jonas was another new discovery, and I gave into it, totally. For all that Jonas was this sweet, gentle, hippie-giant, when you got him in bed he was fairly rough as lovers go, pushing me around into different positions, intent on his personal satisfaction. He wasn't cold, though – the sex wasn't cold. It was emotional and intense, and Jonas wasn't embarrassed to be that way, so it allowed me to be too, a little. I guess the guys I'd slept with before hadn't been that passionate, or if they had – I'm thinking of Michael – they were too shy to show it. Jonas and I were a little nervous of anybody knowing at first, especially friends of his from back home, because of Elizabeth. People kept asking Jonas if she was coming up for a visit. And the secrecy made everything extra potent, of course. I remember, right at the beginning, sitting in the back seat of my car one afternoon, on a cold day with the car heater left on, pressing up against each other, kissing, rubbing, just gone. We had driven into town to get some ice-cream for everyone back at the ranch. It was raining. The windows got all steamed up and my whole body felt like one big nerve ending. Or another time, when we were cooking a meal together – there were lots of people around, and he came behind the kitchen table, where I was standing chopping some carrots, and as he passed by, wiped one hand between my legs, under my dress, swiftly tracing the line of my cunt with two fingers, without stopping on his journey to the sink. I had to hold myself upright. God. God, it was exciting.

Anyway, at the end of the apple-picking season, Jonas and I couldn't stop it, so we drove down to North Carolina in my car. He lived in Durham, in a big house with seven other people, including Elizabeth. I didn't know what was going to happen when we got there. Jonas hadn't said anything about me in the two letters he'd written to Elizabeth, or on the phone the one time he'd been near a phone booth in town. But he was too responsible a person to shirk his duties to either one of us; the more I got to know him, the more I saw the sexiness of Jonas was sort of an aberration, something a bad fairy had bequeathed to him to mess with his inherent sense of fair play. Because in everyday life, he was painfully moral. He loved me, and he loved Elizabeth – we would just have to talk it out. So, the morning we arrived in town, I dropped off Jonas at his house, so he could see Elizabeth on his own first, and drove to a nearby shopping street.

The first store I went into was a dusty old drugstore called McDonald's, the kind with a soda fountain and round swively chairs. I was greeted by a hoary old man and what looked like his equally wintry sister, though it could have been his wife. Or maybe they weren't related at all. Maybe they just looked really old, and to a twenty-year-old, two such ancient faces were as undifferentiable as Asian faces to most Caucasians.

'Ice-cream soda?' the lady peeped at me, with a feeble smile. Her face hardly reached the counter.

'No thanks.'

She nodded as if she understood, and I walked

around. It was a great store; there was nothing on the shelves for people under seventy. Packet after packet of those white donut things that protect corns, medicated foot powders, incontinence diapers, un-explainable rubber objects, with tubing, or with handles to grip on each side. In one corner, a tower of shiny Zimmer frames, stacked up precariously. Even the candy at the cash register looked years out of date, peppermint candies wrapped in stiff cellophane, card-board boxes of Hershey bars. I glanced out of the window to make sure this was still the 1980s.

I felt like I had to say something eventually because I could feel their kindly gaze on me wherever I went, full of expectancy.

'Do you have any diapers for babies?'

'For babies? No, I'm sorry, miss, I can't say we do,' said the man. 'You should try the Rite-Aid across the street. They're bound to have some.'

'How old is your baby?' said the lady.

'What?' I'd been looking at the man, and thought it was still him talking, until I noticed his lips weren't moving. Grandma was smiling at me. 'Oh, they're not for me – they're for a friend. I don't have a baby.'

'Not yet you don't!' She waggled a tiny crooked finger at me. They both kept nodding and smiling while I backed out of the door.

This place made me think of Barbara – we always had these kind of random encounters with *Twilight Zone* people – and I realized I'd sort of forgotten about her. I was scarily capable of just forgetting people: out of sight, way out of mind. Like mother, like daughter. Anyway, I wished that Barbara had been there to see these two oldies and their store. She would have made me laugh. What would she have thought of Jonas and his hippie friends? It was fall again now and she must have started at music school in New York just as I was leaving. I'd never written her. I wondered if she'd known I wouldn't. Maybe she hadn't gone to New York in the end. Maybe if I'd written her, she would have written back. What a fuck-up I am. But just thinking that about yourself doesn't fix it.

After killing a few more hours in two different bookshops, I ended up in an ice-cream place, nursing a tea and reading *Anna Karenina*.

Jonas turned up at about 4.30.

'Hi.' He kissed me and sat down in the dainty ironwork chair, his long limbs reducing its proportions to doll-house size. 'Are you OK? Did you get lunch?'

'Yeah, I'm fine. A little fatter after sampling every flavour of ice-cream they got here – yum yum. Just kidding.'

He smiled and reached over, touched my face. He was always quietening me down that way.

'So how about you? Did you talk to Elizabeth?'

I had decided before he came that if he looked away after I asked him whether they had talked, I should begin thinking about where I wanted to drive to next. But he didn't. He looked right at me.

'Yup. We talked. But it took me a while to find her – that's why I've been gone so long. She's moved out of the house – she moved to Chapel Hill. A few weeks ago.'

'Out of the house? Without telling you?'

He nodded. 'She's allowed.'

'Aren't you hurt?'

'Sure, a little. But it's not like I haven't been acting a little independently myself.'

I looked over at the counter. 'Do you want something?'

He shook his head and took my hand under the table. I smiled and looked away, then jiggled my foot until the clog I was wearing fell onto the floor and made a loud noise.

'Sorry.' I picked up the shoe and put it back on.

Jonas pulled at my hand. 'Are you going to stay?'

'What? Here?'

'Come on – you know what I mean.'

'I don't know. Do you want me to?'

'I do.'

'At the house with you? Won't your friends feel weird about it?'

'About what?'

'Us. You know, me living there, instead of Elizabeth.'

'Sure, it will be a little strange, at first. But we're all grown-ups – the house is used to a certain amount of change. It's not as if it's your fault – me and Elizabeth. I mean it's not down to you. Everybody knows that.'

'Even Elizabeth?'

'Especially her.'

I felt a little weird, but excited. Domesticity. 'Are you sure about this?'

'Are *you* sure? I mean, what do you want to do? I don't want to run your life for you.'

What did I want to do? I didn't care. I could get a job here – I could get a job anywhere. I wanted to smell Jonas's skin, lie around on a big bed with him, reading and eating while he smoked his little roll-up cigarettes. I wanted to have sex with him a lot.

'It was my birthday last month,' I told him.

'It was? When we were at the farm?'

'Uh-huh.'

'Why didn't you tell me?'

73

'We didn't really know each other.'

'So how old are you, now?'

'Twenty. I'm twenty.'

'OK then, twenty. Happy birthday.' He leaned across the table and kissed me, softly, romantically. Me, I wanted to grind the length of my whole body against those lips, though maybe not in the ice-cream place.

'I think I'll stay,' I said.

Jonas stood up and pulled me off my chair. In the movie of my life that was still rolling as I watched, this was only the hippie phase, and part of me knew it. And even though I also recognized that me and hippie were about as mismatched as body-slamming at a charity square dance, I didn't want to acknowledge this. I wanted to be on the committee; I wanted to be able to sustain it. I wanted to be like them, because I thought life would be so much simpler if I were.

I wondered if the postcards would find me here.

There were eight of us in the communal house after I moved in: me and Jonas, Peter and Cindy, C.J., C.J.'s brother Erik, Steve, who had moved in that fall, taking the room of Jonas's actor friend gone to New York, and Laura. Laura was the unofficial house president, partly because she'd founded the house two years ago and arranged the lease, but partly just because she was like that. Steve – we called him Stevie – had a girlfriend named Mary, who was also around a lot of the time. Peter was the oldest, twenty-seven, and everyone else fitted in somewhere between, down to the youngest three, me, Stevie and Mary, all twenty. Jonas, C.J. and Erik worked at the health food supermarket which had a café attached. Peter was a musician, played bluegrass guitar and banjo, and Cindy was a kindergarten assistant. Laura was getting a degree in environmental management, and Stevie and Mary were both studying at UNC-Chapel Hill, something to do with agriculture. And that was the family.

A few days after I arrived, I got a job as a checkout girl at the same health food supermarket as the boys. It was run co-operatively, which meant everything was decided by committee, even our salaries. If the profits went up, so did our pay. Lots of workers' meetings. It was a good place. Why was I tempted to be sarcastic about it?

Life was easy in North Carolina. The house was big, with a wrap-around porch and a nice green lawn. When we weren't at work, we just hung around. We'd stay up all night round the kitchen table, talking about stuff that had nothing to do with anything. Peter played his guitar; he taught me to play a little. Jonas cooked and smoked and read, looked at me over the candles. Cindy and I used to talk a lot; she'd been really good friends with Elizabeth, still was, but it never stopped her from being my friend too. I liked her; she seemed calm and wise, and I tried to act like her. Stevie and I got along pretty well too. We shared a slightly harder taste in music than the rest of the house – most of them were into folk/bluegrass or Southern rock – so Stevie and I would go out for drives and crank up the Talking Heads or Prince, bop around in clubs, feeling mildly contraband. I never really talked much to Erik. He was sweet, but sort of slow. I don't mean retarded or anything, just very, very simple. A hillbilly.

Laura was bossy.

Of all the people in the house, the person I respected most was C.J. We were never best friends, but C.J.

approved of me because I did my cleaning rotas well and on time, and I approved of him because he was honest. He wasn't smiley; he didn't give everyone hugs all the time. He lived in a sun room at the front of the house, a little garden room never designed to be a bedroom, and he needed time to himself so he let people know, and he got pissed off when people didn't pull their weight in the house. Pissed off in an obvious way and told them so right then, instead of bottling it all up and then kind of hinting at it later in a house meeting. I trusted C.J. We weren't close, but what we were, we really were, all the way through.

Although I was curious, I figured Elizabeth would keep her distance from the house for a while, especially since I'd moved right into her former room. Instead, she turned up on only the third day after I'd arrived. Can't you just tell from the name? It wasn't Beth, or Liz. Elizabeth. Saint Elizabeth of Hungary, the patron saint of bakers. Not of my baker, she wasn't.

I'd slept until past eleven that morning, on Jonas's futon, under his thin sheet and battered second-hand quilt. The sun woke me. Even though it was November, North Carolina felt like spring. There was a tree outside our window and the light was moving through its leaves, flickering gently onto the surface of the wooden floorboards near my face. I had nothing to do, I didn't know what I know now – life should have been such an easy thing. Jonas had got up earlier, giving me a kiss on the neck as he went and tucking the sheets up over my bare shoulders. I threw them back now, pulled on some underwear, jeans and a T-shirt and went to look for him in the kitchen. Chances were he'd be cooking something, Bob Marley on the tape player.

He was, it was, and at the table, drinking some juice, sat a small, perfectly formed woman, with short blond hair cut like a boy's. Jonas had never mentioned that she was a dancer. Yeah, sure. North Carolina School of the Arts. Then Duke University. Now she was choreographing.

They were talking together, Jonas with his back to her, cooking something. When I said 'hi', he turned around and smiled at me, but he didn't come over to me, lift me off the floor in a hug, like he usually did whenever he saw me, desperate to get his body pressed against mine. He just said, 'Hey', and smiled.

Elizabeth turned around in her chair and smiled at me too.

I stood in the doorway. 'I guess I missed breakfast.'

'Meg, this is Elizabeth. Elizabeth, Meg.'

'Oh! Hi,' I said, and waved, like some stupid four-year-old.

She stood up and came right over to me and hugged me, before I had the time to defend myself.

'Welcome to the house,' she said.

Shit, I thought. Was it me? Was I too much my father's daughter in that I didn't trust this woman, or wasn't it weird that an ex-girlfriend, a recent ex-girlfriend, would be so nice to the chick who had just emerged from her old bed? I felt badly for not trusting her. Maybe if she'd been a little less beautiful, I would have warmed to her right away. I was sure she was being maddeningly kind about me to everyone and the thought of that made me even more on edge.

'I just came by to pick up some of my records – the last of my stuff.'

'That must be a relief. I mean, getting the last of it moved.' Fuck, what was I saying? I was babbling.

'Have you got everything you need in your new place? I mean, is it going all right, settling in?'

'I love it.' Jonas, who was gazing at Elizabeth as she spoke, smiled. 'It's right in the middle of the woods – this sort of geodesic dome a friend of mine built, and he's gone to Japan for the whole year, so I get it.'

'Wow. Sounds great.'

'It is. I wake up to the sound of the birds and the smell of wood smoke, and that's all. You wouldn't believe what meditating's like, out there,' she said, to Jonas.

Meditating? Did Jonas meditate?

'Wow.' I said. 'How excellent. That sounds great. I'm just going to make myself a coffee – do you want one?'

'No thanks. Meg.' She smiled sweetly.

From then on, Elizabeth was always sort of around, and everyone was so nice about it, and they liked me and they liked her, and if Jonas was able to be so level-headed and, uh, democratic, about a past love affair, then what did the present love affair matter in the whole scheme of life's flowing rivers and all that? I wanted him to be more fucked-up than he was, which was fucked-up on my part. I know.

The first Christmas in North Carolina, Jonas took me back home to his parents' house in Asheville. Alice and Todd's. These two were like the Adam and Eve of classy hippies. She had very long, greying hair and gentle blue eyes and walked around like a female Moses, parting the seas of loving grandchildren. He had a white beard and dirty sneakers and a sexy smile, like Jonas. They played musical instruments together and kissed in public. I instantly loved them, and I wanted to be their daughter more than anything.

'Your parents must be missing you this Christmas,'

said Alice, on Christmas Eve when just the two of us were sitting in front of their wood-burning stove, drinking red wine. I think Jonas was outside in the hot tub with his dad.

'I guess so.'

Alice must have intuited something, or else she was psychic, which I wouldn't have put past her. She asked if my parents were still together.

I shook my head, lifting the glass to my mouth.

'Are you in touch with them?'

'My mother's dead.' I hoped to God I wasn't jinxing my mother in some way with this lie, but it's what I had told Jonas months ago, because I hadn't wanted to make up some long story, and this had seemed the simplest way to stop any more questions. We'd just finished this great sex session and I really hadn't wanted to go to motherland right then.

'Oh. I'm so very sorry, Meg.'

'Thanks. Don't worry, it was a long time ago.'

'All the more reason – that's no age to lose a mother. Not that any age is good. I lost mine five years ago and it still hurts. I'm always thinking about what she would have said if she heard this, or how cute she would have found something one of the grandkids said.'

I wanted to curl up in this woman's lap.

'I know what you mean.'

'And your dad?'

'He remarried a couple years ago.'

Alice nodded. 'Todd was married before – it's a hard thing, stepfamilies, even when it's for the best.'

'But Jonas is your son, right?'

'Right. There weren't any children in Todd's first marriage, which made it a little easier, I suppose. It's

79

the children who get their hearts broken, often. I just thank God Todd and I are the soul-mates we are.'

'That's great. Jonas is lucky.'

Alice smiled and patted my arm. 'So are you, love – we all are, really.' Usually I would have balked at such a totally ridiculous statement, but somehow I didn't mind it coming from Alice. 'You just don't know what's around the corner. Half of luck is recognizing it when it comes, don't you think?'

She almost made me believe it.

Before we left Todd and Alice's, I tried to ring James, one morning, when everyone was out walking in the woods and I'd begged off because of my period. It had been over a year since I'd tried to call home on Michael's phone. After five rings, my dad picked up the phone.

'McCall's residence. Hello? Hello, can I help you?'

I heard Janine ask, 'Who is it, honey?' in the background. It would have been pretty early in the morning back home – probably James was getting ready for school.

'Nobody there,' my dad said, and he hung up.

The first thing I did when I heard that Dad was going to marry Janine was go and find James. He was in his bedroom playing complicated games of Dungeons and Dragons with himself, all the little figures laid out and James writing down data in a tiny notebook. He was always looking up little facts in medieval history books and writing them down. He'd tried to get me interested once, but I couldn't see the point of it. I closed the door to the hallway.

'Look, James. I'm making up a box of things, private things, and I'm going to get it out of the house before

80

she comes, and hide it somewhere safe. If you want to put some things in too, you can.'

'Why?'

'Because there won't be any place private once she moves in. You know what she's like – remember when she stayed for the weekend? She'll be in our rooms all the time, cleaning.'

'I won't let her in my room.'

'What are you going to do, stay home from school every day? She'll go in, even if she says she hasn't. Mom used to do it too.'

James hated it when I remembered things about Mom that he didn't. He frowned.

'You don't have to. I just thought that if there's anything you don't want her to find, anything you want to keep safe, you could put it in the box. Then when you leave here, when you're older, you can go and get the box and take it with you.'

'Take it where?'

'I don't know – wherever you go. You're not going to stay *here* all your life, are you?'

James thought about this for a while, leaning against the door to his closet.

'OK.'

Very early on the morning of the wedding, James and I stole out of the house with our two boxes in plastic garbage bags, and a shovel hidden under my coat. I had bought two metal boxes, each one about the size of a bread-box, with integrated locks on the front. I didn't know what James had put in his – he did it in his room, on his own, but it wasn't incredibly heavy.

We walked to a field that was behind our house, about a quarter of a mile away, across a ditch that always flooded every spring, through a little line of fir trees. It was a cold morning, very quiet except for the sound of birdsong, and the ground was wet with dew, a little frosty in places.

'Where should we bury them?' I asked James.

'Somewhere we won't forget,' he said.

'Obviously.'

We looked around.

'Under this tree?'

'No,' said James. 'Too many roots – we couldn't dig there.'

'Well, where then? We'd better hurry. Dad will wake up soon and wonder where we are.'

Thank God they hadn't planned a big wedding, just a quick trip down to the town hall, or wherever.

'Come on,' said James. 'I know a place.' He started to run towards the far side of the field, and I followed, carrying both the boxes in their garbage bags and the shovel. I kept tripping up on the stubbly grass. It was the kind of field where there might be rabbit holes, and I didn't want to step in one and break my ankle.

James pointed to a corner, near the old highway road that ran along the opposite edge of the field. I worried about people in the cars passing by, whether they'd wonder what we were up to digging a hole, but there was hardly any traffic along that road anyway, especially this early in the morning.

'There,' said James. He stopped by the let-out of a drainage tunnel which ran under the road.

Neither one of us realized how hard it would be to dig a good hole or how long it would take. While we were digging, we hid the boxes in the drainage tunnel, because we figured they made us look suspicious. Several cars did pass by, but not a police car, and nobody even slowed down. I wasn't sure how well they could see us anyway, because the road was slightly elevated. I let James do his share of the digging, though I knew I could have done it faster, and it was hard not to be impatient. We took off our coats and then our sweaters, and everything got smudged with mud, our hands, shoes, jeans, faces. We were going to have to make up some story for Dad – he'd definitely be awake by the time we were finished. In the end, we didn't dig as deep a hole as we should have, but it wasn't like we were hiding a body, and what were the chances of someone coming around digging in this exact spot? We'd have to keep an eye out for developers, that's all. And floods.

James put his box in first, with the plastic bag around it, to keep out the damp. He nodded seriously to himself and said 'OK' in a quiet voice. I wondered what he had in there – a couple of old pictures of Mom? The Sunday school book she had marked with smiley faces? I'd put the Labor Day colouring book in mine, and a Julie London record she used to listen to all the time. I stepped in front of James and put my box next to his. I was glad he couldn't see my face, because I was crying. I felt sadder than I had for months, as bad as I ever had.

'Here, I'll just do this quickly,' I said in a choked voice, grabbing the shovel and filling in the hole. When it was done, James asked if we should mark it with anything, then answered the question himself.

'Better not – we'll remember where it is. Have you got the keys?'

I took the key to his box out of my pocket and gave it to him. We walked back to the house, deciding what excuse we would use.

'Barbara's coming over for the weekend,' I said. 'We can go wild while Dad and Janine are away.'

'OK,' said James.

In the spring, Laura decided the women in the North Carolina house should start getting together once a month, to talk.

'Hey, thanks for doing this,' said Laura as we joined her in the living room with our cups of herbal tea.

'You know, don't you, that Jonas and Peter are sitting in that kitchen right now, making jokes about us,' said Cindy.

'Well, up theirs, frankly, if they're threatened. Do they think we're going to waste our time talking about *them*? No, seriously, I just thought it would be nice if we all hung out together a little. And I know if, at least this is true for me, if it's not scheduled, it ain't ever gonna happen. Kind of interesting our first get-together's on Mother's Day.'

'Why? Is somebody going to be a mother?' said Mary.

Laura didn't get it. 'I don't think so. What do you mean? Is someone pregnant? I was just making an observation. Cindy?'

'Don't look at me,' said Cindy.

'I was just joking, Laura,' said Mary.

'Oh.'

Laura was one of those people that if you said anything slightly off the wall, like 'I'm going to scream if I have to eat even one more grain of brown rice', she'd take it literally and ask you if you really felt the rotation of meals cooked by house members was getting a little dull and did we need to look at ways of livening it up? She was earnest. For some reason, she took it upon herself to be responsible for everything in

84

the house, which of course was too much to cope with, and every three months or so she'd get totally stressed and go around slamming doors without knowing she was. Slamming them so hard you thought she was going to bust them.

'I just mentioned it, I guess, because my mom died on Mother's Day. When I was eight. I guess that's why it sticks out. I know it doesn't mean a lot, Mother's Day that is, just another way to get people who can't afford it to spend money on cards – waste of trees, really.'

'Whoa,' said Mary. 'I didn't know your mom had died, Laura.'

'I'm sorry,' said Cindy. 'That must have been so hard for you.'

They both looked at me.

'Did you make her a card?' I asked.

'A card?'

'On Mother's Day. Before she died.'

'Oh. I suppose so, yes. I don't remember, actually. I don't know if we did.'

I nodded. 'There was probably too much else going on. Me and my brother used to put on plays for my mom.'

'Plays?'

'Yes. On Mother's Day.'

'You did?' said Cindy. 'How fantastic. I haven't even called my mom today – y'all are making me feel guilty.'

'What were the plays about?' Mary asked.

'Our plays? They were about mothers. Famous mothers, like . . . Marmee in *Little Women*, or the mother in the Bible whose son gets brought back to life by Jesus. Actually, you wouldn't believe how many stories there are where the mother is dead – think

85

about it. All the fairy tales, the mother's either a step-, and therefore totally wicked, or she's dead. So sometimes we'd make them up. I'd always be the mother and my little brother played all the other characters.'

'Where would you put on these plays?'

'In the living room. Or in the garage. Depending. My brother liked making the sets and sometimes he got really elaborate, cutting out these cardboard back-drops and taking hours to draw on them with magic markers.'

The three women were staring at me. I guess this was longer than I'd ever talked about anything.

'It was no big deal. You should have seen the things she did for *us*, on holidays She was majorly into holidays.'

'Have you called her today?' asked Laura. Guess Jonas hadn't told them she was dead.

I shook my head. 'No.' I guess you could say Mom and I were pretty incommunicado these days. It had been five and a half years.

The week before though, at work, I'd received post-card number 3, the first North Carolina postcard. It didn't really surprise me when it came. Somehow I'd figured it would only be a matter of time. I did wonder why it had been sent to me at work, when whoever had sent it probably knew my home address too. Maybe they didn't approve of my new friends. This one was of Saint Marius, invoked against head colds apparently, and the question of the moment was *Where are you going?* Maybe the FBI were on the case now – maybe they'd been checking the payrolls across the country – maybe Janine had got them to print my face on the side of a milk bottle. I wouldn't put it past her.

I'd put this postcard with the other two, tucked into the pages of *Saint Days*.

'What did your mom die of, Laura?' asked Cindy.

'Cancer.' She nodded her head. 'Of the cervix.'

'That's tough.'

'Yes, it was. So get your pap smears, everyone!' Peter and Jonas burst out laughing at something in the kitchen. 'But hey, look, I didn't mean to bum everyone out. This is meant to be a good thing, getting together – it's supposed to be fun. Maybe we should go to the Catacomb, for a beer. Get out of the house.'

Laura would have been a great camp counsellor; you could just see her with a clipboard and a whistle. She was a tiny bit like a hippie Janine, but how could I hate her after I found out she'd lost her mother?

That summer, Elizabeth went away for two months to Japan, where she was learning a new sort of movement technique, sort of a cross between martial arts and contemporary dance as far as I understood. She wrote Jonas a few times from Japan, little cream envelopes with her tiny, pretty writing on them. I looked for these letters sometimes, in the piles of Jonas's things, but I could never find them. If I had found them, I'd like to think I wouldn't have read them, but face it, why was I looking for them? I didn't realize until she left how much more relaxed I felt with her gone, when there was no possibility of finding her in the kitchen late at night, sunbathing in the garden, laughing with Erik and C.J., helping them fix their truck, looking all cute and gorgeous-dancerly in her dirty overalls.

It's not that she didn't try hard to be my friend. And there were times I really liked her, times I thought we were becoming friends, but even this was a little too self-conscious. I could see the things about her that other people loved. I could. But the truth is she didn't really want to be my friend, any more than I wanted to be hers. And in the end, you don't do things you don't want to do – you just don't. All that niceness making our smiley teeth ache.

Once, the September she got back from Japan, she really blew it. Coming up to the first year anniversary of my arrival in North Carolina, Jonas and I had talked about going apple-picking again. In fact, we had planned on it, because we felt romantic about the place and wanted to go back, but then Jonas hurt his back lifting something at the store, so we had to cancel. Apple-picking was too much hard work, if you weren't feeling a hundred per cent. One night Cindy and Elizabeth and I went out to see a movie – a documentary about retired people who sell everything up and hit the road indefinitely, in giant RVs. Little did I know I was kinda looking at my future life up there. Anyway, afterwards, we went to the same ice-cream place where I had sat waiting for Jonas, my first day in town. We were sitting around with our teas – Elizabeth didn't like sweets and Cindy didn't eat dairy – and Cindy asked where we would all go in the world, if money were no object. Cindy wanted to go to New Zealand with Peter, and hike a famous trail on the South Island. Or maybe the North, I forget. I couldn't really think of anywhere. For all my nomadic tendencies, I'm not really a tourist. I don't have that hunger to see far-off places. But just for the sake of it, I said I wouldn't mind going to Europe, to see some of the places I'd read about in novels.

Elizabeth said, kind of dreamily, that she and Jonas were planning on going to Japan together some day.

She caught herself almost immediately. 'I mean, we *used* to talk about it. Before I went there myself, when he knew I wanted to go – he used to say it would be fun to go together. I'm sorry, I didn't mean anything by that, honestly. I was sort of spacing out, to tell you the truth. I was thinking about something else.'

She slapped at her forehead, to imply she was a complete knucklehead, and Cindy right away changed the subject, asked her how her new dance piece was going. But it was obvious Elizabeth felt I was just a little blip in the straight line of her and Jonas's life together. I wanted to video our fucking and stick her right down in front of the television to watch it. I wanted to prove her wrong.

The problem was, I myself sort of suspected I was only a little blip in everybody else's lives. I was the curl in the lifeline before it got back to normal again. I was the wild oats.

'I'm just going to go browse in the bookstore for a while,' I said, standing up from the table. 'Come find me when you're ready to go.'

From the very first day of apple-picking, back in New Hampshire, I had started to chameleonize myself, and even by the time Jonas arrived, the persona was already pretty firmly in place. Not that there weren't some real things about me that I shared with Jonas, some true things that I said. There were. But I was so mixed up. All I could compare it to was sorts of food. I was pretending to be a sweet dish, when in fact I was a savoury. I was sort of burnt. Some kind of salty, crunchy thing, like grilled sardines or roast potatoes, burnt. But that's not to say I didn't have sweet elements in me, either, and that's what fucked everything up. The problem was I tried to pretend to Jonas and all those good people that I was sweet through and through, that I was a simple, home-made pudding, and in the end all the other fucked-up, over-complicated ingredients in my insides leaked through and ruined the dish. I only knew who I really was when I was alone, not that I was even sure then.

Still, despite all this, occasionally – very occasion-ally – someone came along who saw right through any persona, who seemed to get me, no matter how much I tried to put them off the scent. Barbara had been like that, and Michael to an extent, though he never said anything. In November that year, an old guy called Chicken began working at the health food store, and he was one of those people too.

I didn't say two words to Chicken until New Year's Eve. That Christmas, Jonas and I didn't go to Todd and Alice's; everyone in the house stayed home, so to speak, because Laura, and some others too, had come up with the idea of us all creating our own Christmas ritual together. A new sort of Christmas, totally un-dictated by the existing conventions. We were each going to decide what Christmas really meant to us, and celebrate it accordingly, with no pressure to conform. We were going to explore all the different traditions of celebration at this time of year, not just the Western-world Christian thing, and pick and choose what we felt resonated with our own very private and unique spiritual practices.

'What's the deal with your spirituality, Meg?' Peter asked me, over his mandolin, during a house meeting in December.

'It's in here somewhere,' I joked, patting myself just above the belly button.

'Yeah, you always joke about it like that.'

A couple of people nodded. Jonas didn't say anything.

'You haven't contributed much to the planning,' Peter continued. 'I'm worried you'll feel left out. Do you feel embarrassed to offer suggestions, or do you just not care?'

I shrugged. 'I don't not care,' I said. 'I just don't . . . care. I guess. Care enough.'

Jonas laughed. A couple of other people nodded their heads, not as if they knew what I meant, more as if they had suspected that was what I was like.

Well, giminy. What a mess it turned out to be, anyway. Laura went around door-slamming. Jonas got pissed off because he stressed himself out preparing about thirty different dishes people had requested for the Christmas Eve meal, and half of the house ended up having issues with each other, or were going through their own last-minute spiritual retreat things, so didn't turn up for the meal.

By New Year's Eve, I needed alcohol and a place of my own.

'Can we skip the party, Jonas?'

'Sure.' He was still a little annoyed about the non-shows on Christmas Eve, some of whom had never even apologized, though they had no problem eating up the leftovers. 'What do you want to do instead? Go to my parents?'

'No, let's go out in town somewhere. Get trashed. Isn't that Irish band playing at the Brown Toad?'

'OK. Can you look it up? I'm working until ten.'

'That's cool. I'll meet you at the store, and we'll go from there.'

Come ten o'clock, I was well on my way to oblivion,

thanks to a bottle of Scotch I'd bought at three in the afternoon. I'd been drinking it with 7-Up in my bedroom, the 7-Up being the liquid I presumed people in the house would most disapprove of, and I didn't want to go into the store now, in case someone clocked me weaving down the aisles, but also in case the ever-present odour of nutritional yeast in that place made me throw up, so I sat outside at one of the picnic tables, the bottle of Scotch in a paper bag.

Chicken was sweeping up around the patio tables, emptying the trash bins. He had these super-duty gloves on, blue and puffy, and they made his hands look enormous. He turned around and stared at me.

'What're you drinking there, girl?'

'Scotch.'

'Could you spare me a plug? It's cold work out here.'

'Sure. Those are some pretty impressive gloves you got there. You want a hand?'

'Nope. Pretty much done.'

He leaned his broom against the wall and came and sat down opposite me, reached for the paper bag. No problem sucking down an eighth of the bottle.

'Nice stuff,' he said. 'Thanks.'

Chicken was even older than he looked, though I didn't find that out until later. He had longish white hair, never combed, and snow-white stubble on his cheeks. Eyebrows like fireworks shooting off. Little green glints at the centre of receding eyes, like the lighty-up eyes on a malicious action toy. I was drunk.

'Who you waiting for?' he asked.

'I'm waiting for . . .' – I couldn't remember his name for a moment – '. . . Jonas.'

Chicken reached for the bag again. 'May I?'

'Sure. You know Jonas?'

'The cook, right? Tall one?'

'That's right.'

By the time Jonas came out fifteen minutes later, Chicken had finished off the bottle.

'Happy New Year,' I called to him, as Jonas and I walked away across the parking lot.

'Sure,' he said. 'Go wild.'

'What's his name? That guy.'

Jonas turned and looked.

'Who, him? That's Chicken.'

Like I said, to Chicken, I was transparent as Scotch tape.

'How long you been working here?' he asked me one day. He'd shuffled over on a break, to the fresh flowers section where I was manning the counter.

'About a year. Why?'

'No reason. Why do you act like you're happy all the time?'

'Excuse me?'

'You're always smiling – gets on my nerves.'

I laughed. 'Sorry it bothers you. Just a happy sort of girl, I guess.'

Chicken snorted. 'Uh-huh. And I designed the Brooklyn Bridge.'

After I'd gotten to know Chicken a little better, it wouldn't have surprised me if he'd made out he had designed the Brooklyn Bridge.

I changed the subject. 'You just started a couple months ago, huh?'

'Nope. Wrong again. I've been working here, on and off, about fifteen years. Just in the winter, though. Last year I missed it, worked all through my other job.'

'What's your other job?' I asked. I imagined he was

going to say something like maybe driving a truck, or some kind of farm work.

'I work in a circus.'

'A circus?'

'That's what I said.'

'That's not what I expected you to say.'

Chicken laughed, and then started coughing, which is what he always did whenever he laughed. 'Yeah. Fucking conversation-stopper, that one.'

'What do you do? In the circus.' I had this vision: Chicken's spindly body in a pair of shiny tights, hanging from the trapeze.

'I'm a canvas man.' He was still laughing, coughing and hacking his lungs out, as if he himself found this ridiculous. 'I fix the canvas. The big top.' He was coughing so much by now he had to bend over. Maybe he was sick.

'Do you need a drink of water?'

He shook his head.

'Why do you have to fix the big top? What happens to it?'

Chicken sighed, coming down from his coughing. 'Shit. Hell. My lungs are going to hell. It gets ripped up by rocks and stuff on the ground, that's what happens, when they're laying it out. And when it's up, the wind works at it.'

'And you work for the same circus every summer?'

'Not the same circus necessarily. But I've been with the same one for the last two years, and I'm going back again this year. Pay's good, free food, owner's all right – so I'll be back. Unless something happens, of course.'

'What could happen?'

He looked at me like I was an imbecile. 'Shit, girlie,

94

what do you mean? Anything. Anything could happen. At any time.'

'Oh. Right. I guess that's true.'

'What about you? What are you planning?'

'When?'

'This summer.'

I shrugged. 'Nothing special. Maybe Jonas and I will get away for a few weeks, go to the beach. I haven't really thought about it.'

Chicken got out a cigarette, but he must have known he sure as hell couldn't light up in this place. He got one out anyway, and stuck it dry between his chapped lips.

'Which one's Jonas?'

'Jonas? The cook. The head cook.'

'Oh yeah. The one with the girlfriend.'

I laughed. 'Yeah. Me. I'm the girlfriend.'

'You are?' Chicken grinned at me. His smile was like a ferret's, and his teeth were whiter than his skin. 'I'm playing with your head, girlie. Don't worry about it.' He put his plastic cup on the corner of my work surface and shuffled out the exit doors.

'Those things will kill you!' I called after him, but I don't know if he heard. A lady hovering over the calla lilies looked up and smiled indulgently.

'He's quite a character, isn't he?' she said.

'Yes.'

'Does he wander into the store a lot?'

'He works here.'

'Oh. Goodness. I thought he was a . ...'

A bum, you thought he was a bum, lady, except you'd never say that. If you ever finished the sentence, you'd say something like homeless person, or unemployed, but what you'd really be thinking is bum.

She bought her lilies at six dollars a stem and left.

'What's the story with Chicken?' I asked Jonas that night, as we were driving home in the big old station wagon he'd brought so he could load it up with fresh produce from the farmers' markets. The interior smelt of green wet, of lettuces and mud, the inside of pea pods.

'Chicken?'

'Yeah. He told me he's been working at the store for years. Is that true?'

'I think so.'

'What's the deal? He just gets re-hired every year?'

'Well, he's Mary's brother-in-law, for one.'

Mary was the original owner of the store. She'd started it in 1965, and now there was a whole bunch of these stores all around the Southeast, so she'd sold up and retired. She still lived locally, and she came in and shopped. At the start of the baseball season she'd throw in the ball for the first staff game, stuff like that.

'Mary's brother-in-law? Who's Mary's sister?'

'She's dead – a long time ago, I think, just after the first store opened. Somebody told me all this once, but I can't remember. I think it was something weird, like hepatitis, that killed her.'

'And ever since, Chicken's come back every winter?'

'I guess so. He wasn't around much when they were married, I don't think. He's always worked in circuses.'

'Where does he stay? At Mary's?' Mary lived in a big farmhouse, about ten miles out of town. We'd all gone there for a staff picnic last June.

'At Mary's? No way – don't you know where Chicken lives?'

'No.'

'He lives in the parking lot. In that red camper van.'

'In the van? I thought someone had abandoned that thing.'

Jonas laughed. 'No, that's the Chickenhouse. You should get yourself invited over some time – we'd all like to see inside it.'

When we pulled in the driveway at home, Elizabeth's little white Honda was parked next to C.J.'s truck. Funny how things like that can put you off for life. I'll never buy a Honda.

'We should have him over for dinner some time, don't you think? Chicken? I mean he must get sick of take-outs.'

Jonas turned the ignition off and looked at me. 'Sure. If you want to.' He put his hand on my knee. 'That's a kind thought.'

I opened the car door and slid away from his hand. 'I didn't mean it as a kind thought.'

At first, Chicken turned the offer down flat.

'Why would I want to go hang out with a bunch of out-of-date hippies?'

'We're not hippies – do I look like a hippie? Just because we share a house? I'd think you'd be the last person to criticize people's alternative living arrangements, anyway. What's the big deal? There'll be free food. Wine, beer. All you have to do is come, eat and drink, and then you can leave.'

'How old are you?'

'What? I'm twenty-one.'

'Twenty-one. Legal in every state.'

'Well, it depends what I get up to, I guess.'

'Where do you come from?'

'The Midwest.'

'What, Chicago? Detroit?'

'Not far off.'

Chicken nodded. 'I've probably been through your town some time, with one circus or another.'

'Maybe.'

'Do you want to know what *I* was up to when I was twenty-one?'

'Sure. Tell me.'

'I was in Morocco. 1926. Shooting at Frenchmen.'

'Shooting at Frenchmen? Why?'

He shrugged. 'Because they paid me to – the Moroccans, that is. Then I went to China, same sort of deal.'

'What, to shoot at people there?'

'Yeah. When I wasn't stealing things. A lot of jade and ivory in China back then, just lying around on the ground.'

Chicken was like me, and a liar can't fool a liar. But also like me, I suspected there were little bits of truth woven into every fabrication. Impossible to tell which was which, really.

'Wow – I guess I haven't lived yet. What am I doing here stocking shelves, when I could be shooting Frenchmen for a living? On the other hand, surely there are a few Frenchmen around here I could start practising on.'

Chicken waved his hand at me and started to walk away, down the dry goods aisle.

'I'm sorry – hey, come back! Come on, won't you come to dinner? Won't you accept my kind invitation?'

He kept on walking. 'I'll come. Just make sure there's plenty of free food. And none of this vegetarian crap.'

'OK. I will.'

It was the first social thing I'd organized in the house, so maybe that's why the attendance was so good. Maybe some of them got the wrong story and thought Chicken was my dad or something, that it was my dad was coming to visit. Of course, Elizabeth was around when I was asking people about their Saturday night plans, so I had to include her. It ended up becoming this whole-house activity, inviting over the interesting old guy.

'Wouldn't he like to stay the night?' asked Laura. 'We could make up a bed in the living room – it must be cold in that van.'

C.J., at the sink washing dishes, coughed. 'More like he'll be dying to get back to that van. Some people aren't used to so much company.'

I smiled at C.J.'s back. 'Yeah, I think he's pretty happy where he is. No-one should treat him like a charity case. That's not why I asked him over.'

'No, no, of course not, I would never do that. He's actually living a very responsible life, it sounds like, ecologically speaking. How old is he, anyway? Jonas said he's ancient. He doesn't have any family to look after him?'

I wondered if Laura's dead mother had possessed the same organizational leanings. Being sick with cancer must have been extra hard for someone like that.

'I don't know – I don't think so.'

'Do you want me to pick up some beer?' C.J. asked, dish-washing done, truck keys in hand.

'Yes. Lots. I'll come with you.'

When I was a teenager, Barbara and I dreamed up this imaginary society called the Tripping Society. We used to take acid together – in fact, she was the only person I ever took acid with – and the Tripping Society came out of the experiences we had under the influence. Which were rare and surprising. So surprising at times that we decided there had to be people out there, calm, dark-suited undercover types, who took care of everybody's trips, by placing in front of those under the influence the more curious wonders of our world: a real fur coat made of orange fur never seen on any living creature; a cat called Timmy who when commanded, would put himself to bed in his basket, even pulling a little tartan blanket over his hind legs; a house built to look exactly like a ship in the middle of a city block, hundreds of miles away from water; a man in a pink suit, running down the street singing in Polish or German or some Slavonic language, who suddenly turns 180 degrees and puts his face five inches away from yours, then whispers 'Bon Voyage'. These were all things Barbara and I experienced under the influence – the cat was in a bar downtown – and we felt sure they were being provided by somebody for our viewing pleasure.

There were unpleasant things too. I remember travelling on a freeway once, under the influence, and seeing this teenager's face in the window of the next car: hazel eyes, pale white skin with a few faded freckles left over from a more innocent age. He smiled at me – it was as if we were alone in the same room – and then suddenly, if suddenly can happen in slow motion, he sort of floated away, as the car he was in with a whole lot of other teenagers fishtailed on some ice and started to plough across the central verge on the freeway into oncoming 60 m.p.h. traffic. He had been smiling. Barbara, who was in the front seat, didn't see, and Barbara's mum, who had picked us up from the museum, just kept on driving.

I didn't look back, because I knew it wasn't safe. Not while I was tripping.

I didn't do drugs now – hadn't since I left home, not since I'd been on my own – but I still kind of believed in the Tripping Society. Those people that came along at just the right moment, for better or for worse. I guess other people just called it Fate. Were these encounters organized by someone? Probably not, of course not. But life is weirder than fiction, that's for sure. The night of the dinner, as I sat there letting everyone battle it out, I had the feeling that the Tripping Society had sent along Chicken.

Jonas made vegetarian chilli, and we all sat around the long kitchen table. The whole house: Jonas, me, Peter and Cindy, Laura, C.J. and Erik, Stevie, and Elizabeth, who'd bought flowers for the table. Only Mary was missing, away for the weekend, visiting a friend in Boston. At first, Chicken was as good as his word, shovelling down chilli – no-one told him it was vegetarian – like he was at an as-much-as-you-can-eat buffet in a Ponderosa, unable even to grunt yes or no when someone asked him a question. People thought it was endearing, this hungry homeless man. I felt ashamed of myself, but part of me wished he'd bothered to wash up a little bit before he came, maybe just his hands, which looked like they were covered in a fine layer of wet sand and oil. I didn't want people to be able to pigeonhole him quite so easily. And it was this embarrassment on my part, as if Chicken was my trained seal or something, that got me saying things I never should have. I guess I'm not a natural-born hostess.

Stevie was all over-excited at meeting a circus performer, and he kept asking Chicken lots of questions about it all. Stevie was the most talkative of any of us, anyway, and he had made me feel welcome when I first arrived. Chicken wasn't going to budge an inch, though. In fact, he didn't even answer, and Stevie would glance at me and then ask the question again more loudly, presumably thinking Chicken must be a little deaf. I kept my head down, close to my bowl of chilli.

'Chicken,' said C.J.

To my surprise, Chicken answered right away, though he was still putting food into his yap. 'Yeah?'

'Stevie asked you a question.'

Chicken turned and looked at Stevie. 'Oh yeah?'

'Yes. Hi. I was just wondering what it is you do exactly, in the circus?'

'Work like a fucking coal-miner,' said Chicken, and went back to his chilli.

'Chicken's a canvas man,' I said, like some kindergartener at show-and-tell. 'He sews the canvas of the big top, when it gets rips in it. He has this hat that he wears with a load of waxed cord wrapped around it where the hatband would usually be, and a big needle stuck through the brim.'

I hadn't actually seen this hat, but Chicken had told me about it.

'Wow.'

'How interesting.'

'That's great.'

Everyone jumped on this little titbit of information, like conversational vultures.

'Where did you learn to do that? I mean the craft of it,' asked Cindy.

I didn't know the answer to that one, but luckily I didn't have to – apparently Chicken could hear Cindy's questions as easily as C.J.'s.

'I learned it on a boat coming out of Sweden, going

102

to Portugal, in 1937. I'd got stuck in Sweden, and this boat was the first step to getting home. An old-fashioned sailing ship, square-rigged. They took me on, taught me all about it, patching sails, splicing, the lot. I learned everything I needed on that one journey.'

'Sounds like you've done a lot of travelling,' said Jonas. Chicken started sucking back his beer and didn't say a word, or even turn his head that way. Jonas was one of the undead.

'Yeah, he's been all over.' Me again. 'Morocco, China, Mexico.' Shit. As soon as I said it, I knew what people would ask, and I saw where this could go to, and I wanted to take it back. Please let Stevie ask about it, or Jonas. Or Elizabeth, at whom Chicken had taken one long look – as she greeted him, reaching out her hand and saying 'Welcome to the house' in that pure, sweet tone she always used – then snorted and turned his back to check out what was cooking on the stove-top. I had to admit he had a nose for bullshit.

Unfortunately it was Cindy who asked. 'My goodness, what were you doing in all those places? Working?'

Chicken reached for a hunk of Jonas's home-made garlic bread and another beer, and grinned at Cindy. 'Yes, ma'am. I was working.'

Don't ask, don't ask. 'What sort of work?' she asked. Cindy was a Quaker.

'Shooting people.'

In a matter of seconds, everyone got so quiet you could hear the sound of Chicken's beer in his throat.

'Did you say shooting people?'

'Uh-huh.'

'You were in the army?'

'You could call it that, I suppose. Pretty dis-organized outfit, though.'

103

'In which war? Gosh, I'm not very clear on my history, I guess.'

'Whichever war was going, sweetheart. Whoever had the cash to pay me – I've never been picky. Moroccans getting out from under France. Pancho Villa's men in Mexico. Spanish Civil War, fighting for the Moors, though I ended up in prison for most of that. China, Saudi Arabia, same deal, shooting at somebody or other's enemies. Everyone's got enemies, don't they? It was a pretty steady line of work; I tried not to get too involved in the politics. In between, though, I worked circuses, in Europe, back home, wherever I could. Of course, the money for fighting was a lot better, five hundred, sometimes a thousand a week. Which was a fortune back then.'

Nobody said a thing. Chicken knew exactly what he was doing. For the first time since we'd sat down, he stopped feeding his face and sat back in his chair. He looked around at all of us, no-one really looking at anyone else, and no-one eating any more, except Erik, and no-one saying a word, then he tipped his chair back and started doing his laugh-cough thing, chuckling and hacking up bits of God knows what, which he wiped away from his mouth with a chilli-stained thumb.

C.J. began clearing people's plates. Jonas, looking tense around the shoulders, got out his pouch and started to roll a cigarette.

'Why are you laughing?' asked Elizabeth.

Chicken smiled at her. 'Because you all look like a bunch of stunned bunny rabbits.'

'Well, murdering people for money as a career choice is not something we run into very often.'

'Uh-huh, I know it, that's why I'm laughing. You all

kids don't have a clue, about the way things are for some people.'

'Excuse me? We don't have a clue? My uncle died in Vietnam.'

Chicken scratched the back of his neck. 'Your uncle? Well, he was a poor sucker. I wouldn't have gone over to that war if they'd offered me a *million* a week. Fucking jungle – as good as committing suicide, trying to kill anyone in that mess. Lucky thing I didn't need the money by then – came back in the thirties and bought bonds, a couple shares of US Steel, for peanuts, and what do you know, the war comes, I'm rolling in it. And I've been comfortable ever since. Pretty comfortable, thank you, relatively speaking.'

He burped, and if I'd been the director of this television drama, I'd have told the actor the burp was overkill.

'How nice for you,' said Elizabeth. She said it quietly, but it was interesting to hear a timbre I hadn't heard before in her voice, a *touche de bitch*, veiny, like the pepper in a peppermint candy. Mind you, she had every reason.

'Well, yup, it is. It is nice. Because the thing you don't understand, sweetie, what none of you all can understand, is that I wasn't doing the work for fun. I wasn't doing it for kicks. I was doing it for the money – and I couldn't have got that sort of money anyway else. The only things I knew how to do back then were ride horses a little, and shoot things. So, so what if I took a job that paid me to do those things? That's what I did. And y'all can judge me from now to forever 'cause it's easy to do so, but ain't none of you come a hundred miles near the poverty line, I figure' – his eyes flicked over to Erik, who was sitting there staring at his hands in his lap – 'and especially not you, little miss saint.'

Elizabeth looked like she was about to cry.

'Hey,' said Jonas, standing up and pushing his chair away from the table. 'Lay off.' He took a drag off his roll-up and crossed his arms in front of his chest. 'So you're telling me being poor gives you an excuse for killing people? Bullshit. Look at Gandhi, look at Jesus. Hell, look at half of the world living near starvation, the ones who aren't going around murdering other people—'

'They probably don't get the opportunity – and I bet a lot of them would do it if they figured they could buy a bit of bread for their family with the money they'd get. As for Jesus and that Gandhi guy, I never said I was a saint.'

'And what family did you have to feed?' said Elizabeth. 'Who were you doing it for? It's not like you were doing it to feed your wife and kids – you only had yourself to worry about – you didn't—'

'You don't know duck shit about my life, honey.'

'Don't patronize her,' said Jonas.

At this point it was as if the sound got turned off, and I just sat there watching the faces moving around, Elizabeth's face, oval goodness like a Nilla wafer, Chicken's face, stratified, grainy, like the cut-open side of a cliff, and Jonas's, the earnest leading man. But just like when you turn down the sound on your television you get a whole different perspective on the acting performances, on this occasion, as I sat there watching them arguing, watching their expressions passing through all types of weather, the words they chose, and their emotions bending their mouths into particular shapes and angles, their eyes squinting and

106

flexing, I saw that Chicken was telling the truth, as brutal as it was, and Elizabeth and Jonas were not. Chicken knew things they couldn't know, and he was telling the truth about these things. Elizabeth and Jonas didn't know about these things – they knew about other things – but they acted like they knew about everything. And the biggest thing they didn't know, or they were pretending not to, but which was pretty obvious from where I was sitting: Elizabeth and Jonas were made for each other.

I gave Chicken a ride back to the store. I told Jonas I felt kinda responsible for inviting him over, and so I couldn't just give him the cold shoulder, and Jonas understood.

'Sure,' he said. 'You're probably a better person than me for it. "God in all of us", right? I just can't handle it.'

'It's OK.'

What Jonas didn't know was, I felt like Chicken was the first real friend I'd made in a while.

'This is a nice little car,' said Chicken, as we drove off. I knew he wouldn't talk about what had just happened. 'Done a lot of miles?'

'Some. It got kinda parked for a year, in New York.'

'New York City?'

'Yeah.'

'I lived there in the forties. When I had a lot of money.'

'Uh-huh.'

I pulled into the empty parking lot in front of the supermarket and stopped the car.

'That was pretty fucked-up,' I said, almost to myself, really.

'Aw, forget it. It's not like it'll keep them up at night. So was letting you give me a lift home sort of like turning the other cheek?'

107

'Shut up.'

Chicken opened his door and hauled himself out. 'You staying?' he said, leaning back into the car. 'For a nightcap?'

'Where? In the van?'

'Where else? What, you scared? Think I'm gonna jump on you?'

The van was spray-painted sort of salmon-coloured, except in places where the rust had turned it copper. When Chicken slid back the side doors, I expected chaos. It wasn't too bad. A single mattress on the floor, sheets a little crumpled but they looked clean. Sure there was a lot of equipment stacked around, tool-boxes, cables, but it also had a kind of homely feel, with a wicker armchair in one corner, sagging to one side, and a portable TV opposite, sitting on top of a fancy antique coffee table.

'Where'd you get that?' I said, pointing at the table.

'My mom.'

Chicken pulled a cassette tape out of a cardboard box near his bed and put some tunes on. Bluegrass music, which was pretty much all Chicken ever listened to.

'What do ya fancy?'

'To drink? I dunno – what do you have?'

'Whole store's worth.'

'Whole store's worth?'

Chicken smiled and reached for a key hanging off a hook in the dividing panel between the driver's seat and the back. 'Come on.'

I followed him across the lot and we went round to the delivery entrance where he let us in with his key. 'Best leave the lights off,' he said, 'but the cold stuff's in the fridge and they're all lit up in there.'

'You're a thief.'

'Nah – my family built this store. And you don't think they pay me to work here, do you? Not a cent. Mary and I got a little understanding going.'

Chicken took a six-pack of Miller and I got a few cans of raspberry soda because I didn't really feel like drinking any more. I wasn't entirely sure I should relax.

'Have a seat,' said Chicken, back in the van, and he took the mattress while I settled down on the iffy wicker seat. We just sat there, drinking, not talking, and Chicken seemed fine with that. He was lying back, listening to the music, I guess. Along the whole length and width of the side wall, opposite the sliding door, ran a collage of taped-up pictures, photographs, large and small, scraps of paper, newspaper articles, letters, bottle tops, postcards.

I hadn't received a postcard in a while – the latest one had come on my birthday, a picture of a big pink cake with burning candles and Happy Birthday preprinted onto the back. That had been the only message, which came as a relief, because I'd been dreading the next probing question.

'What's all this on the wall?'

Chicken raised his head and looked where I was looking. 'Memorabilia.'

'Is this your circus?' One of the largest photographs was of a large big top, striped in purple and red, with a peaked top and flags sticking out of the roof.

'That's it,' said Chicken, without looking up this time. 'At least that was it the last two years. We're getting a new top this season.'

'A new top?'

'Sure, they don't last, you know, more than one or two seasons.'

'Who makes them?'

'Guy called Leaf made that one.'

'Leaf?'

'Yup – lives in Sarasota, Florida. He makes most all of the good tops you see around.'

'All by himself?'

'Uh-huh.'

'How long does it take him?'

'Hell if I know.'

A lot of the pieces of paper stuck up on the wall were maps, or just typed directions to a place, with handmade drawings along the margins.

'What's your circus called?'

'It's not my fucking circus.'

'You know what I mean.'

'Sherman Brothers Circus. There's a poster up there somewhere, if you use your eyes.'

'Oh yeah. So when will you be taking off again?'

'To the circus? March – meant to be at winter quarters end of March, but I might take off a little early. I wanna visit my daughter.'

'Your daughter?'

Chicken kicked a girlie magazine off the mattress to make more room and put his feet up. 'That's what I said. I always try and get in a visit, either end of the season.'

'Did she grow up around here?'

'Nope. Look, you're talking too much – I wanna get some sleep. Get going.'

I laughed and kept looking at the gallery wall. There were a couple of matt-framed photographs up there; looked like they'd been taken in a family photographer's studio. I guessed one of them would be his daughter.

Chicken sat up. 'I'm not kidding, girl. Get lost.' He picked up a dirty T-shirt and threw it across the van at me. 'I'm too tired for any action. Give it up. Go home.'

When I got back to the house everyone had gone to bed, including Jonas, but he was still awake.

'You OK?' he asked, in the dark.

'Sure.'

'What'd you talk about?'

'Not much. I got to see the inside of his van.'

Jonas turned around and I moved into his arms.

'How about Elizabeth?' I asked. 'Was she OK?'

'She's OK. She's staying over, in Stevie and Mary's room – she didn't feel like going home by herself.'

He started kissing me, and despite feeling pretty alienated, I couldn't resist. After he'd come, the weight of his body felt like a comforter. If only I could have just pulled up the covers and never come up again. I traced my fingers across his back, along his shoulders and arms, took a deep sniff of his neck.

'Jonas?'

'Yes?'

'You know when I was in New York?'

'Uh-huh.' He was falling asleep.

'I used to have sex with men there.'

Jonas didn't say anything.

'Did you hear me?'

'What?' He turned his head my way. 'Sorry. I was dozing off.'

'That's OK. You know when I was living in New York?'

'Yes?'

'I made my money having sex with businessmen. Well, some of it. Actually I didn't make very much, because it was all pretty badly organized.'

111

Jonas rolled onto his back and laughed. 'Are you making this up?'

'No. Why would I make it up?'

He turned on the bedside light; he was still chuckling. 'I want to see your face – I still can't tell if you're kidding or not.'

'I'm not kidding.'

He was leaning up on one elbow, looking down at me. He frowned a little and went very still. 'So why are you telling me this now? Are you sick?'

'What, do you mean do I have AIDS or something?'

'No, I didn't mean that. I meant I'm worried about you. That's a pretty intense thing to have gone through – are you starting to remember it all of a sudden? You can tell me.'

'I never forgot about it. It's really not a big deal, to me. But I thought it might be for you.'

'I think it's probably more of a big deal than you want to admit.'

'No. Really. It's not.'

Jonas sat up on the edge of the bed, ran his hands through his hair. 'This is freaking me out a little bit, Meg. It's like Chicken got to you. Are you trying to be tough or something? This isn't you. I mean, I know you – this is just some sort of weird act, for somebody's benefit.'

'It's for nobody's *benefit*, believe me. Anyway, forget it. Forget I said anything. I shouldn't have. Just go back to sleep.'

'Just go back to sleep?' He stood up and walked over to the window. 'I can't just forget it. Is it true about the sex for money or not?'

'No. It's not true. You were right, I was just trying to shock you; I just wanted to see how you'd react. I'm

112

sorry. It was Chicken tonight. I was a little weirded out by this whole evening.'

Jonas looked at me hard, as if he was trying to see inside me, then he got back into bed, with an air of bravery like he was getting back into an unheated swimming pool. 'Yeah, well. So were we all.' He took hold of my hand. 'Are you feeling insecure about anything? Elizabeth was saying tonight she's worried you've always felt like an outsider here. In this house.'

I took my hand away and lay back on the pillows.

'She said that?' I shut my eyes. 'Yeah. I'm probably a little insecure still. That's probably it.'

Jonas turned off the light and took me back in his arms. 'You don't need to be insecure. I love you. Everyone thinks you're great.' He kissed my shoulder when I turned the other way. 'You know, even if that stuff is true, the stuff in New York, even if it's true, you don't need to worry. No-one would judge you here, for your past.'

'Thanks. That's good to hear.'

When I asked Chicken if I could go with him, in March, in his salmon-coloured van, he laughed and said, 'Sure, if you pay your own way.' He didn't seem that surprised.

Circus Land

'So where do you want me to drop you?' asked Chicken, a few miles down the road.

'Drop me?'

'Well, I'm not planning on adopting you or anything. Don't you have somewhere to go?'

'Nowhere I want to.'

He laughed and spat out the open window. 'You're a real long-goner, aren't you?'

'A what?'

'A long-goner. Hank Williams song. Long-gone daddy, long-gone baby, long-gone girl. Bet you never say goodbye. Bet your family has no idea where you are.'

Just to prove him wrong, somewhere in Tennessee, I started trying to write a letter to James.

Dear James, I am running away to the circus. How could I explain? *Dear James, Heard from Mom lately?* Not likely. *Dear James, How was graduation?* James was eighteen now, since February, and I hoped he was having the most normal adolescence ever. I wanted him at junior proms, hanging around with the guys, in the car park after football practice, kicking a hackensack, cracking the books after supper because he was

114

going to attend the university of his choice, kissing a sweet sixteen-year-old who tells him she loves him for ever. I knew he wouldn't be this way, though. He was probably the kind of kid who got home from school, closed the door to his bedroom and wasn't seen again until the morning.

'What are you going to do for money?' asked Chicken.

'I don't know exactly. What about the circus? Do you think there'd be any jobs going?'

'The *circus*! Jesus Christ. What sort of experience you got? It's not like some scout club you can just walk up to and join. Circus families been in the business for generations and they don't like outsiders. What do you think you're gonna do in a circus?'

'Sell popcorn?'

Chicken snorted. 'Hoxie usually gets some of the young kids doubling up on that – about anybody can do it. Don't worry,' – I must have looked sort of worried – 'I'm not gonna drop you in the middle of nowhere. I suppose I'll have to take you along to Mary's.'

'Mary's?'

'My daughter. I told you I was planning a visit.'

Chicken's daughter lived in Lawton, Oklahoma. When we got about an hour away, Chicken called her up from a phone booth. Her number was on one of the pieces of paper taped to the van wall.

'I don't want to get in your way, Chicken. Why don't I just wait in the van? Or go get a sandwich somewhere. You can drop me off in town.'

'You can get a sandwich wherever you want. I'm meeting her in a Denny's.'

'Oh. With her kids?'

'Kids are in school – guess I didn't give enough notice.'

'Well, we can – I mean you can stay for a while, can't you? If you want to. I can take off on my own.'

When we got to the Denny's, Mary wasn't there yet, so we sat at the counter together and I ordered a milkshake.

'I still think I shouldn't be here,' I said.

'Will you stop your whining! Christ. It's just my daughter! I'm not meeting the fucking Queen of England! Get lost, if you want to. Just stop yakking about it.'

I went and got a free *USA Today* from the stand by the door and hid myself behind it. When his daughter came in, Chicken acted like he didn't know me, and I played right along. Mary had red hair, sort of medium-length – maybe Chicken's had been red once – and she gave Chicken a big hug when she got to him, which I hadn't exactly expected. I guess I'd been counting on dysfunction.

'Why don't we get a booth, Dad?'

'Sure,' he said, and they let the hostess take them to a horseshoe-shaped booth at the back. I tried not to look over too often, but when I did, things looked happy enough. Mary got out some photos; at one point she was writing down something Chicken was telling her. Chicken didn't look transformed by the situation; he still had pretty much the same sardonic expression, but he laughed a couple times and they shared a piece of pie at the end of the meal, one plate, two forks, which I figured someone wouldn't do with somebody they resented. My dad and I used to go out to breakfast sometimes, on Sunday mornings when neither one of us could face church. We never shared pies, though.

I'd start making a racket, in the car going to church, and then Dad would lose his temper, or pretend to, and when we got to Saint Boniface's, he'd sigh and say to my mother: 'Look, I can't take this. I'll drive her around till she calms down – you go on inside with James. No point all of us missing church.' Then we'd head off to the International House of Pancakes where I could have blueberry syrup if I wanted, while Dad read the paper and smoked.

When Mary got up to go, I thought Chicken and she would walk right past me, but they stopped. I wasn't sure if I was meant to look up from my Grand Slam breakfast plate or not.

'This is Meg,' said Chicken, standing by my stool, 'or that's what she likes to call herself. Meg, meet my daughter. Mary.'

'Hi. Pleased to meet you.'

'Pleased to meet you. My dad's giving you a lift, huh? Don't let him bully you.'

'OK.' Mary's dress was made out of seersucker, a blue and green checked pinafore, with a white short-sleeved T-shirt underneath. She looked like a kindergarten teacher. I bet she was a kindergarten teacher.

'Are you thinking of joining the gypsies then?'

'The gypsies?'

'The circus.'

'Oh. Well, I don't think there's a job going, it sounds like.'

'What?' Mary swatted at Chicken's shoulder. 'Oh, don't let him stop you. I'm sure they'll think of something. Last time my kids visited, Hoxie had them hocking programmes before they knew what hit them. Child labour, I called it.'

'Thanks for the tip.'

'Sure. Well, see you, Dad. If you want to come for Thanksgiving, it'll be fine, but Mom's coming too, and you have to be nice to her or I'll kick you out, you know I will.'

Chicken mumbled something and put his driving hat back on, a shapeless old fisherman's hat.

'Bye then, Meg. Good luck.' She turned and walked out of the restaurant.

'You finished with that?' said Chicken, looking at my plate. 'I want to get going.'

As he started up the engine, I tried one more time, though I suspected I'd get my head bit off.

'You really sure you don't want to stay any longer?'

'What is your problem, missy?'

'Well, you were only together for about an hour.'

'I'll see her in November. Besides, it's quality, not quantity.' He started to back out of the parking space. 'Quality, not quantity – when it comes to family. You know that by now, don't you? Seems like you must do.'

The only time my mother ever got angry with me was when I ruined the Easter egg hunt. I was seven years old, and instead of waiting for my brother to finish his big-boy pee-pee, I ran out to the back yard on my own and scooped up every single piece of confectionery in about ten minutes. James tumbled out a few seconds later, zipped up, button-snapped, hands washed, eyes wide open, and I was sitting there on the cement step, with chocolate-covered fingers.

I giggled. 'Uh-oh, James. Too late.'

My mom let go of James's hand and slowly walked around the whole yard, just making sure. Then she came over to where I was sitting.

'Have you actually not left him one single piece? Have you act-u-ally done that?'

I started to get this scared feeling. Mom was looking at me with an expression of total disgust, as if I'd made a bad smell or something.

'Well, if he hadn't taken so long—' I started to say, then stopped. Something was building up in her, something I could feel like the pressure in the air outside, before a storm.

She knelt down and put her face right up to mine.

'You are a horrible, *horrible* person! And I don't even want to look at you.'

She scooped up the bewildered James and she was off, crossing the yard like a bee that doesn't know where it's going, wearing the pale yellow Laura Ingalls sunbonnet she wore every Easter, muttering so I could only hear the occasional word. She shifted James from one hip to the other, James who probably wasn't quite sure whether he was crying because he'd missed the Easter egg hunt or because Mom had turned into this Fury and was taking him along for the ride. She went around ripping down all the yellow crêpe paper from the tree branches, kicking at the little green confetti nests she'd laid around the lawn, tearing up the cardboard bunnies stuck to sticks and planted in the lawn.

I sat there on the edge of the cement patio, turned to stone. I couldn't swallow the chocolate in my mouth. I wanted to take it back; I wanted to take it all back. My mother didn't love me any more.

'I'm sorry,' I said, too softly for Medusa mom to hear. I stood up, and without saying a single word went around re-hiding each of the chocolate eggs still uneaten. In the grass, between the roots of tree trunks,

119

only in places where James would be able to see them and find them, easily.

'Mom?' I said, more loudly this time, when I had finished. Now she was standing completely still in one corner of the yard, looking out over the three-quarter-height fence my dad had put up, looking out across the empty field behind our house. She had put James down, and he was quiet, leaning against her legs, his face pressed into the material of her dress. She was just standing there, turned away from me, like she was looking at something out there which had completely captured her attention.

'James,' I whispered to him, kneeling down. 'Come here, James. What's that? What's that, James? In the grass.'

James turned his head against Mom's legs and squinted at me.

'Look, there's an egg there, isn't it? Isn't that one, Jamie, under the tree? A chocolate egg for you?' He looked where I was pointing and began to tentatively detach himself from Mom.

'Where's your basket? Is this Jamesie's basket?'

I went and got his basket. Mom had left it by the sliding glass doors, where it had been waiting next to mine when I'd first come out. I took it over to James and together we started looking for his eggs, hand in hand. I don't remember my mother turning around, but she must have at some point. I mean, she obviously forgave me at some point.

When we drove into the Sherman Brothers winter quarters, basically a big dusty field outside Albuquerque with a few trailers and some farm buildings where they housed the animals, Chicken told me I was on my own.

'What do you mean?'

'Well, I'm not holding your hand. I gave you a lift. If you want a job, you gotta get it yourself. Go and see the lady in that trailer over there. Name's Shirley.'

Shirley was sitting wedged in behind the little banquette at one end of the trailer, with a whole bunch of paper piles spread out on the table in front of her. Looked like credit card receipts, probably ticket receipts, I figured. A phone was resting underneath her right hand, and while we talked she drummed her long, cherry-red nails on it, absently.

'What can I do for you, honey?'

'I was looking for a job.'

'You'll need to talk to Mr Sherman about that – you an artiste?'

'No.'

'Oh. I thought maybe you'd come from one of those circus schools – all sorts of young folk turning up from those circus schools. How'd you find us?'

'I'm a friend of Chicken's. I'm his granddaughter, actually.'

'His granddaughter!?' I figured Chicken would forgive a little lie, if anybody would. 'Never knew Chicken had a granddaughter, or maybe Hoxie did mention it once. Chicken here? Did he bring you? 'Cause we're expecting him.'

'Yes. He did. Ma'am.'

'Well, best thing to do is wait around till Hoxie, till Mr Sherman gets back. Truth is, he's in and out like a sewing needle this week, so I can't really tell you a time when you'll get him for sure. He's picking up an animal right now. Why don't you just sit down and wait? Or did you bring your own trailer with you?'

'No. I didn't bring a trailer. Chicken brought me.'

121

'That's right, you said. Well, whatever you want to do, fine with me – hold on.' The telephone rang and she started taking what sounded like a ticket booking. I looked around for a place to sit least in the way, and got a book out of my bag.

'What're you reading?' asked Shirley, when she'd finished on the phone.

I showed her the paperback. '*Anna Karenina*.' I'd picked it up at a Salvation Army shop in Durham; there was a picture on the front of a woman on a train station platform, half obscured beneath steam from the train's funnels, wearing a dark bonnet, her hands plunged into the roll of a white, furry muff.

'Romance, huh?' said Shirley. 'I like a good romance. Any good?'

'Not bad.'

'Only not bad? I know books like that, where you start skipping ahead about three pages in, trying to find the good bits. Have you skipped ahead yet?'

'Sort of. I've read it a few times actually.'

'Well then, you *must* like it.'

A vehicle pulled up outside and Shirley drew back one of her gingham curtains to see who it was.

'Here he is,' she said. 'Hoxie Sherman. The one you want.'

Hoxie was a fat man in a three-piece suit. He had a stick pin of a stripy hot-air balloon on his lapel. It turned out hot-air ballooning had once been his all-time passion, but he didn't have any time for it now. Also, I figured, at his weight it would be a bit of a hazard. He had a wide, doughy face, with a nose that looked like the start of an elephant's trunk, and hair brushed sideways over his head, from one ear to the other. Most of the time, I would learn, he wore a hat.

'What sort of job you looking for?' he asked, when Shirley had explained.

'She's related to Chicken,' Shirley added. 'His granddaughter.'

'His granddaughter? That so? What's your name?'

'Paul. Well, Pauline, really, but my friends call me Paulie.'

Hoxie shifted his weight and looked me over. He scratched his neck. 'You seem pretty nervous. Am I making you nervous? Are you on the run or something?'

I coughed into my hand and tried to look less nervous. 'No. Chicken brought me.'

'That's right. You said.' Hoxie chuckled. 'First time Chicken's brought anything more than attitude. But don't worry – I'm not going to chuck you out. It's none of my business; *everybody* works here got some sort of secret.' The phone rang again, and Shirley picked it up. 'Why don't you go outside and wait for me? I got something to do, then I'll show you around.'

I climbed down the trailer steps and stood on the dusty ground. I looked across the way at some of the other trailers – there was a woman sitting on the steps of one, reading a paper, big German shepherd at her feet. No sign of Chicken, or his van. I could hear a television going somewhere. God, I hadn't watched TV in a long time; needless to say, TVs had been frowned upon back in North Carolina. Boy, it would have been great to watch a little *Jeopardy* right now. Or an episode of *The Brady Bunch*.

I wondered what Chicken would make of my new name.

About fifteen minutes later, Mr Sherman stepped outside and asked me if I was hungry.

'Excuse me?'

'Are you hungry?'

'Uh, sort of. I mean, I could eat, but I'm not desperate or anything.'

'I've gotta pick up a snake. In Phoenix. Thought it would be a good chance to get to know you better. And besides, it'd be useful to have another body around, in case the snake gets out on route and starts sliding around the inside of the car. Have you ever been to Phoenix?'

'I should probably let Chicken know—'

'Chicken's gone. I sent him to Texas to pick up the new top from the train station in El Paso. He'll probably get back about the same time as us tomorrow.'

Hoxie walked away in the direction of a little hut that stood next to the large generator; keeping the trailers' televisions going, I guessed. I followed him.

'Chicken's gone?'

'Uh-huh. Funny thing is he didn't mention you.' He pulled an enormous bunch of keys out of his pocket, must have been about fifty keys hanging off it. 'Hell, if I can remember which of these little biddy keys fits this padlock. But I should, since I locked it up myself last night. Didn't want anyone stealing my mice.'

After a few false attempts, he found the right key and squeezed himself through the door. It was starting to rain. When he came out, he was carrying a large glass cage with nothing more than chicken wire on top, sort of duct-taped on.

'Little cuties, aren't they?'

Inside the cage there was a whole tribe of white mice, running around, tumbling over each other. 'Appetizers. For the snake. Don't want him getting hungry on the journey.'

124

He laughed, his stomach jiggling the cage around.

In the middle of the night, somewhere over the border in Arizona, Hoxie turned down the radio, on which we'd be enjoying a non-stop assortment of Vegas performers, Frank Sinatra, Tony Bennett, Sammy D.

'You know . . .' he said. 'You awake?'

'Yes.'

'You know, we'll be looking for someone to handle the snake in the side-show. My wife can run you up a costume. Have to have bare arms and legs for it to curl around – it's a boa constrictor. You interested? It's good money. Well, as good as anybody else gets. You're not going to be able to just loaf around you know, if you're planning on travelling with us – most people do one or two jobs at least. It costs a lot to run a circus – you gotta earn your keep.' He took his eyes off the road for a second and looked at me, hard, as if he were making sure I'd heard. 'Snake-handler's the only vacancy going. So what do you say?'

I didn't say anything, for about fifteen seconds. I was trying to think what to say.

'Well, I could give it a—'

Then he exploded, a great pudding of laughter. He could hardly speak for laughing, and he pulled at his seatbelt where it was too tight across his belly. 'Shit . . . your face . . . Oh my Lord . . . as my mother used to say, the look on your face!' He turned the radio back up, but kept on laughing for about a mile.

When we got to Phoenix about 4 a.m., we drove through a fancy suburban neighbourhood. Sprawling, new-built houses surrounded with bright green lawn like cake frosting, right up to the doorways. Hoxie turned the truck into the driveway of one with a forty-foot-long, pink-sided mobile home parked outside. It was a monster, that mobile home, could have been six bedrooms inside, at least.

'What do you think of her?' said Hoxie, meaning the pink thing.

'Pretty amazing. Is it yours?'

'Well, the wife says it's hers. Come on.'

We got out of the truck and walked the two or three steps over to a door in the side of the mobile home. I noticed that the house in whose drive we were parked seemed empty, no lights on anywhere and the curtains left open, but then again, it was four in the morning.

'I'm going to get some shut-eye,' Hoxie said, in a low voice. 'Do you think you can get some sleep on this thing?'

He pointed to a padded bench running along the wall of the kitchenette we'd come into.

'There's a blanket and some pillows over there, I think, in that cupboard.'

'Sure. No problem.'

I'd dozed quite a lot during the ride, figuring I'd better not on the return journey, once the snake was on board. So I wasn't that tired. I curled up in a blanket, read a little, sat there watching it outside getting lighter and lighter. Maybe I'd never see anyone I knew again. This felt miles away from anybody.

About 8.30 the next morning, Hoxie's wife, also called Shirley – funny thing – came out from behind the door through which he had disappeared a few hours earlier. She was dressed in a quilted dressing gown, pastel blue. Her hairstyle was immaculate, the kind of hair only movie stars have when they first get up in the morning.

'Hi there. You must be Chicken's friend.'

I stood up, uncurling from the blanket. 'His grand-daughter – yes. How do you do?'

'That's right, his granddaughter. Pleased to meet you. I'm Shirley, Mr Sherman's wife.' She held out her hand and I shook it. It felt like it had just been moisturized. 'Do you want some coffee?'

'I don't want to be any trouble.'

'It's no trouble. Have you ever worked for a circus before?'

'No. I haven't.'

'Well, we're not usually early risers, unless it's a moving day. Especially not the performers.'

'Are you a performer?'

'Not any more. I used to have a horse act, but my hip got too bad. Arthritis.'

She didn't look old enough to have arthritis: she looked about forty-five.

'There you go,' she said, handing me a mug. 'There's milk in the fridge. I'll see you later. Make yourself at home.' She went back through the door with a little tray, two cups of coffee on it, and the pot.

I didn't see her again though, that day. When Hoxie came out, hair wet from a shower and smelling like aftershave, we got straight in the truck and went off to pick up the snake.

The snake was packed tight in a wooden crate, and we picked it up in the kids' play area of a highway rest stop. The deliverer looked vaguely like an animal guy, I guess – he was dressed in dark green trousers and shirt, with a brown leather belt from which bunches of keys were hanging. He could have been a zoo-keeper.

'She's been fed,' he told Hoxie as he handed over the paperwork. 'Yesterday.'

'I've got some little mice in the truck.'

'Won't need them – they only need to eat 'bout once a week. You've got a qualified snake person on the crew, right?'

'Yeah. Lily Johnson. Her old boa died over the winter – just old age, she figured.'

The guy nodded. 'OK then, if you'd like to sign here and here – how will you be paying?'

'Cash. It's all in here.' Hoxie produced an envelope.

'Make sure you tie it down – I wouldn't want her crashing around back there.'

'Sure thing, Saul.'

When we came out of the back of the truck again, after securing the crate to the inner side bars with some wire cables, Saul was gone.

'OK,' said Hoxie. 'Let's get you back to your grandad.'

I'd never been to a circus. In fact, there'd been a big circus parade in my home town every year and one year at school we'd all been invited to join this after-school clown club run by our woodwork teacher, who was a part-time clown, I guess, on the weekends. At the end of the year, we were all going to get to be in this parade. Well, I didn't last long. One look at Mr Sendik in his white face and outsized red lips sent me scurrying home to Mama, seriously disturbed. And ever since then, I'd associated circuses with depressed-looking animals in urine-soaked cages, and psychopathic clowns that come up out at you from sewer gutters, which is actually a bit from a Stephen King novel. How would Chicken fit in?

Chicken was standing in a group of about six or seven guys when I found him, a few of them leaning against the open back-end of a truck with all kinds of junk spilling out of it, bits of old engines, scaffolding, tent piping, batteries. He was wearing a vest, and his shoulders were bare; his shoulders looked pretty good for an old guy.

'Hey, Chicken – how was Texas?'

He turned around, and right away when he saw me, he began laughing.

'Jeeeezus,' he rasped, 'you still here?' The other men fell silent, standing around, staring, waiting to see how the situation went.

'Hi there, guys,' I said to everybody, wading right in. I knew this was do-or-die, this was me really joining the circus or not. 'I'm Chicken's granddaughter.'

'My what?' Chicken was coughing so much he brushed his lit cigarette against his own arm and it burned him. 'Shit.' He threw the butt-end down onto the grass. 'My granddaughter – oh yeah. That's right, my granddaughter. Well well well, what a surprise, honey.'

'You always said I should come and visit, didn't you? Any time. Mr Sherman says he thinks he can find me a job.'

'Does he now? What do you know.' Chicken put his arm around my shoulder and pulled me in, hard against the side of his body, so it hurt me. 'Gentlemen, I'd like to introduce you to this here my granddaughter – what'd you say your name was again, sugar? I didn't quite catch it, last night in the bar.'

He winked at his friends, and they all cheered.

'There you go, gramps,' said one of them.

'Got yourself a nice little girl,' said another.

I pulled away from Chicken. 'The name's Pauline, actually.'

129

'Pauline? Oh yeah, Pauline, this here's Pauline. Paulie, I've always called her, since she was knee high to a grasshopper.' He gave my butt a slap.

'Hey! Cut it out. Grandad.'

Chicken raised both hands to the sky. 'Sorry. It's just what I *used* to do, you know, when you were a tiddler, running around butt-naked all the time. Didn't bother you then. But I guess you're all grown up now.'

'That's right.'

Some of Chicken's cronies were looking sorta confused now – was I his grandkid or not? Chicken could sure give as good as he got in the lying department.

Hoxie walked by just then, along with Terry, the company manager.

'OK, guys, I think there's a tent to raise,' said Terry. 'Fun's over. Elephants were dying of thirst, Joe, last time I looked.'

'Made it out of jail, I see,' said Hoxie to a gangly blond guy wearing a Sherman Brothers T-shirt and muddy black sweatpants.

'Sure, no problem,' said the man, standing himself upright. 'Got back yesterday. Those guys didn't have a single witness.'

He chuckled, but Hoxie didn't. Hoxie had a panama hat on now and he pulled it down to shade his eyes from the sun. 'Chicken,' he said without looking at Chicken. 'I don't want any trouble with this one. What's she going to do for us, anyway? Could you use an assistant?'

Chicken looked me up and down like I was a piece of cattle he was thinking of buying. I expected him to say no.

'I guess she can help me with the canvas, Mr

Sherman, sure,' he said. 'And a few other things. Round the house.' The men chuckled again.

'We'll get her selling, too, half-time. OK with you, Pauline?'

I nodded, and Terry took a note of this as they walked away.

And that's how I became a canvas girl.

The Sherman Brothers Circus was a three-ring, well-oiled, big-business entertainment source. After the sparseness of their winter quarters – there had been no quarters, basically – I had expected a sort of motley travelling medicine show, with a dwarf riding a Shetland pony and maybe some lady dressed up in a beard. But this thing had been going for almost twenty years, run by Hoxie's uncle, Henry Sherman, before Hoxie took it over five years back. This shit was Disney. There were elephants, a whole pack of them who helped raise the top, and tigers, and an equestrian act. We had a canteen and a short-order grill; we had a laundromat and a sort of circus post office. We had Sid. Sid used to be shot out of a cannon, until he missed the net and broke his back. Now he manned the grill and organized the site parking each place on tour. He was a real little Hitler, a bitter shit. The first time he saw me he spat out a big hunk of yellow phlegm that landed an inch away from my feet, and said 'not *another* one'.

'Not another one' referred to the number of women, ladies and girls who turned up out of seemingly nowhere each season, and then trailed along. Circus groupies. Who knew? Free labour more like. I was totally insulted to be taken for such, but of course nobody knew different. It was clear after about a day, no-one was buying the granddaughter thing, and Chicken made no attempt to keep up his end of the story.

'Why you calling yourself Pauline now, anyway?' he asked. 'Get some work gloves if you don't want to fuck up your fingers.'

I was having my first lesson in sewing and it was hard enough work already, just pushing the thick needle through the bit of canvas Chicken had given me to practise on.

I shrugged. 'Just wanted a change.'

'What was your name? Before? Hell if I can remember.'

'It was Meg.'

'Oh yeah. Sure. Meg. Stupid name anyway. So what did your boyfriend think of you hitting the road?'

'Who, Jonas? He was cool.'

'He know you were leaving with me?'

'No. Fuck.' I sucked at my finger where I'd pricked it.

'So where does he think you're at?'

I didn't say anything.

Chicken laughed.

'He expecting you back?'

Again, I said nothing.

'Shit. Maybe you are circus material.'

Chicken wasn't doing anything to help me, or instruct me – he was just sitting there, parked on a plastic deckchair lounger, next to the van. The van was like some sort of Mary Poppins carpet bag; the things Chicken produced out of there were impressive, including his collection of banged-up garden furniture. I leaned my head down close to examine the stitches I was making. They looked like shit, all loose and wobbly, nothing like the tight little waterproof suckers Chicken made.

'But you better not have your eyes on my job, little girl. I'm not teaching anyone anything, if they're planning to get me laid off.'

Chicken did teach me, though. He taught me everything he knew, which he didn't have to do. He must have thought I was OK, I figured, because he wasn't the type to suffer fools, or to put himself out for people who bugged him. For all his sarcasm and his dirty, drunken ways, Chicken was kind to me. But there wasn't really enough canvas work to go around, and that was obvious, so I got roped into other stuff too, barkering, selling programmes, usher work, all the girlie groupie assignments, which made me hate doing them more than I'd minded if some of the regulars did these things too. I did make sure that if I was going to work I got paid for it, and after a fair bit of grumbling, Hoxie agreed. There was nothing he could do. Chicken told me the crew had unionized themselves last year and now Hoxie didn't get away with as much shit as he used to.

'Sid's the union rep.'

'Sid? Great. Does he believe in votes for women yet?'

I used to wonder how young Chicken thought he could pass for; he probably pictured himself about twenty-five and handsome, instead of pushing on eighty. Because he definitely still had an eye out for the ladies. He even tried it on with me once, pretty early on, but I suppose I had that coming. Since half the crew figured something was going on already anyway. Word had got round we arrived together. And I was still sleeping in his van.

It happened on tour, in Iowa City, and we'd been

getting along pretty well, considering. He was letting me work on the tent now instead of just little bits of canvas, and I knew it made his job easier, however much he complained. It was back-breaking work, leaning over and working on the tent when it was rolled out on the ground, and ladder work did your neck in. It must have been hard on him. On the Friday of that week, he said he knew a great place to eat and, since I'd just got my very first canvas-girl pay packet, a handful of bills in a used envelope, he suggested we should go out and celebrate. The restaurant was called the Iron Horse.

'Nothing like good American food,' said Chicken, opening the door for me.

'Let me order. I know what they do best,' said Chicken.

'Ever had a sloe gin fizz?' said Chicken. 'You'll like it.'

'The lady'd like a steak – medium rare,' said Chicken.

After we'd stuffed ourselves on fried cheese appetizers, pepper steaks, mashed potatoes with gravy, and corn on the cob baked in aluminium foil, we went and sat at the bar adjacent to the dance floor. There was a billiards room too, as they called it, but it was a long wait for the tables so we watched the dancers giving it a go instead. The band was playing easy-listening jazz standards, smoky music, I'd have called it, smoker's music. It made me want to smoke, anyway.

'Bet you don't know how to dance,' said Chicken.

'What do you mean?'

'Younger generation, never dance worth shit – everybody knows that. In my day, any girl you cared to

134

look at automatically knew how to dance. That was the way people got to know each other.'

'So you used to go out dancing, did you? When you were young?'

Chicken snorted, and shook his head. ''Course I did.' He drained his glass and then lifted it to let the bartender know he wanted another.

'Where?' I asked.

'Where what?'

'Where did you go dancing?'

'All over the place – Europe, New York, Chicago, Paris, Lond—'

'All right, all right, Mr Astaire.'

'Shit, you've got no idea. You've never even left this country, I bet.'

'That's right. I still gotta get some shooting practice in, before I go. I guess you used to fit the dancing in between bumping people off.'

He looked sort of confused then – I wasn't always sure Chicken remembered the stories he'd told. Because I felt sorry for him and because I must have been drunk, I told him I wouldn't mind dancing with him, if he wanted to risk it. I wasn't really wearing dancing clothes. I'd changed into some clean jeans, at least, but they were still jeans.

He looked me up and down, and blew some air out between his lips. Then he got off his bar stool and offered me his arm.

It was actually fun for a while, until during a slow number he started to rub along the side of my breast with his thumb, and when he pressed himself against me I could feel an erection through the fabric of the only clean pair of trousers I'd seen on the man.

'Hey. Grandad. Simmer down.'

He backed away, just far enough so he could grin at me, leery-like.

'I'm not your grandad.' We kept on dancing and he leaned in and whispered in my right ear, 'You sure you don't want a little?'

'A little what?'

'A little Chicken? A little Chicken in your mouth?'

I cracked up at this remark, which was a good thing, because I guess I could have been really grossed out or offended. Chicken acted a little offended himself, what with me standing there in the middle of the dance floor, hooting and pointing my finger at him.

'Come on,' he said, dragging me by the arm, 'let's get out of here.'

When we got back to the grounds and stood there outside the van as Chicken looked for his keys – he never left the van unlocked, said you couldn't trust anybody, least of all the people in a circus – I wondered what I should do. Maybe I should sleep out-side tonight; drag my mattress out in the grass. Christ, it was hot enough, and it would be a lot cooler outside of the van. Chicken climbed inside first and went straight to his own bed, threw himself down and assumed the sepulchral sleep position he always adopted. I sort of futzed around, collecting some stuff, clothes for tomorrow, my toothbrush, and then I started trying to drag the single mattress Chicken had found for me out the door without disturbing him. Chicken leaned up on one elbow and asked what in the hell I thought I was doing.

'I thought I might sleep outside tonight.'

'Jesus Christ. I'm not going to rape you, girlie. You're too butch-looking for me anyway – why don't you grow your hair long or something? Or lose some

136

weight. Gain some weight, even – you're skinny in all the wrong places. When you going back to your hippie boyfriend anyway? Old Noah, or Moses, or whatever the hell his name is. Peace-boy. Get yourself back to peace-boy, that's where you belong.'

He lay back down again and we never said another word about it.

It was definitely hard work, the circus, with no monetary compensation. People who'd been working with this outfit for ten, fifteen years, since the start even, some were still on $180 a week. Everyone got depressed a lot, including the animals. A horse trainer once told me her trick with lacklustre ponies: she administered a raw ginger suppository, and it perked them right up. They would lift their tails up as they pranced around the ring. But I never needed a suppository – I had a career now. I felt like I'd been walking in a forest and suddenly I'd found this path and it was good and it was clear and it was my path. I felt like I could tick off at least one area of my life with a giant Biro: CAREER, Tick, canvas girls of the world unite. And for me, all the travelling was rejuvenating. If ever I felt gloomy, it was during a week-long stand, when we were stuck on some muddy lot, and the generator was breaking down, and there was no water, and your clothes never dried out, and the inside of everywhere smelt like damp wool. But as soon as we were pulling out again, my spirits would lift. I was so oddly optimistic, as if the next place we went to was really going to be amazing. As if suddenly we'd pull off the Interstate in Lovett, Texas, and it would be like we were in Bali H'ai or something. When I was travelling, I was sure that everything was for the best;

what I'd left behind was better left, because what I was going towards was what I was meant for.

One day I was paging through my *Saint Days* book and happened on Saint Marina, the patron saint of sleeping children. I remembered how James used to fall asleep so suddenly when he was little, in his high-chair, mid-swallow, or on the rug, his head colliding with the wooden truck he'd been busy pushing across the floor, two seconds before. Right then, right after I read about Saint Marina, I went and found the letter, in my backpack, the letter I'd started writing him in Tennessee, and I finished it before I changed my mind or got too busy and then never got round to it. I didn't tell him about the postcards. I sent him the circus schedule.

He wrote back almost immediately, which frankly amazed me, as if I hadn't really believed in the mail service, as if I'd thought every letter you posted got air-blown to Santa's workshop and had just as much chance of being answered.

Dear Gert, he wrote.

Wow. Working in a circus. This is not what I had imagined you were doing, all these years. It sounds cool. Dad and Janine asked me lots of questions about your letter – I hope you don't mind if I told them that you're OK and what you're doing, well as much as I could. Life here is fine, pretty much the same. As you guessed, I'm graduating this year and guess what? – you won't believe this – I'm going to seminary in September, to become a priest. I know, a little freaky, considering everything, but it's what I want to do. I hope you won't think I'm too weird. It's the helping people side of things that attracts me – think of me like a paramedic, for the soul, I guess, if that helps . . . A paramedic for the soul? Cripes. I didn't think I believed in souls. But I couldn't blame James for anything, or judge him. After all, two of us had walked out on him – he was entitled. Despite the priest thing, he sounded OK; he sounded like a good person, not crazy, not some religious freak. And the letter wasn't written on religious stationery or anything, with little crucifixes all over it; there wasn't a Bible verse printed at the bottom. He didn't even sign off with 'God bless'. He just wrote, '*Keep in touch. Love, James*'.

He didn't mention Mom, but I figured he would have, if he'd heard anything.

So this is what my mother did. A week before my fifteenth birthday, she ran away with the priest from our Episcopalian church. The church was called Saint Boniface's – the patron saint of brewers, which was pretty appropriate as the city we lived in was famous for its beer – and it looked like a Swiss chalet. An A-frame modern building, with wooden beams sticking out at the end of its roof either side. It was on Rural Route 54, just sitting there, near the road, with a gravelly parking lot, and a replica Swiss chalet house next to it where Father Bill lived, my mother's adulterous lover. Father Bill, father of our congregation, cautious supporter of women priests, but not a condoner of homosexuality. Father Bill, father of one toddler and another kid on the way, and husband to lovely Diana, to whom he left a note saying that he had fallen in love with my mother and that he could therefore no longer be a moral leader for this community, and that he hoped Diana could find in her heart, as a Christian, to forgive him. The runaways didn't tell a soul what they were going to do, not even my mother's sister, Ruth. And my mother didn't get in touch with me and my younger brother James just to say she was OK. Not in a few days, not in a week, or a month, not in the next year, or the next, or the next. They must have had a fatal car crash that night, on the freeway leaving town – that's what I used to figure, anyway.

'I can't believe she's done this,' my Aunt Ruth said over and over, for years afterward, shaking her head. 'I wouldn't have believed it of her. If someone had told me that my sister would . . . I would have said "no, not my sister, she'd never . . ."' Aunt Ruth would look up at my father, tears in her eyes. 'I thought I knew her, Don.'

And he'd just shrug every time, and mutter 'Women', exactly like Grumpy the dwarf does when Snow White tries to get all of them to take a bath.

I didn't know why Mom had gone either, and I hated how Aunt Ruth never actually said that she had run off, abandoning us all. She always let it hang in the air like that, dot dot dot. It wasn't as if James and I didn't know all about it, as if we hadn't noticed or something, like 'Gosh, where's Mom? We haven't seen her in a few days!'

I used to wonder where she was, every single day.

But James and I never talked about it. I remember one day, the summer after my mother left. I was sitting on a deckchair in our back yard, looking at the clouds. The clouds were proving so interesting mainly because of the tab of acid I had ingested three hours before. It was very humid, like it gets in the Midwest, and the rubber slats of the chair felt sticky against the back of my bare thighs.

Suddenly I realized James was standing next to me. He was eleven years old, a blue-eyed kid, with a heavy dark-blond fringe that lay flat against his forehead. His breath smelt of chewing gum, the sweet kind.

'Hi, James.' Did my voice sound funny, or was I just imagining it? 'I'm just looking at the clouds – they're amazing today.'

James glanced up at the sky.

'Yeah.' He sat down on the grass. 'Dad's gone to McDonald's. He's getting you a cheeseburger.'

'Wow. Great.' The thought of a cheeseburger was a little alarming, yet sort of fascinating as well.

I noticed James was holding a small red notebook.

'What you got there?'

'I found it under my bed.'

'Yeah? What is it?'

'My Sunday school book.'

James had been in my mother's Sunday school class when she left. Now I had this wild idea that she'd written him a note inside the book. Up to now, there'd been no note. The one she had left Dad the night she went contained nothing but a description of the supper that was in the oven. I knew because I had fished it out of the trash the next morning.

'Oh yeah? Can I see?'

He handed it over. On the pages inside, there were the usual assignments: a carefully copied-out 23rd Psalm, coloured-in pictures of Jesus with his apostles, Jesus with the fish and loaves, Jesus suffering the little children to come. Over a two-page spread, James had cut out pictures of animals from magazines and pasted them into the book in twos, all making their way across the margins to a crayon drawing of the ark.

'You're good at drawing.'

James nodded.

'Maybe you'll end up being a cartoonist or something.'

Mom's handwriting was all over the book. Mom's smiley faces drawn with a pink felt pen, the little gold stars she posted near to especially good work, her little comments. One said 'Great work, sweetie-pie'. I had to stop myself from leaning over to smell the ink.

I closed the book and handed it back to James.

'Neat.'

I didn't know what else to say. I could see that James was about to cry and I was worried about losing it myself, especially because of the acid, and if I really thought about it all right then, if I thought about my little sad brother, I might start sobbing and end up having a bad trip, like you heard about. Then Dad would come home and realize I was taking drugs and I couldn't let that happen. I needed to get out of there. But I didn't want to abandon James, still staring down at the red Sunday school book in his hands. I didn't want to leave him like Mom had. I still couldn't believe it, that she had. It was obviously all some big misunderstanding. For sure.

'Dad's getting me a chocolate shake,' James said and went inside. I heard the television going on.

After I got James's letter, at the circus, I tried to make it a habit to send him something, every other week or so, from wherever we were, postcards mailed in an envelope so that Janine didn't read them first. I did mean to visit back home some time. Maybe one Thanksgiving, after the season, the way Chicken organized it. Give 'em all a shock.

In July, the gangly guy who'd just got out of prison had ended up in prison again, for starting a fist-fight outside a bar, and before I knew where I was, Terry had recruited me into the ring crew.

'You can wear Stanley's old costume – he worked for us last season.' We were standing in the office, Terry pulling red satin trousers and a jacket from a cardboard box next to the filing cabinet. This Stanley must have been a funny shape: the trousers were at flood level on me, while the shoulders stuck out stiff and wide like a scarecrow.

'I don't know, Terry,' I said. I didn't want to do it. I don't like being in front of a crowd of people at the best of times: 'the best of times', whatever that means.

'Nothing to it,' said Terry. 'Just do whatever Tex tells you to do – all it will be is setting up some props along the edge of the ring, and lifting the flaps, occasionally, for the animals. Holding a few ropes steady. Mostly you have to stand around looking like you're enjoying the show. You can do that, can't you?'

'I guess.' Truth was I hadn't really been to the show much, but I wasn't sure if Terry knew this. It might have seemed strange, to be travelling with a circus and after three months, not to have really watched the show, but the people I was hanging around with never seemed to watch it, so I'd taken my cue from them. Besides, I didn't know circus from circus; what did my opinion matter? Obviously I could hear it going on, and I'd seen bits of it through the entranceway when I was waiting with my cotton-candy stand before the interval.

For Chicken and his gang, show-time was play-time. Off-time, fuck-around-time. The one part of the day where they weren't expected to be doing something, the one time there was nobody checking up on them. This was when they got drunk. Or if they did have a job during the show, like selling hot-dogs or standing holding the animals' leads outside the tent, then those jobs precluded them from watching the show anyway. None of them ever mentioned it, or anything else about the performers working the crowds twice a day. It was as if they worked in a parallel universe.

'There's one set of rules for performers and one for us,' said Chicken, when I mentioned this to him. 'That's why you don't get a lot of mixing between the two camps.'

'Not a lot of mixing? What are you talking about? We're practically sleeping on top of each other. Everyone seems to hang out together.'

'Well, there's together and there's together. I mean you'll never catch a performer getting up at 5 a.m. to lend a hand with the tent-down, or cleaning up their own horses' shit-pile in the ring.' He grunted as he cut through a loop of cord. 'And I don't seem to get a lot of time for oil-painting either.'

One of the performers, an aerialist called Manuel, had a penchant for sitting on his home-made veranda in the afternoon, before the first show, surrounded by his potted plants, re-creating scenes in oil of circus life on canvas. He had a lot of time for this, since his act lasted about fifteen minutes, as far as I could tell. I knew this because his trailer was parked near Chicken's van, and I'd watched him pass by in his baby-blue dressing gown during the shows, go into the tent, do his stuff, and come out about that amount of time later. Fifteen minutes twice a day.

'But they take a lot of risks, don't they? And performing in front of all those people – along with the danger – it must be pretty exhausting.'

'Must be,' said Chicken.

Anyway, for whatever reason, I hadn't watched the show much. So I was worried about making a fool of myself. What had made Terry choose me, of all people? Everything went smoothly, until halfway through the first half when I had to stop a man wearing a brown suit and purple running shoes from stepping into the ring. It was during this act where a lady was balancing all sorts of things on her head, like a table with glasses of wine on it and lighted candles, and all of a sudden the ringmaster and the rest of the ring crew started rushing around – except for me, because I didn't know what was going on – looking for this bit of saw-horse, something they apparently needed to prop up a ladder for the lady so she could climb up onto a tightrope still balancing this table on her head. Circus acts are absurd. Of course all I could think was that it was my fault in some way, that I'd forgotten to put this thing somewhere. So when this weird-looking man from the audience got up and sort of wandered forward, offering to help, I was the only one who noticed him, and I thought I'd redeem myself by stopping him from reaching the ring. He was speaking really loudly, in a nerdy voice, with some kind of accent. When I tried to restrain him he did this comedy double-take and then, when I still wouldn't let go, he got up close and whispered, in a totally different voice: 'It's OK. I'm part of the show.'

Oops. How was I to know? The ringmaster, this guy called Tex Hamilton whom I'd never even spoken to, gave me a dirty look when he came over to 'see what the trouble was, folks!' He probably wondered who in the hell I was. Anyway, the show must go on, as they say. What followed was obvious: this 'guy from the audience' turned out to be a complete weakling, and every time the lady performer climbed up and down the ladder, he only just managed to prevent it from becoming completely horizontal, à la Stan Laurel. It sounds pretty cheesy, but the performer was great because he just played it completely straight, with never a whiff of finding himself funny. He really played the tragedy of it, of what a loser he was. To my amazement, as I watched – I completely forgot about being ring crew, I might as well have sat down in the audience – I started getting the hots for this guy. For a clown. I couldn't believe it. But there was something about him. Performers will do that to you. All through the rest of the show, he kept turning up again to 'help' in other acts, equally unsuccessfully. He wreaked havoc on a juggling act. He got tangled up in a deckchair. You felt sorry for him, even though you knew he wasn't real.

Later on, after the show was over, I sort of hung around by the tent, probably waiting to be congratulated by someone or something, just drinking beers with the rest of the ring crew. Chicken wandered by, back from a bar in town.

'How'd she do?' he asked.

'Pretty good—' I started to reply.

'Except when she tried to stop an act from coming on!'

'I didn't know—'

'Only the star clown. She didn't know – practically threw him out of the tent!'

'You should be a bouncer,' said someone else. 'Doesn't know her own strength.'

'Yeah. I reckon she'd take him in a fight, don't you think? Wadda you think?'

'Hey!' I said. 'No-one warned me about him. I didn't

know there'd be someone coming from the audience.'

'So it was you that tried to stop me,' said Matt. 'I wondered who it was.'

All the time we'd been standing around, blowing down the necks of our beer bottles, talking crap, there'd been this skinny guy sitting on one of the musician's stools, a little bit away from the group. He looked sort of depressed, tired. I'd never have recognized him.

'I'm sorry I got in your way.'

'That's OK. It was kind of nice for a change. A little variety.'

We didn't talk again that night. I noticed he didn't much talk to anyone. A few minutes later he stood up, said 'Goodnight all', and when nobody really said goodnight back, he wandered off. Chicken and I went home for a nightcap, to celebrate my introduction to show business.

A few towns later, Peoria, Illinois, I ran into Matt near the Portakabins. Needless to say, there was no toilet in Chicken's van – why would he need a toilet? – so I had to use the customer ones. Matthew didn't see me at first, because it was late, but when I said his name, he turned around and put a hand over his eyes for a shade, as if that would make him see better in the dark.

'Who's that?'

'It's Paulie – Pauline. The one who stopped you from going on.'

He came closer. 'Oh, it's you. Hey, why haven't you done it again? It set me up in just the right mood that night.'

'I haven't been on the ring crew again. Joe's back. Terry bailed him out of prison.'

'Oh, right.' I could tell he didn't know what I was talking about. 'So what do you do normally, then? I mean for the show.'

'I'm Chicken's assistant.'

'Chicken. Who's that?'

'The one who sews up the big top. The guy with the hat?'

'Oh, right. The old guy. He's got an assistant? I'd like an assistant.'

'Well, I – I'm pretty new. There wasn't a lot else I could do.'

'Did you enjoy it the other night?'

'What?'

Matt laughed. 'The show.'

'Oh. Yeah. A lot more than I thought I would.'

'What do you mean?'

'Well – no offence – but I'm not such a circus fan.'

'I'm not either.'

'You're not?'

'Well, not if you mean most of the shows touring around the US calling themselves circuses. Real circuses, yes, I love them, the kind they have in Europe.'

After he said that we just stood there, the chemical smell of the Portakabins sort of destroying any atmosphere.

'I thought you were great, though. Really. Great.'

'That's nice of you to say.'

'I'm not being nice, believe me. I mean, you surprised me. Because I'm *really* not into clowns. To me, most clowns are like kiddie perverts who—'

'Do you want to get something to eat? I thought maybe you'd like to come with me – my treat.'

'You don't have to treat me. But sure,' I shrugged, 'I'd be up for that.'

We walked out of the fairground towards town. It was late, past ten: we'd been starting the second show an hour later in this town, so as to attract a different kind of crowd, according to Terry. I wondered if it was working.

'So, have you got one of those fancy RVs?' I asked this because I couldn't think what else to say. Most of the performers had these souped-up, individualized Elvis-trailers.

'Are you kidding? No. I just left Clown College. But give me another few seasons – I'll be there.' He turned and pointed back to the tent. 'See that truck, parked around the back? You can just see its end sticking out. That's Clown Alley. All-purpose dressing room, props storage, rehearsal space if it's raining, and my house – I'm sleeping in there.'

All alone? That was the question, but I asked another one.

'There's really a college for clowns?'

We ate in a Mexican restaurant, and we downed a pitcher of Margaritas before the food arrived, which I would later learn was totally uncharacteristic of Matthew in the middle of a run of shows. The truth was, off-stage he really wasn't a barrel of laughs, especially if you got him on to the subject of clowning, which of course I did that night, because it seemed a natural thing to talk about. And it's what he liked to talk about more than anything else.

'So what made you decide to go to Clown College?'

Yikes. Get him started. He talked about clowning like he was on some mission. Like it was brain surgery or something, quantum physics. Come on, you're a *clown*, I wanted to say at one point. You're not reducing the Third World debt. He was taking it way too seriously.

Still, I knew I came off that way to people too, sometimes. Too serious. Too intense. So I gave him the benefit of the doubt. Maybe he was just nervous with people, offstage.

After a while, even Matthew ran out of things to say about clowning and the conversation started to choke and stall. He seemed a little distant. I wondered if I was boring him.

'Another pitcher?' This was my circus good-time girl personality. One of the guys. When in doubt, try alcohol.

'No thanks.'

Oh, well. I didn't know what to talk about either.

'Should we head home?'

On the way back, we walked along this fakey riverwalk, with little lamp-posts and old-fashioned iron benches the city had obviously put in as some sort of downtown beautification scheme. Just as we were passing under the arches of a low bridge, the kind of place stage-managed for this sort of thing, the kind of place you get in a Gene Kelly–Audrey Hepburn movie, Matt stepped in my path, took my face between his hands, drew it towards his, and kissed me.

Woo-wee. Quite a long kiss, actually.

Then he let me go and we kept on walking.

'So you like what I do?' he said. 'In the show? You think it works?'

My pelvic floor had turned trampoline, and someone was bouncing up and down on it, but I played it cool. 'I did. Yeah. It was great because you seemed such a loser. I mean, no offence.'

He laughed. 'No, that's it exactly – I love that you get it. He *is* a loser – it's really sad how he tries. I never

150

feel funny when I'm playing it. I feel embarrassed, and humiliated.'

'Uh-huh.'

It was pathetic. He was treating me like one of those twelve-year-old kids who wins an evening with Rickie Lead-Singer-Dropped-Trouser Guy of the Boys R Us band. And, per usual, I was falling right into persona number 152.

We stopped walking again. Of course I knew he was going to be high-maintenance, this guy – it was obvious he was attracted by the ego prop of my admiration. But I didn't mind. It was actually a relief, after Jonas, to be with someone a little off balance, someone needy. Someone who wouldn't have the time, or the inclination, to notice all my problems.

Of course Chicken acted like I'd gone over to the dark side.

'You know he comes from Connecticut,' he said.

'What does that mean?'

'He's a fucking phoney, that's what it means. He comes from this family of bankers, fucking stockbrokers.'

'What have you got against stockbrokers? I thought you had your own little portfolio, in steel?' Chicken looked blank. 'You know, those investments you told me and Jonas about, back in North Carolina? The ones you made after the war?'

'I'm not saying stockbrokers don't have their purpose. Jesus Christ. But you don't see them deciding to come down here and have a try on the tightrope.'

'So you're saying clowns can't be rich.'

'They can get rich – some of the famous ones have, the ones that end up on TV – but they can't start out that way. If you want to understand the circus, that has to be it – there has to be nothing else. You can't have a net. What this guy has is a big fucking net. A million-dollar fucking net. And anyone can see it in his work.'

'Oh, come on. Have you even seen his act?'

'I've seen it. I've seen more than you'll ever see, missie. I've seen enough to know.'

After I started sleeping with Matt, Chicken made it clear I should find somewhere else to sleep in between times. I was cramping his style, he told me – he hadn't got laid for months.

'Sorry,' said Terry, 'dormitory's full, unless you can find someone female to sleep with . . .' Ha-ha, thanks, Terry. 'Tell that clown boyfriend of yours to buy himself a real trailer. He's got the money, doesn't he?'

In the end Shirley, Hoxie's wife, turned up in her long pink trailer, and she offered me a tent their grandkids stayed in when they came to visit.

'Won't they be needing it?'

'They're all at summer camp this year, and they'll be there right up to school starting, so it's yours until the end of this season if you want it. It might get cold come October. You can't depend on the weather by then, no matter how south you are. There's a guy comes round every year – I'm surprised he's not turned up yet – does some great deals on second-hand trailers, mobile homes – you can get them on credit. If you're thinking of sticking with this outfit, you should start saving your pennies. Especially for a young lady,' she looked me over, 'it's not good to be without a place you can lock the door of, if you know what I mean.'

I took the tent and hoped for something better to turn up. Maybe Matt would buy a trailer from this guy and he'd ask me to live with him; maybe Brigid the

152

hand juggler would trip and break her wrist and have to go home to Bratislava, so I could have her place in the female sleeper. Maybe the Tripping Society would provide. Maybe it would be the hottest October in recorded history.

Come September, people started talking about what they were going to do at the end of the season, where they were going to go. Matt already had a job in NYC, working for a circus in a schools education outfit. I wondered if he'd be living in some flashy apartment. I wondered if he'd want me to come along. He still hadn't admitted his background to me, but I was the last person with a right to ask questions. Chicken made it clear I was on my own over the winter, as far as he was concerned. He was going back to North Carolina anyway, I guessed, and that was one place I didn't want to go.

One day I was hanging around near Manuel's trailer, putting a new coat of paint on the frames of the circus parade wagons. Manuel was the aerialist who favoured oil painting, and who liked to grow flowers in little pots in front of his trailer. He beckoned me over to his veranda.

'I hear you're looking for a home,' he said.

I wasn't quite sure what he meant at first. He was wearing his baby-blue dressing gown and the black makeup lining his eyes had blurred a little.

'You mean a trailer?'

He looked around again and beckoned me closer. 'Take mine. It's pretty old, but the engine's fine. She should last a while yet.'

'And what are you going to do?'

He leaned over his little picket fence, because I wasn't standing close enough.

'I'm blowing,' he whispered. 'Tonight, or maybe next week. Soon, anyway. Real soon.'

I didn't get too excited. People were always talking this way around here; I had learned not to take it too seriously. 'Why not stick it out till the end of the season? There's not so long to go now.'

'I've been offered a better job, that's why. With another circus – pay's three times as good, and the rehearsals start next week. In Vegas.'

I could tell he'd been dying to tell someone this. I guess he'd chosen me because I was the closest to a stranger, the person with the least reason to tell anybody else. He was right. I didn't care. I had no allegiances and I was very good at keeping secrets.

'I'm gonna to get myself a new trailer. On the pay I'll be getting, I figure I'll buy a Winnebago, something big.'

'Sounds great, Manuel,' I said.

'You bet it is. It's fucking fantastic.'

'Why would you give me your trailer though? I mean, don't you want to sell it to someone?'

'No. There's no-one. Besides, I like you. I've watched you this season. You're a good girl, and you're all on your own. You take it.'

'Thanks.' I didn't know what else to say. 'What are you going to do about your flowers?'

His eyes flicked over to me and then away, to check if I was making fun.

'Well, I haven't figured that out yet. I can't take them with me, can I? Not on a plane. I thought maybe I'd plant them out, in that little grove of trees, across the road. You see where I mean, right over there? Unless you want to keep them.'

I still didn't really believe he was giving me his

trailer. 'To tell you the truth, I probably wouldn't be the best person to leave them to. I don't know if I'd be that reliable.'

Manuel was stroking the leaves of one of his best geraniums. He nodded. 'Yeah. I understand.'

'So you're leaving soon, huh?'

'End of the week,' said Manuel. 'End of the fucking week.'

Manuel meant what he said. Two nights later he slipped away, and I drove his trailer to the next site. I was expecting a lot of awkward questions, especially from Terry and Hoxie, but Manuel must have been a little less discreet than I had figured, because it seemed like the details of his defection had already got around.

'You lucked out there, didn't ya?' said Terry.

'Woo-hoo!' said Matthew, jumping up and down on the double bed.

Even Chicken came by, poked his head in, during the show when he knew Matthew wouldn't be around. 'Not bad,' he said. He turned over some canvases Manuel had left leaning against the wall. 'Hope you're not going to take up painting.'

The Bluebird

My new house wasn't a palace; it wasn't anything. It wasn't clean, it wasn't flashy, it wasn't big, it wasn't small, it was just a thing. It did have sort of a cool retro shape, like a rectangle with curvy corners, and a nice broad stripe running around the outside, smoky blue, which looked good against the cream background, especially after I took it through the car wash. You had to find special car washes for trailers. Inside, there was lots of storage and luckily, because I didn't have any money to be buying these things myself, Manuel had left almost all his kitchen supplies and utensils, including about fifty cans of pork and beans, a heavy skillet, and the thingamajig you use to lift manhole covers when you need to dump your toilet tank down the sewers.

Two days before the season ended, a postcard finally found me at the circus. I'd been beginning to think the postcard-writer had lost me, and whenever I'd thought about this, which I tried not to, it made me sad. So postcard number 5 came right on time. It didn't freak me out by now to get them: it made me feel like someone was checking up on me. I didn't need to know who. The picture on the front was of Saint Julian, and

I'm sure at least five people read it before Terry delivered it to me in the canteen. 'Drive carefully', it read. I ran right back to the trailer and looked up Saint Julian, who it turned out was the patron saint of travellers, especially circus performers. I put it with the other postcards, tucked between the pages of *Saint Days*.

Drive carefully to where? Everyone else seemed to have places to go: Hoxie and Shirley back to her parents' driveway, in the pink palace. Matt to New York, Chicken to Jonas country. The very last night, after the show, while I was waiting for Matthew to get out of the shower in my trailer, I took another peek at the Saint Julian card. The post office stamp said New Orleans; the ink wasn't even mildly blurred.

'You gonna head home tomorrow?' called Matt from behind the bathroom door. It was pretty indicative of Matt's character that this was the point at which he'd begun wondering what I was doing during the winter break. I shoved *Saint Days* under my mattress as he came out of the bathroom, rubbing at his hair with a towel, naked.

'I don't know. I'll probably pay a visit. Sure.' I'd told Matt my parents lived in Ohio and that my father was a dentist. He was easy to lie to because he wasn't that interested.

'You should come and see me in New York, if you get the chance.'

It was another one of those little moments I'd imagined – imagined it would feel great to be asked. But when it came to it, it turned out to be also one of those moments where you get a flash of self-knowledge, like God's swinging a flashlight on a rope and it's suddenly hanging south, right over you. I knew right then I didn't really want to be Matt's girlfriend any more.

But I slept with him one more time anyway.

The first thing I would need to do, wherever I drove to, was get a job. Unless I was planning to live on pork and beans all winter. Hoxie, and Chicken, had both told me I could come back next year, so I only had to make it to the third week of March. I took a southern route, through El Paso, San Antonio, skipping around Houston and over the Sabine River into Lousiana. Down into New Orleans. It's not that I thought the postcard-sender would be there to greet me or anything, holding up a huge billboard-sized postcard of a saint as I coasted down into the flood plains. But if by any chance it was the Tripping Society sending these things, maybe they were giving me a hint, telling me where I should go. Besides, tracing the postcard trail to New Orleans was like letting go of any responsibility, my favourite thing to do. This way I was only doing what I'd been told, and frankly anyone could have told me to do it: an anonymous postcard, the lady giving traffic reports on the radio, a talking pigeon.

I didn't want to own my decisions – they weren't decisions. I wasn't reacting; I wasn't looking for anyone; this was just one way instead of another way, for no reason, nothing to do with nothing. So the fact that I ended up working in Kate Keefe's Bluebird Bookstore and Café was just one of the fattest pieces of good luck I ever encountered.

Anyway, it never ceases to amaze me how I cheer up when I'm on the freeway and a great song is playing. It doesn't even have to be a happy song; sometimes angry ones are the best. On really dark days, for instance, when I wonder what the hell I'm doing with my life and why I am still such a fucking loser, the fact that 'Revolution Rock' by the Clash can get me slapping the steering wheel for joy, my heart swelling up like a whoopee cushion about to blow, this proves to me there's a reason to go on. Because there *is* joy, like a secret lake, somewhere inside me. I've no idea why. Was it something to do with Mom? Because I didn't see much of it in Dad. Had she planted it inside me, pushed a bean down my ear while I was sleeping, hoping it would sprout, would take root and grow, pull me back from the ledge if ever I needed?

I thought about Mom a lot, driving around in my new trailer. I used to imagine we'd just passed each other, not right close by, but maybe going opposite directions on an Interstate, at night, one of those headlights that catches you in the eye. Those kind of close brushes with people you know happen all the time, don't you think? It's not that big a world. I imagined she and Father Bill were living in one of the hick towns I was always driving through. Maybe that was their house right there, the yellow tacky box with aluminium siding, sitting in the middle of an empty concrete yard, the house just past the Smytheville town limits sign. She was standing in the dark kitchen right now, drinking from a glass of water as the beams of my headlights moved across the wall behind her and were gone.

I thought about Mom, and nuclear holocaust. Every skyline I was driving towards, every opportunity going, I pictured the bruised purple of a mushroom cloud rising up before me. What would it be like? If it happened right now. Would I have the time to see it before I felt the blast? I guessed the heat would come pretty instantaneously, depending on how far away you were when it hit. Maybe I'd see the missiles coming in, and after wondering if it was a plane or a space shuttle gone wrong, I'd probably get this scared feeling that deep down I knew what it really was already, and I'd have just a few seconds to think. Think about what? Would I pray? Would I call out 'Mom' in a quiet voice inside the cab of my trailer? Just some left-over basic reflex really, from when you're little and you have nightmares but you know all you need to do is wake up so you call out to your mother to fix it. Then maybe if I had any time left, I'd realize that if the bombs were falling here, on Route 61A, in Broadwater, Michigan, they were probably falling all over, and so therefore on James, and on Dad and Janine, and on Mom. Were they thinking of me? In their last two seconds? Were they calling out *my* name?

The first night in New Orleans was rough. Parking up the trailer, when it wasn't part of a mini-city of similar vehicles, was conspicuous and not very safe. I ended up in a vacant lot near the Mississippi, where I thought the police would leave me alone, at least for one night. But some time around midnight a few gunshots went off nearby, and then twice, between two and four in the morning, somebody came round the trailer and checked all the doors. This was not a comforting thing. I don't know if it was the same person twice, but each time I lay still as a board and then when they'd gone away for a second time and I thought enough time had passed by, I crawled over to the driver's seat and started the engine, still huddled over in case of gunfire. I didn't know where I was going, but after getting on the freeway and then off again, and making a magic number of left and right turns, I ended up in a residential neighbourhood. At the corner of a little intersection, I parked in front of a fire hydrant. It was quiet and I fell asleep as soon as my head hit the pillow.

Next day, when I stepped out into the southern sunshine, like Dorothy stepping into Oz, the first thing I noticed was the hyped-up, Gothic stone entrance to the graveyard opposite. It was the sort of place where they bury their dead above ground instead of under, something I later learned was to do with the flooding, but my first thought was, what did they do about the smell when it got hot? The second place I noticed was the Bluebird Bookstore and Café, on the corner, diagonal to where I'd parked. It had a tin sign hanging from a bar over the screen door, with a bright blue bird on it. The wooden shingles of the store face were painted pine-tree green, although the original colour had faded a lot in the sun. I had forty-two dollars left and I figured that allowed me a breakfast. Not that I'd ever walked out of a bookstore without a book, either.

'Hey,' said the woman behind the counter.

Hey what? Had I done something, I thought, until I realized she was just being friendly. There was no-one else in the book part of the shop, but quite a few customers in the café at the back.

I pointed towards the restaurant. 'I just came in to get some breakfast.'

'Sure,' she murmured, turning a page of the paperback she was reading, without looking up. Was she pissed off?

'But I'll be back to look at the books.'

She still didn't look up. 'Great.'

'You can bet I will.' I think I had gone too many days without talking to anybody.

After my waffle and eggs, a hot chocolate, and a few Isak Dinesen short stories – I'd noticed you were allowed to bring a book to the table with you, so I grabbed the chance – I did go back into the bookstore to browse. An hour and a half later, I was still there. The woman I'd seen when I first came in found me crouched down by the History section, thumbing through a book on Tudor England.

'Excuse me?' she asked. 'Is that your trailer outside?'

I stood up straight, with stiff knees from crouching down for so long among the shelves.

'I think you just got a ticket.'

I walked out of the store and sure enough, I now owed the City of New Orleans forty bucks, which, after breakfast, was about five more dollars than I had. I walked back in, staring at the ticket in my hands.

'Did they get you?'

I nodded.

'I should have warned you – they come by pretty regular, every morning around now.'

I didn't know how they'd find me anyway. The trailer was probably still in Manuel's name. I'd certainly never signed any papers or anything.

'Are you on holiday?' asked the lady behind the counter.

'Not really.'

'Do you live in that thing?'

'Uh-huh.'

'All by yourself?'

162

I looked up from the ticket. 'Uh-huh.'

'Sorry. It's none of my business.'

'That's OK. You don't know of any jobs going around here, do you? I'm looking for work.'

'Work? Not that I can think of.' She stopped to serve a customer and I started browsing through the seconds on the sale table. 'What sort of work you looking for?'

'Anything. Waitressing. Cleaning.'

'What kind of experience do you have?'

She was sitting on a stool behind the counter as she asked all these questions, turning a pen over, top to bottom, bottom to top, in her hands. She had bushy brown hair with a lot of grey in it, pulled back into a loose ponytail. She looked sort of like a witch in fact, the day I met her, a witch in a denim shirt.

'I've been a waitress. I've been working for a circus the last six months.'

'For a circus? Waitressing?'

'No. Backstage, helping out.'

I didn't know what more to say then, and she didn't say anything either, so I kind of drifted away. I went out to the trailer and put the ticket back under the wipers, figuring I had another day at least before they'd give me another one. I took a walk around, looking at the houses and the little kids running around in a playground. Then after an hour or two, I wandered back into the Bluebird, hoping I'd been away long enough to make it OK. About five o'clock, I was sitting in an armchair leafing through a biography of Marilyn Monroe when the lady behind the counter approached me again.

I stood up. 'Sorry. Are you closing?'

'No, not yet. Look, if you really need a job, you

could probably do some work for me – this is my store. Can you run a coffee machine?'

'Sure.' I couldn't.

'Someone will teach you anyway. What's your name?'

'Frances – Fran.' Patron saint of writers.

'OK, Fran. My name's Kate. Seems like you like books, anyway. Unless you just don't have anywhere else to go.'

'I like books a lot.'

'It's not a prerequisite. OK then. You want to start tomorrow? Or do you need a day or two?'

'Tomorrow's fine.'

'Minimum wage, cash-in-hand. You'll have to find a better place to park your trailer.'

For about a month I moved the trailer every day, parking whenever I could in front of largish family houses, so people would think I was somebody's relative staying for a short visit. It meant getting up early, of course, to move spots, and I became an expert on which sides of the roads were illegal on which days. One day, when I found a space right outside the bookstore after lunch, having gone to move the trailer in my lunch hour, Kate asked me where I was living.

'In the trailer.'

'Where are you parking it?'

'I just move it around. I haven't really found one particular place.'

'And you sleep inside it?'

'Uh-huh.'

'That's not so safe. New Orleans is a pretty violent town.'

'I try and pick the nicer neighbourhoods.'

'Have you got a good lock on it?'

Later that day, when we were building a pyramid in the window of some new paperback fiction, Kate asked if I wanted to park the trailer in her back yard.

'In your back yard? On the grass? Won't it sort of trash your lawn?'

'The driveway goes around back of the house. There's plenty of space there, on the concrete.'

'Oh. Well, thanks – it's really nice of you, but I wouldn't want to get in your way.'

'You wouldn't. I've thought about it. I mean we'd have to have some ground rules. I'm not asking you to move in with me. But I've got a pretty big yard.'

Kate was forty-five. She'd grown up in New Orleans, in the house she still lived in, and she'd graduated from the local university with an English Lit. degree. 'The plan was to become a teacher,' she told me, 'but I couldn't handle it.' There was something sad about her, something separate. She seemed lonely, though she never would have said so. She had lots of friends – quiet, sort of nerdy people that she helped in various ways – but no-one special. I don't think she was gay; at least I never got that vibe off her. She didn't talk about any exes. Who knows? Maybe she had a really active sex life and she just kept it all secret, kept her cards close in to her chest. The only people she really talked about were her family. She had about sixteen sisters, it seemed like, and after I started working at the Bluebird she used to take off sometimes in the afternoons to visit her mother in a nursing home.

'How come you know so much about saints?' she asked me one day, after I'd told her to pray to Saint Hervé to help with her eczema. Saint Hervé, the patron saint of allergy sufferers.

'I've got this book. It's sort of a hobby.'

165

I didn't have to worry about Kate asking lots of follow-up questions; she never did. I guess she realized pretty quickly I didn't like to talk about myself, so she left it alone. Which was lucky because I found I really didn't want to lie to her. I saw her as a sort of kindred spirit, both of us full up with our secrets, and I didn't want to insult her intelligence by trying to con her. Neither one of us was the talkative type.

But of all the jobs I'd had so far – beer tent cutie, female escort, apple-picker, supermarket cashier, canvas girl, popcorn seller, ring crew – this was right up there at the top, along with canvas girl. I could read and eat most of the day. But I didn't just loaf around. I wanted to do a good job for Kate, like I'd wanted to for Chicken. With my first wages, I'd gone to the Goodwill and bought myself some new clothes, clothes that hopefully made me look a little more respectable and bookish. It wasn't as if there was a dress code: Kate wore jeans most days, so I really didn't have to dress up, but I felt like I was playing a new part, once again, and I needed a costume.

One day in December, I was unpacking some glossy coffee-table books for the Christmas display and I came across a book on James Audubon, the man who painted lots of pictures of birds and animals. I didn't think much about this, except whether it would be more appropriate to put it in the Local Interest section rather than Nature, because he'd lived in New Orleans and there was even an Audubon Park named after him just down the road. While I was pondering this, I turned the book over and looked at its cover again. Michael Roethke was the name of the author. Michael Roethke – what was weird about that? It took me more than a few seconds to place the name, in this context.

'Michael.'

'What?' Kate was passing by with a tray of dirty coffee cups.

'Sorry. Nothing.'

'Something wrong with the book?'

'No.'

What the hell, I knew I'd be going back to the circus in a few months, even if she didn't. Why not tell her?

'I used to know this guy. The author of this book.'

'That so?'

'He lived in my building, when I lived in New York.'

'Did you know he wrote books?'

'Sort of – he wrote for newspapers.'

'Give it here.' Kate took the book from me and opened to the flyleaf. 'It doesn't mention any other books. Says he writes for the *New York Times* – no picture. How'd you get to know him?'

Kate was curious because she was always interested in writers; otherwise she'd never have been so nosy.

I shrugged. 'We just ran into each other in the hall one day. He was in a wheelchair – he'd had an accident.'

I read Michael's book over the next few days, in between customers, sitting at the counter, nursing a big round mug of tea. It was a great book. Really interesting, not dry and factual, like you would expect. I would never have picked up something like this usually, let alone finished it. But I could hear Michael's voice all the way through, slowly pronouncing the more obscure bird words, over and over, loving them.

On Christmas Day, Kate invited me over. She was having the whole family over for dinner, which was not a problem because her house was huge. I was worried she was just asking me out of charity, but on the other hand, I wasn't going to act like some sort of martyr, sitting a few yards away in the back yard, eating my eggs and ham out of a skillet. It would have made me too conspicuous.

'What can you bring for the meal?' Kate asked.

'I can make some bread, if I can use your oven.'

'Sure – come over the night before.'

Late on Christmas Eve, after the bread was finished, I curled up in bed with some instant cocoa and a couple of loans from the store. I'd started reading Charles Dickens, on Kate's recommendation, and was halfway through *Great Expectations*, really getting into it. I started thinking about all the Christmas pasts in my life. Last year, I'd been with Jonas and the gang – ducking the flying Christmas rituals – and the Christmas before that with Todd and Alice, Jonas's parents, stoked up in lovin' Asheville. The year before that, in New York, Michael had come over on Christmas afternoon with a video of *The Red Shoes*. We were just starting to get to know each other. I'd served store-bought eggnog and donuts with red and green sprinkles. The year before that, back home with Dad and Janine, there'd been a colour-coordinated, ribbon-tied tree from hell, little twinkly lights framing our front door and every window, and James at fourteen, caught smoking some pot by me, in the shed where Dad kept the lawn-mower. And four long years before that, on what would be our last Christmas together, me and Mom locked ourselves in her and Dad's bedroom and I got to help her do all the present-wrapping, like we did every year. She always left it to the last minute, and she was an impulsive gift-buyer too. She'd root around in the plastic shopping bags, bringing out item after item, a Transformer toy for James, a new alarm clock for Dad, and handing them to me to wrap. I loved being in on all the secrets. Then at a certain point, every year, she'd say, 'OK, my girl, time to go', and I knew that meant all the bumps and lumps left in the bags now were mine. What did I give her in return? I can't even remember one thing.

I wasn't sure if I was looking forward to tomorrow.

It turned out there was nothing to be nervous about. I felt right at home, because it was such a circus. Kate's house was like the Addams Family house, with lots of back staircases and large square rooms, painted in mute greys and dusty browns, high ceilings, long church windows. Even in all that space, we were a crowd. I lost count at eight aunts, and the only one who stood out was Aunt Sylvestra, because she asked me if I'd ever been to Scotland, and when I said I hadn't, she kissed me and told me I must go and that her Christmas kilt was from Aberdeen. I now saw why Kate had told me to make what seemed like a week's supply of bread. We were twenty-eight around the dining-room table, and that was just the grown-ups; the kids had their own table, in a separate room. To be fair, there were a few other hangers-on like me: friends of siblings, friends of friends. Occasionally, we non-family sort of waved at each other across the chaos. No-one much asked me about me, which was how I liked it, and there was no tight family unit to envy or despise – it was impossible to sort out who belonged to whom. One of Kate's teenage nephews had obviously been told by Kate that I'd worked for a circus, because he asked me if I'd seen anyone fall off the trapeze.

'There's usually a net,' I told him.

I think it was one of Kate's sisters who drew the curtains back on the window over the kitchen sink and asked, 'What is that thing out there in the yard?' She probably wasn't asking me – I was drying some glasses that were needed for the table – but I felt it was my responsibility to explain.

'That's my trailer.'

'Oh, it's yours! Well, *that's* all right. We all thought maybe Kate was planning a big road trip or something.'

Another reason I remember Aunt Sylvestra is because she inadvertently explained to me how Kate, on her bookstore earnings, had ended up living all alone in this huge house.

'My God, when is she going to take that off the *wall*?' said Aunt Sylvestra, waving a flabby arm at an oil painting of a pond with some geese flying over it. 'I've hated that picture all my life. I hated it when I was a child, and I hate it now, and I'm sick to death of looking at it, every single family get-together.'

'Did you grow up in this house?' I asked.

'Sure I did. What's crazy is,' she said, lowering her voice, 'now that Martha's gone into the old folk's home, Katie's ended up with it. No children and never going to be any, but everyone loves her so much, they won't ever kick her out.'

I felt a little jealous hearing that, and for the rest of the night nursed a little grudge against Kate for having a family that loved her so much, if it was true. I could see why they would love her. She wandered around in the middle of them all like some sort of gentle servant.

After dinner there were games, and people danced, and I made my excuses at about 1 a.m. As I walked

170

across the yard, digging in my pocket for the trailer key, I felt something I hadn't felt since I was a really little girl. A tiny sense of disappointment: the thought that it was all over for another year, Christmas come and gone. The next day, back at work, I bought one of our store postcards, and wrote to James. He was probably home with Dad and Janine for the holiday season, if he wasn't working in a soup canteen, doing good somewhere. There were lots of things to say, but in the end all I wrote was 'Spending Christmas in the Bluebird Bookstore and Café, New Orleans. Wish you were here.' I stuck it in an envelope, walked down during my lunch break to the mailbox on the corner, and sent it off.

On New Year's Eve, about 7 p.m., someone knocked on the aluminium door of the trailer. It was Kate.

'Hey. What are you up to?'

'Nothing. Do you need help with something?'

'No. I just wondered if you feel like going to a movie with me. I'm not a big one for New Year's parties.'

We went to see *Postcards from the Edge*, the flick about an ageing film star and her drug-addicted daughter. I guess there are some mothers you wish would run off. The film was OK, sort of funny in a wise-ass way, and I loved going to the movies. I hadn't been in a while. Me and Barbara used to go all the time in high school, at least one night every weekend, usually to this arty house cinema downtown, see double features of weird films. Barbara was really into it; I think she used to go by herself, if I had a date.

Afterwards, driving home in Kate's car, I felt sleepy – she had the heat on and the classical radio station was playing low. We were going down one of those double-laned strips you get on the outskirts of almost every American town: Shell gas station, Sunoco gas station, a video store, McDonald's, with a Burger King right across the street but never right next door. Every window and rooftop was strewn with Christmas lights and electric Santas, yet not a spoonful of snow. This wasn't how it was meant to be.

'What's your favourite book of all time?' asked Kate, when we were stopped at a red light. 'Do you have one?'

I'd been dozing, so I was kind of slow to answer. 'My favourite? I don't really have one. I haven't read that many books, to tell you the truth.'

'Yeah, right – you never stop reading. Anyway, I didn't ask how many books you've read.'

Just to say anything, I told her the first title that came to mind, which was probably somewhat accurate if you believe in the power of the subconscious. '*Anna Karenina.*'

'*Anna Karenina*? Why do you like that one so much? I have to admit I've never read it. Doesn't she jump in front of a train at the end?'

'Uh-huh.'

'So you like that kind of high tragedy.'

'I dunno. There's happy people in it too. Not happy exactly, but, you know, they have these sort of joyful times, in wheat fields.'

'The happy peasants, you mean.'

'What's your favourite, then?' I opened my window a crack, because it was so hot in the car.

'Usually whatever I'm reading at the time. I was just thinking though, about why we connect with certain stories, or why we don't. Why people come into the store and always head to the same section. I'm sure it means a lot. Obviously it does.'

She still hadn't told me what her favourite book was.

We turned off the main road into the darker tree-lined roads of Kate's neighbourhood, and a couple of teenagers, walking hand in hand, caught my attention. The girl had bare legs under her denim skirt – must have lost all sensation in this weather – and he was wearing a floor-length navy blue overcoat, looked like a navy captain's coat on a ten-year-old. They were walking fast, eager to get somewhere, to a friends' party, maybe, or somewhere they could lie down together for a while. It might have been the way they were passing directly under the streetlight just at that moment, like being caught in an alien spaceship's tractor beam, but as I looked, I had a strong sense of this second of their lives which would never come again. Like my gaze was a camera shutter – opening, the light flooding in, shut again, darkness – freezing them there, at that age and that temperature. And in front of this moment, I imagined two very long lead reins were pulling, pulling them along by their snowy noses, pulling them apart eventually, apart and along-side other people, all those people's lead reins, held slack but somehow never getting in a tangle. My own lead rein. Pulling me towards my calculable future.

Would I ever see these two again and not realize it? Or had that been their and my lives' one and only point of intersection, done and gone? Totally stupid thought, really.

'Do you want to come in for a drink?' said Kate, turning off the engine. 'Or maybe you're tired.'

'I'm not tired. But I thought you hated New Years.'

'I do. I just thought it would be a distraction.'

'Why don't you come over to *my* house for a change?'

As soon as I'd said it I kind of regretted it, because the trailer was really messy. Actually I'd been a little down lately, because of the holidays, and I hadn't been too good about doing the dishes or anything. Kate had never really been inside. She was so careful not to look around too much, not to pry. So much so, it got on my nerves a little. I wanted to tell her it was OK – she could look at the titles of my books if she wanted. Seeing it through her eyes, I noticed how completely neutral the trailer was, no pictures up anywhere, nothing to mark it as my own, no trace of the circus except for a framed snapshot on the wall, of Manuel in the middle of his act, which he had left behind. We sat squeezed in at the tiny laminate table, self-consciously, and drank a bottle of wine her family had given me at Christmas. We talked about what we could – the bookstore, the Christmas sales, a book fair she was going to next month. I was never sure how much money Kate had. She lived rent-free, presumably, but she probably depended on the bookstore for her everyday expenses. Or maybe she didn't.

'I think I'm going to have to sell the house,' she suddenly said, as if she'd read my mind.

'Really?'

'It's a waste, isn't it? Living in there all by myself.'

'Doesn't anybody else in your family want it?'

'Sure, but nobody has the money, and it's still my mom's house technically, until she's gone.'

'Too bad.'

'Well, it's about time I got out of there. Look at you, you're independent. You've lived nine times the lives I have, I bet.'

She talked about her family, per usual. She told me how one of her sisters was getting a divorce, and that her mother was all upset about it, except her mother couldn't keep straight in her mind which son-in-law it was she was losing, and there was one son-in-law she liked and one she hated, so depending on the day and the sharpness of her faculties, her judgement would fluctuate. Her mother's health was deteriorating fast. Any day Kate expected the doctors to set a time limit.

I looked at my watch.

'Sorry, it's late,' she said, standing up and zipping up her down parka. She blew on her hands and looked around. 'Look, Frances, can I say something?'

I had this weird feeling she was going to tell me how unhappy she was.

'I don't know if I can let you sleep in here tonight. It is, pardon my language, effing freezing in here. Isn't it? You'll freeze.'

Southerners. New Orleans was having a cold spell, but it wasn't that bad, not like they were making it out on the weather reports. Give them anything below fifty degrees and they acted like it was the coming of the Ice Age. We'd had winters back home where the temperature never went above freezing for weeks at a time, never mind a wind-chill factor of sixty below. Still, I had to admit there was frost building up on the inside of the trailer windows.

'It is pretty cold, I guess. But you shouldn't worry about me.'

'You're going to catch pneumonia. And die in my back yard, and that could end up being very expensive, because I'll be sued by your family.' She paused, as if she'd said something wrong. 'Really, please come stay in the house. Just for tonight. Otherwise, *I* won't be able to sleep, imagining you freezing solid out here.'

175

I couldn't say no to her. The bedroom she took me to was Amy's – the youngest of Kate's sisters, I think – and whatever age Amy had reached by now, it was still designed for a twelve-year-old. A powder-white vanity table, laid out with mini-sample perfume bottles and little wicker baskets overflowing with hair accessories. Garfield-the-cat pyjama container lying on the pillow. Scotch-taped on the wall above the bed, pages ripped from *Sixteen* magazine and *Teen Mademoiselle*.

'I'm sorry it's a little childish in here. Amy went away to boarding-school when she was thirteen, and what with one thing and another, we've never really dealt with this room.'

'That's OK. It's warm, anyhow.'

'Exactly. I don't heat all of the house in the winter – too expensive – and this is the only bedroom, besides my own, where the heat is on.'

She was standing in the doorway, still wearing her down jacket, with one hand up against the frame and her hair slipping out of its habitual ponytail. I suddenly saw her as a teenager, standing in that same doorway, in her sensible pyjamas, telling her younger sister to shut up and go to sleep. I wondered if she was a virgin.

'You're close to your family, aren't you?'

She turned and looked at me, didn't answer right away, as if I'd woken her from a deep sleep.

'You all get along.'

She laughed a little. 'Most of the time!' Then she looked down at her foot tracing a pattern in the hall carpet. 'I mean they're it, really. For me. Aren't they?'

I felt like I'd reminded her she was a loser or something, and I didn't feel that way at all. I admired her closeness to her family; I wondered how she'd

176

achieved it, how she maintained it. It was like a language I didn't speak.

She slapped her hand once, lightly, against the door frame. 'Anyway. Sleep well. I'll see you in the morning.'

'In the New Year.'

She smiled. 'Don't say it. In the New Year.'

The cold snap didn't last, but without ever speaking about it, I sort of moved into Amy's room. Some nights I'd still sleep out in the trailer, because I felt a little mean abandoning it, to tell the truth. But five out of seven I'd go into the house after work to do something for Kate, help her move something, or watch a little television, and then we'd end up eating together and I'd crash on Amy's bed. Kate didn't seem to mind – she seemed to like the company. We tried not to get in each other's way.

One day in February, when I walked into the store after my day off, she pulled out two pieces of mail from behind the counter, a letter and a package.

'Don't shoot the messenger,' she said, handing them over. Saint Simon was the patron saint of messengers.

I didn't recognize the handwriting on the package, and there was no return address.

'Does that look like New York City there, on the stamp?' I was thinking of Matt.

Kate barely glanced at it. 'Could be.'

The letter was from James. I recognized his handwriting right away. I wondered how he'd found me until I remembered the Christmas card I'd sent him. He must have tracked down the Bluebird's address.

'Thanks.' I put both items of mail away unopened, on the little shelf hidden behind the counter where I kept my wallet and keys. 'Want me to start un-boxing those self-help books?'

Later on, all alone in the trailer, making myself wait until every scrap of my Chinese takeaway had been eaten, I pulled out the package from New York. Inside, wrapped in newspaper, was a small hand-bound book, leather ties at the binding, with a letter tucked into its pages, addressed to Queenie.

Hail to your Majesty.
I remember you once told me I should begin making up my own words – new words – instead of becoming perhaps irreversibly clogged up with more antiquated coinage. You may not have said this last bit, but it was, for me, implied. I have followed your advice, and though no-one now understands me, I am happy. As I no longer have a use for this collection of old words, I wondered if you might find them efficacious, and so am making a gift of them, as a way of thanking you for your sound advice, as well as much else. Please forgive this presumption, if it is one, but it seems that as opposed to being occupied, as I am daily, with trying to imagine a future, you may, by necessity, be pursuing the illumination of your past, for which old words can be useful. I shuilwend you, as always and as ever.
Michael

I put the letter back in its envelope.

The pages of the book were filled with tiny lines in his hand, straight-backed, smooth, no cross-outs, tidy as a printed manuscript, in direct contrast to the domestic chaos in which I know he would have been writing. It was a dictionary. A diary, from A to Z presumably, of words once adored, once eaten, once rolled between the teeth, see-sawed on the tongue and swallowed at leisure. Michael's exes, so to speak, a catalogue of his semantic romances.

A is for abbey-lubber, a lazy monk.
A for abeyance, the state of suspension or temporary inactivity. Now use it in a sentence – 'My life is in abeyance.'
A for abigail, a lady's maid. A for ablutomane. That's a good one. Janine – see Janine clean – Janine is an ablutomane.
A for abodement, a foreboding, an omen.
A for aboulia, a loss of willpower, the inability to make decisions.
For Abreaction: the resolution of a neurosis by reviving forgotten or repressed ideas of the event first causing it.
For Acatalepsy: the unknowableness to a certainty of all things.

Jesus. I couldn't read any more. I didn't understand how he had found me. Maybe it had been Michael sending all the postcards. I'd never once considered him. But then why would he have chosen to sign his name now? Kate's face had looked sort of guilty when I asked about the stamp, now I thought of it. Maybe she'd contacted Michael's publisher, tried to get a message to him. The one thing she was openly passionate about was writers. But no it wasn't like her. The truth is I didn't care to know how he'd found me, how anybody had found me. I suppose most people would have wanted to get to the bottom of something like this, find out who was sending the damn postcards, for instance, right away. But I didn't want to know, because I had this sixth sense, this certainty, that the answers would be painful.

I got out of bed and brushed my teeth and when I was tucked up and ready, I tore open James's letter.

Hey, sis' – how are you? Thanks for your Christmas postcard – I'm really sorry I've taken so long to write back.

So, I'm confused – have you dropped out of the circus for a while? Maybe this is like your home base when you're not travelling with the circus – I hope this will reach you, anyway, or someone will know where to send it on. I can definitely imagine you working in a bookstore – no surprise there. Or maybe you just know someone who owns the bookstore. Anyway, I'm here in Seattle now, still doing my priest-training, and working part-time in this clinic for drug abusers, of which there's more than a handful around here. It's hard work in the clinic and pretty intense – last night I went along on a call-out to a lady who wanted to jump off the roof of a ten-storey apartment building, and her eight-year-old son was standing there watching the whole time. She was Catholic and she wanted a priest there right away, and since I was standing around in the hospital that night, they hauled me out in the ambulance, too.

Thank God she didn't jump, but I don't think it was much to do with what anyone said. Anyway, I was thinking about you in the ambulance afterwards, when we were taking this lady to the hospital, out of her head on something – that sounds weird, let me start again. I don't mean you're like this lady, or that

*she reminded me of you. I was thinking about Mom,
actually, and the little boy who'd been standing on
the roof watching his mother, held back by police-
men. It all got jumbled up in my head, what was my
life and what was somebody else's. Some of my
memories seem like that – a lot, actually – like they're
not really mine, like they're from somebody else's life
– do you get that ever? I mean Mom never acted
crazy, did she? What's me, and what's somebody else?
It's happening a lot at the moment. Weird, huh?*

*Sorry to get so depressing – things are really fine. It
was just an intense night last night – they tell us to
expect to get a little traumatized ourselves now and
then, so I guess I shouldn't be surprised. You know
you can call me here if you want – I don't know how
the phones work in the circus, but maybe at the
Bluebird – if you're still there – it's easier. I've got a
phone in the hallway right outside my cell – that's
what we call our rooms, ha ha – so you could ring me
direct, day or night, on the number below.*

*God bless you. Or whatever. I hope you don't mind
me saying that.*
James

I got out *Saint Days* and tucked in James's letter,
next to the postcards. When I was ten, I'd had this pen-
pal from Sweden for a while, through a project at
school, and Mom bought me a pack of my own
stationery and some of those special airmail envelopes
with the blue stripy edges. We went out and bought a
book about Sweden too. In fact, Mom was so enthusiastic she decided she would start writing as well,
to my pen-pal's mom, hoping to get her own grown-up
pen-pal, I guess. Whenever a letter came with a

Swedish stamp on it she would wait for me to get home from school before she opened it, even if it was for her. We promised we'd visit Sweden together some day – 'when you're in college', she said. Well, I hadn't gone to college yet, so maybe it would happen.

When March came around, time to head back to Sherman Brothers, I was a little torn. Was it just the home comforts? I mean it was a pretty great thing I had going on here, even though I knew I couldn't park the trailer in Kate's back yard for ever, and if I didn't have anywhere to park it I'd probably have to sell it, eventually, and that's the point at which the decision was not a choice to be made. The trailer was my get-out clause, the key to my self-sufficiency. And besides, I missed Chicken, and even reading and eating got boring if it was all you ever did.

When I told Kate that I needed to go, she seemed OK about it.

'I was wondering if you were going to get restless. Don't worry. Truth is, I can't really afford you, not all year round.'

'Thanks for all the help,' I said, 'with the trailer space and everything.'

'Sure. But look – if you want to come back again, any time, on a casual basis or whatever, go ahead. You're trained up and everything now, so it'd be no problem. Are you going to go back to the circus?'

We looked at each other, both of us aware this was the kind of question she never asked.

'It would be nice to keep in touch.'

'Sure. I'll probably go back to the circus, yeah.'

'Well, if you get another break next winter, come on back.'

'That's really nice of you. I'm not always very dependable when it comes to revisiting places. But it's a great offer. Thanks.'

Kate looked away like she was embarrassed. She got busy with some books she was wrapping.

'Do what you have to do, of course. It would just be kind of quirky, that's all – a winter employee. Nice way to differentiate the seasons.'

'What, you mean, like "It must be nearly Christmas, honey! The trailer's out in the back yard."'

She looked up. I think she was relieved I was making a joke of it. 'Exactly. A phenomenon of nature.'

At least I felt better about myself this time, leaving with somebody's blessings.

The High Wire

Of course there isn't a Saint Wanda, but I wanted there to be one. The saint of Michigan, the saint of kick-ass, the saint of shoppers and woman athletes.

The first time I saw her, neither one of us was at our best. It was opening day again, on the fairground in Albuquerque, and it was bucketing down. Horizontal rain. This year, Hoxie had put me on the big top crew as well as helping out Chicken, and I still hadn't got the hang of raising the tent with the elephants helping. I always felt like I was going to get in an elephant's way and be flattened, especially when we were all, humans and beasts, slipping and sliding around in the mud. To top it all, the new elephant trainer had been drunk since he arrived ten days ago. In the midst of this chaos, tent halfway up the centrepole, sagging at the quarterpoles, strung up round the circumference and looking like a Bundt cake which had refused to rise, Wanda appeared. Two hard suitcases, kinky hair plastered down the side of her flushed cheeks, and a Mexican embroidered top that was leaking its colours down the front of her jeans.

I saw her ask for directions and someone pointed

towards Terry, who was trying to repair a split jumper rope. When she tapped on his back, he spun around, ready to bite off the head of whoever was bugging him. Everyone was in a shitty mood. Instead, when he saw it was her, he hung onto the rope with one hand and shook her hand with his free one, then pointed in the vague direction of the female sleeper and she wandered off.

I didn't think about her again until the dress rehearsal that night. Per usual, the crew had all been invited – told, more like it – to come, since this would be our last chance to sit and watch. Matt had brought a friend back from New York, another clown he'd met there and convinced Hoxie to hire, and all winter they'd been working up a new double act based on this bit from a Laurel and Hardy movie. Matthew was doing the Stan Laurel part, and he was really enthusiastic about it. Maybe this lessened the blow of me telling him it was over between us, because he didn't seem that upset. And what do you know but a few weeks later he surfaced screwing the Hungarian handbalancer. Performers should pretty much be with performers, I reckon.

The show started with a husband and wife bicycle act – they'd been around last year – and a new juggler, who was OK but seemed sort of nervous, and then the first of the palomino slots, the shorter, easier programme, a build-up to the really impressive second-act slot where they all waltzed around in formation, one after another, like choreographed dancers. I could never figure out how they taught these horses the dance steps, never mind how they got them to wait for each other and do all the steps in sequence. Tex made lots of appearances in between, keeping the crowd happy and, just like last year, the first act finished with the elephants. But now, just before that, came Wanda.

Wanda was a contortionist. She could really bend her body any which way, there were no tricks to it, no faking going on. She told me later she'd always been that way: 'I came out all twisted up,' she said. She did things that made her middle look like Wonder Bread, Wonder Bread that you had folded all the way over on itself to make a sandwich, yet somehow managed to never split in two.

'Do you think she eats?' I asked the guy sitting next to me during the dress rehearsal.

'Who cares?' he said.

I turned and looked at him practically drooling over every inch of Miss Bendy-Twisty in a leotard, imagination working overtime no doubt.

Her act started with Phil and Jerry from the ring crew bringing this Plexiglas box on stage: it was painted blue and about the size of a large footstool, the size people have in front of their La-Z-Boys. They left it there, sitting all by itself in the middle of the ring, lit by a white spotlight. All at once the lid sprang off, pushed from underneath, the spotlight turned green and a slender arm emerged from the box like a snake coiling out of a snake charmer's clay pot. You're thinking, there is no way a whole person could be in that box – maybe there's a trapdoor underneath the ring, except how could there be? and I knew there wasn't. Then another arm, and then a knee and the calf unfolding, then the feet, both legs straight up as the arms gripped onto the hard side of the box and the legs pulled backwards over the torso, a backward somersault uncurling out of the box, allowing the back, shoulder and finally head to present themselves, right side up at last.

She was dressed in a full-length white leotard with a white turban on her head, but the colour of the spotlight on her was green, so at first she looked like some sort of lizard, an emerald salamander, dish-washing liquid in temporary human form. She slithered across the ring, at least one part of her un-dulating body always in touch with the floor. Near the outer edge, she pulled herself up onto a small, round platform for a sleep in the sun, and suddenly the lights changed to orange and the platform began to rotate. She was an exotic bird, preening, arching, spreading its plumage, stretching its neck skywards except you suddenly realized that what you knew to be its head and therefore you had been assuming in some strange way was Wanda's head, was actually her foot and her face was tucked between her other knee, a baby bird looking out between its mother's wings. Another light change, and at the same moment she grabbed onto a ring which had been lowered and took flight as the ring was lifted again – a yellow butterfly. Pure sunlight, threading itself through the tiny ring and back again. Light change – blacklight – and she hung herself off the ring like dry-cleaning, a vampire bat asleep in its cave. Then final light change – red – she started the ring spinning and sent her body revolving outwards. The ring lowered to the ground; she ran back to the box and, bending back-wards into it, repackaged herself, replacing every cubic inch of air with the matter of her body. Phil and Jerry came back on, replaced the lid, and carried her off.

One night, the next week in Santa Fe, I asked her how she did it as she was extracting herself from the box in the backstage area.

'I played a lot of hide-and-seek when I was a kid.'
She was out of breath. 'Can you help me with this?'
she asked, pulling at her turban. 'There's a safety pin
in there somewhere at the back – I wrapped it on too
tightly, and it was giving me such a headache out
there.'

'Sure.'

'Man! That's better.' Swiftly she unrolled
the material, rubbing her scalp once it was free. 'The
music's not right, though – it all sounds a bit seventies
light-show, you know?'

'I guess.' Was that what I was supposed to say?

'Do you know if there's a mall around here? Do you
have a car?'

'A car? No.'

She picked up a white fluffy bathrobe that was slung
over a chair.

'I've got a trailer,' I blurted out.

'Your own trailer? Cool. How old are you?'

'How old am I? Twenty-two.'

'Are you rich or something?'

'No – you mean the trailer? Somebody gave it to me.
Last season.'

'Boyfriend or something?'

'No, just this guy. Manuel. He was getting another
one.'

'You never slept with him?'

'No.'

She laughed. 'You must have something special,
girl. What do you do? Around here, I mean.'

'A little bit of everything. I stitch up the tent – me
and Chicken.'

'You and a chicken?'

'No. Chicken – he's a guy.'

'Is he the real oldie who stares at me in my costume like I don't have it on?'

'That's him. He's not that bad really.'

She nodded, but I wasn't sure if she was listening any more. 'I tell you what, though, it's fucking cold. I thought Arizona was meant to be warm.'

'New Mexico.'

'Yeah, well, the whole area.'

'It is still March.'

'Even so. I'll have to get a little heater for my room. Do you like this bathrobe? It's my Marilyn Monroe look, except I shouldn't be wearing anything underneath. Have you seen those photos of her?'

I shook my head.

'Anyway. See ya round. What's your name again?'

'It's Pauline.'

'Pauline? You don't look like a Pauline. Do you wanna go shopping tomorrow morning? There's probably a bus or something. You could help me choose some new music for the act. I can't stand shopping on my own.'

'Hey! Paulie!' One of the crew poked his head out of the artists' flap. The first act had finished and people were coming out of the tent. 'Elephant just stepped on a flap and it's hanging off by a couple threads. Terry wants it fixed before the second half.'

'OK.' I turned back to Wanda. 'Sure, I guess I could go.'

'Great. I'm in the female prison. Come and find me.'

The next day, in town, Wanda and I didn't find any music for her act, but we did have a great time just walking around the mall, window-shopping. I hadn't done this sort of thing in years, not since days with my dad on the job.

'There's a place just like this back home,' said Wanda, as we were riding down an escalator.

'Me too.'

'Most places, I guess. Where'd you grow up?'

I told her somewhere not miles from the truth.

'Wow, you're a Midwest girl! I figured you were East Coast.'

'You did? Why?'

'You're so quiet – you seem sort of sophisticated. You don't gab away all the time, like I do, blah blah blah.'

'Maybe I can't think of anything to say.'

'Yeah, well, somehow I doubt that. Anyway, knowing to say nothing when you have nothing to say is pretty sophisticated.'

I said nothing.

'Oh, look, there's a Limited! I used to love this place when I was in high school. I think my entire wardrobe came from it, or whatever I could afford off the pay cheque from Burger King. Hey, let's go buy some tacky teenage clothes.'

We tried on the most disgusting clothes and finally bought two outfits that were so out of fashion they'd come round the other side and were somehow the height of fashion again, if you know what I mean. Her body, in the changing room, was economical. Light-brown skin, pencil thin, yet strong, not flimsy. Afterwards, we had lunch at a fakey French café place and she asked me how I got into the circus. I just fudged it a little, told her I'd met Chicken working in a supermarket in my home town and he'd asked me if I was interested in working for the circus.

'He asked you? Isn't he kind of old for you?'

'What do you mean?'

'Chicken.'

'Completely. Oh, there was nothing going on.'

Wanda lifted one eyebrow, something I can't do. 'What do you do, put a spell on these guys?'

I shrugged. 'In the right place at the right time, I guess.'

'If you're sure this is the right place.' The waitress placed our bill on the table, face down, as she was passing.

'What about you? Did you always want to be in the circus?'

She shook her head. 'Nope. I wasn't one of those weirdos, if that's what you mean, making little circus models in my back yard at the age of five. I got into gymnastics when I was about three, at a YMCA down the street, and things just kind of proceeded on from there. My mom's cousins were in the circus, so we were sort of aware of it as an option, I guess. I always knew I wanted to do something physical, and you need a shit-load of money to get into the Olympics, no matter what they say. And I like performing in front of people – it was either this or kinky dancing! Kinky dancing's probably what I'll end up doing when I'm forty.'

I was sitting there totally envious of her, because I'm envious of anyone who knows exactly what they want to do, whether it's be the President, or hang from a trapeze, or even sweep up sawdust. The circus was about thirty/seventy: people who had a passion, and people like me, who were kind of lost, treading water. As much as I pretended canvas girl was the be-all and end-all.

'Paulie?'

'Yeah?' I was watching a little kid at another table,

about to lose the chocolate ice-cream off his spoon.

'Your name's not Pauline, is it?'

I frowned at her, trying to look confused. 'What do you mean?'

'It's OK. I mean, my name's not Wanda. Obviously.'

'It isn't?'

'You know it's not.'

I shrugged my shoulders. 'I hadn't really thought about it.'

'But tell you what,' she said, 'don't *ever* tell me your real name. I'm such a blabber, and I'd get confused and call you by your real name sometimes, probably at the worst moment, without meaning to. So don't tell me if you don't want people to know. OK?'

It seemed like, at that moment, I couldn't remember my real name anyway.

'We'd better pay,' she said, picking up the bill. 'I gotta warm up before the show.'

The only sex I had that season was with a mechanic called Nick. Nick had a shaved head and sexy man-knees that showed through the holes in his jeans. And what can I say? – he was a charmer. An English charmer, actually – said he came from up North and sometimes I couldn't understand a fucking word he said, especially when he'd had a few. Probably not half as charming back in his own country, but it worked for me. He lived in the front half of his truck and we did it in there one night, on the sleeper bunk behind the front seat. When the news got out, I could feel this silent approval from the rest of the crew, for choosing one of our own this time. Chicken told me I'd be better off keeping myself to myself.

'Who knows what kind of foreign diseases he's got?' he said.

'He's from England, Chicken.'

'So what's he doing over here? Don't they have circuses in England?'

'Jesus. You're so unforgiving.'

I expected him to say it was nothing to do with forgiveness, but instead he said he knew he was.

'It's one of my faults.'

Chicken never ceased to surprise me.

'Talking about forgiveness,' he added, 'I never did see your ex back in NC this winter, so I didn't get to spill the beans like I wanted to.'

'You mean Jonas? Why didn't you see him?'

'How the hell do I know? He wasn't around.'

'You mean he's stopped working at the store?'

'I don't think so. His locker still had his name on it – he just wasn't around. And I wasn't interested enough to find out why.'

'What about Erik and C.J.?'

'C.J. was there.'

'Did he ask about me?'

'Nope.'

I felt kind of deflated. No-one looking for me then. No-one missing me, except maybe Kate. But I didn't want them to miss me, did I?'

'Are you going to climb up and have a look at this hole *today* some time, or do you want me to fucking do it? It's gonna rain tonight and we don't want any towners complaining about their little Suzie getting wet.'

'Yeah. I'll do it.'

Newcastle Nick got bored with me pretty quick and started fucking one of the so-called *corps de ballet*.

There were six members of this petite ensemble, all from Romania, and call me crazy if any of them had ever stepped foot in a dance class. Mistresses of quick leotard changes, that's all they were, backstage and elsewhere. It was one of my best moments of the season when I was working the backstage flap and I witnessed two of them get the hot-pink feathered plumes of their head-dresses tangled up just as they were about to make an entrance. As they squealed for help like little spangly piglets, their heads craning sideways, hands gripping their yanked-out hairlines, I stepped back into the shadows and let Tex Hamilton sort it out.

After Nick, I sort of swore off sex for a while, and that's when Wanda and I really became a double act. Through Amarillo, Oklahoma City, Tulsa, Springfield, Jefferson City – in every town, a different shopping centre to conquer. It's not that we were so alike: she was a lot more sociable by nature, and she more or less dragged me centre stage in that respect, kicking and fussing. But for some reason, even though I mostly sat around like a stick in the mud, she seemed to like me. No-one had been this focused on me since Mom on my birthdays, and I ate it up. Wanda was fun, like Barbara had been.

We worked a lot on her act together too, which could have been a little like the Matt performer–crew dynamic, but somehow it wasn't at all. Maybe because she wasn't so neurotic, but definitely because she didn't take it all so seriously. Scrounging around the world music section of a Peaches record store in Oklahoma City, I found these recordings of Eastern European women choruses – Albanians, I think. Their voices were haunting and freaky, totally different from any other music in the show, and when we fed their strange throaty cries through the large sound system it was a fantastic effect. At first Hoxie hated it – he'd hired the guy who'd composed all the music – but Wanda could be a bit of a diva, and she was proving a real hit with the audiences, so the new music was in. Pretty soon after, she said she wanted me running her follow spot, because the guy doing it kept missing the colour changes, but in a circus this big these kinds of things are pretty fixed, and Hoxie said I couldn't do it. I took personal care of the props for her act, though, which was basically her box, and the rotating pedestal which had a little foot brake on it she worked herself. And we planned further improvements; at least, she asked for my opinion about anything new. Almost every evening after the show she came back to my trailer and we cooked something on the hot plate. Wanda moved her portable TV into my trailer when she found out I didn't own one.

'There's more room in here anyway,' she said. 'All I want to do is sleep, in my place.' It was true her room was pretty basic, pretty shabby, with dividing walls as thin as balsa.

'Are you two lezzies?' Chicken asked us.

'Oh, Chicken, man, wouldn't you just love that?' shot back Wanda. 'I'm sorry we can't oblige you there. But maybe there's something *else* I could do for you, honey. On my lonesome? What do you think?'

'For me and everyone else. Soiled goods,' said Chicken. 'I'm not into soiled goods.'

'Oh, fuck you, you dirty old man – you'd be lucky for a go. How can you stand to work with this guy?' she asked me as he shuffled away, chuckling because he'd got her riled.

195

But Chicken had a point: Wanda was pretty slutty. She was always pointing out some guy's physique to me and then a few hours later I'd see her eating lunch with the same guy in the canteen, leaning towards him and smiling. She said she just didn't like sleeping alone.

One afternoon, we were hanging around in the trailer watching soap operas during that dip in the day before the first afternoon show, and she picked up my book of saints.

'What's this?'

I'd pulled it out early in the morning to check on the saint of the day – Saint Rita, the saint of impossible situations – and then I'd gone to the bathroom and must have forgotten to replace it.

'Some old book I picked up in a flea market. Last year.'

'Are you religious? My grandma used to always make us go to church, till she died.'

'No, I'm not religious.' What was I going to say? I had to say something. 'I just liked the look of it. It's fun, checking out all the saint names. It's sort of like astrology.' I knew Wanda always read her stars.

'What do you mean? You mean you look up your own name? Does it tell you what you're meant to be like?'

'No. It just tells you about the saint you're named after, what you're supposed to pray to them for, stuff like that.'

'I don't think I was named after a saint.' She flipped back to the front of the book, where my mother's name was written. 'Lydia Harding,' she said. 'I wonder where she is right now. Probably dead, I guess.'

'Probably not. It's only 1962, the date she's written down. Year before I was born.'

The soap opera finished and a preview started running for the talk show on next.

'Hey, look,' said Wanda, 'Aretha Franklin's on *Oprah*. I saw her sing once in Detroit, when I was little. My mom took me.' She was still holding *Saint Days*. 'Shit, we'll have to miss it. Fucking circus, gets in the way of our viewing pleasure! So, *is* there a Wanda in this book?'

'I don't think so.'

'What about you? Is there a Pauline? Must be a list or something, at the back. Nope, no Pauline, but there's a Paul – you must have looked this up already, huh? Page sixty-three. Here we go. Saint Paul, born blah blah blah, one of Jesus's guys, yeah yeah, the patron saint of tentmakers.' She stopped reading and looked up at me. 'Patron saint of tentmakers. You're a smart cookie, aren't you?'

I kept my eyes on the screen like she hadn't spoken. She stood up, laughing, and handed over the book. 'Here, here's your book. You put it away safe.'

'Oh. Sure. Thanks.' I threw it on the bed.

'But I might want to look up someone else's name some time. You know, if I meet Mr Right or something?'

'Sure. Yeah. Whenever.'

Bloomington, Peoria again, Quad Cities, and Rockford, Illinois. May, the onset of a very humid summer.

Land-locked. My home town.

It was bound to happen some time. But there was no reason to see anyone, if I didn't want to. No-one I knew would be coming to the circus, I was pretty sure of that. Unless someone from my old high school saw me and then spread the news, but it wasn't like I was

197

performing or anything. Still, I lay low during show times. If the truth be told, the only one I was sort of curious about was Barbara – I wondered if she was still in New York, if she'd ever gone. It seemed too complicated to just call her house. If she was there, what would we say after we said hello? And even worse, what about the goodbye? 'Keep in touch'? 'See you in another four years or so, maybe'?

'I have to get an electric fan,' said Wanda, the morning after the first night in town. 'I'm not going to last another night – it's like a witch's oven in my place, and I'm going to grab one of the brats in the audience and cook 'em if I don't get some relief soon. I heard there's a monster mall downtown – you wanna check it out? We can walk.'

We were playing in a lot on the lakefront, a few miles away from the baseball stadium where I'd worked with Barbara. This was a site the city regularly used for summer festivals. I'd been to rock concerts here, and beer festivals, an arts and craft fair every spring with my mom. She'd always talked about starting some sort of little career in arts and crafts, something she could do at home while we were at school, but nothing ever came of it. Maybe that was why; maybe she'd run off to some artists' colony where she was weaving wall hangings for the rich and famous. You could see all along the lakefront from the top of our tent: the art museum, a modern-looking boxy building suspended over the water half a mile down, the city hall, and the O'Connor mansion where the story was a heart-broken débutante in the 1970s had jumped out of one of the third-floor windows onto the lakefront boulders below. There were lots of things I kept remembering.

'I bet this lake ices up in the winter,' I said. 'I knew someone who told me the whole thing ices over some time – you can walk across it, state to state, if you ever wanted to. Kids sometimes get killed walking on the icebergs that build up on the lakefront, when the icebergs flip over. That's what this person told me.'

'Get outta here.'

'It's true.'

On the way over to the mall the air was so humid, felt like you were putting your face in the centre of a hot-wet washcloth just walking down the street. The rubber in some of the sidewalk seams squished when you stepped on it. But luckily the mall was air-conditioned. We bought Wanda her electric fan and when we left we used a different exit and came out opposite the City Museum. This museum had been one of Barbara and my favourite places to go when we were tripping – we had spent whole days in there, marvelling at its bizarre contents.

'Hey, the museum!' I said. 'Let's go in.'

'The museum?' said Wanda, holding her new fan in its box. 'You wanna go to the museum?'

'It's great. It has this whole oldie-time display, where you walk the streets of the city as it was around 1900, and there's a policeman, and a lady in her parlour, rocking in her rocking chair, and a cat whose eyes light up. It's a trip.'

'Is that so?' Wanda was staring at me, a big grin on her face, and I realized my mistake.

'Been here before, huh?'

I shrugged. 'Yeah. I guess so.'

'Is this your home town, Paulie?'

'Could be.'

Wanda jumped up and down, still holding the fan in

its box. 'I knew it! I thought you knew your way around a little too well, and all that stuff about the icebergs by the lake. So are your parents coming to the show? Do they know you're here?'

'No, and no. And that's how I want it, OK?'

'OK. Fine. I won't say another word.'

Except she did. She couldn't help herself, I guess. The next two days, she kept bothering me about it, asking me questions about the town, which inevitably led to questions about how I remembered that, or why I did, and whether my family had been there too. Thursday morning, on our way back from eating breakfast out, Wanda went into a phone booth, saying she needed to make a call.

'Come in with me.'

When we were both inside, she shut the door and handed me the phone book on its little chain.

'Call them,' she said.

'Who?'

'You know who. Your family.'

'Come on, let me out. This is stupid.'

'What, you're never going to see them again?'

'Sure I will, some time. Just not this week.'

'When's the last time you saw them?'

'I don't know, a while – three years? Three and a half?'

'Three years?! They'd *love* to see you. Think how happy it'd make them. They don't hate you, do they?'

Wanda's family lived in Detroit. Her dad, who had beat up her mom and occasionally her, wasn't around any more, but her mom and her little sister were, and she talked to them on the phone all the time. They sent her little care packages.

'Look, you say you're going to see them some time.

Well, we're here now. You won't have to make a special trip, you won't have to stay with them, even – it's the perfect time. Very in control.'

She was right. But mostly because I just didn't feel like fighting with her about it for the next three days, I sighed and said OK.

'OK what?'

'OK, I'll phone them.'

'Truthfully? Are you sure?'

'It was *your* idea.'

'Cool. Do you want to call right now?' She handed me the receiver. 'Do you need to look the number up?'

I shook my head.

'Here.' She put a quarter in the slot, and I dialled.

Janine was in the middle of tiling the bathroom. I thought I could hear a sort of thrilled horror in her voice, as if she was speaking to a fugitive or something, but she spoke kindly and asked me how long I would be in town.

'I'm here with the circus.'

'With the circus? Are you? Oh yes, James told us you worked in a circus.'

'Uh-huh.'

There was a pause.

'I'm re-tiling the bathroom – you remember the small one downstairs?'

'Yes.'

'We've had it enlarged, added a shower. But it isn't finished yet. How long can you stay?'

'We're only here another three days. But I live in a trailer, I don't need a place to stay.'

There was another pause.

'I'm sorry I took so long to answer the phone, dear. I was wearing rubber gloves because of the adhesive.'

201

'That's OK.'

'What's going on?' whispered Wanda. I shook my head at her.

'Janine. Is Dad around?'

'He's at work right now, but he'll be back at six. He'd love to see you! He won't believe it's you!'

I put my hand over the mouthpiece and whispered, 'Do you want to go with me?'

'Me? Sure,' Wanda said, trying to play it cool, but I knew she was mega-excited I'd asked her. After trying to keep my family a big secret for the last three years, I suddenly didn't want to see them on my own, not the first time. Wanda was the perfect escort – a bit of exotic. I don't think there'd ever been a black person in my house before. Janine would be far too busy asking Wanda polite questions to worry about my life. And I figured Wanda would keep me laughing, she'd keep it from all getting a little too intense. Maybe she'd even give me a little perspective. Now she knew about them anyway.

We arranged to go over for lunch the next day. That way, I had the get-away excuse of the afternoon show. If I wanted to leave, I could pretend I was irreplaceable in the running backstage, but if, for some strange reason, I wanted to stay for the evening, Wanda could easily get someone to cover for me. People were always blowing the show, or turning up drunk, or disappearing for a few days, so there was no job that couldn't be done by half a dozen other people on the lot. Janine got flustered all over again when I said I was bringing a friend, and then she got excited.

'Oh, how nice. We'd love to meet her. Does she work for the circus too?'

'Yes.'

'What does she do?'

'She's a contortionist.'

Wanda covered her mouth with her hand in mock horror, pretending to be Janine.

'How *interesting*!' said Janine. She was probably expecting Wanda to turn up for lunch in her costume.

'OK, you can come,' I said to Wanda, after hanging up. 'But I'm not answering a lot of questions. My mom's not around – that was my dad's wife, Janine.'

'No problem,' she said. 'I won't say a thing.'

Janine had dyed her hair red. She answered the door wearing a white blouse and yellow trousers, with yellow and cream shoes to match. After commenting on the size of my trailer, parked out front, and showing us the new guest bathroom in the front hallway, which she'd finished decorating just yesterday, she ushered us to the dining room.

'*Please* sit, both of you. I thought we'd have a cold lunch, what with the heat and all. What would you like to drink?' She took our orders, smiling the whole time, and went into the kitchen to fetch them. Wanda and I only had time to make a face at each other across the table, and then she was back.

'You must *love* children,' she said, handing Wanda the iced tea she'd requested. I'd asked for a beer, but Wanda didn't drink before a show.

'They're OK,' said Wanda. 'Though you'd be surprised – a lot of the hard-core circus fans are grown-ups.'

'*Are* they? How interesting! I haven't been to a circus in I wouldn't like to say *how* many years. Of course, I went once when I was a little girl. I used to love the elephants. Do you have elephants in your circus?'

Janine was looking at me. When I didn't reply, Wanda answered for me.

'We sure do. Paulie's always afraid that one's going to step on her.'

Janine looked puzzled.

'They help put up the big top,' Wanda explained. 'The elephants.'

Janine was still looking confused. Then I realized she didn't know who Paulie was.

'They call me Paulie at work, Janine. It's a sort of nickname.'

'Oh I *see*.' Janine smiled broadly. 'Do you all have nicknames?' she asked, neatly swivelling her hostess head towards Wanda.

Kama Sutra was what a lot of the worker guys called Wanda, but I wasn't sure if she knew about it.

'Only some of us,' said Wanda.

'It sounds fascinating. I'm afraid our lives are very dull in comparison.'

Janine was managing to sound interested and yet mildly repelled at the same time. I guess she was just trying to be friendly. Meanwhile, my father, who had been in the middle of mowing the front lawn when we arrived and had kept on mowing the lawn for another ten minutes, after which he'd come into the house, shook Wanda's hand and said, 'Nice to see you, honey' to me as if I lived around the corner and he saw me every day, was now still getting 'cleaned up', five minutes later. How weird was that? Wanda kept trying to catch my eye, but I was concentrating really hard on the wallpaper Janine had chosen for this little room she called the dining room — an olive green background, with what looked like royal blue peacocks parading up and down. What had she done to this house? And how often?

'Could I have a look around?' I asked.

'Before lunch? Why, of course, dear. I mean, your father doesn't seem to be ready quite yet, anyway.' Janine pushed back her chair. 'Shall we show Wendy your old room? It's been changed a little, but I think you'll still recognize it.'

Wendy? Wanda grinned at me and stood up.

'Now this was your room, wasn't it, dear?' Janine said, opening a white door with a fake brass doorknob, the kind of door someone could easily put his foot through with one hard kick. 'I use it for my sewing now, you see.'

I did see. There was flowery fabric everywhere, and little quilted dolls that probably had secondary functions, and striped valances under every piece of furniture, and shades at the window made out of a blue gingham with little strawberries running across. The spotless cream carpet which spread like milky vomit throughout the rest of the house inevitably overflowed into this room as well.

'This isn't how it looked when it was mine,' I said to Wanda.

'I figured.'

'Oh, she had posters everywhere, didn't you? Movie stars, I think, or musicians, and that strange modern painting over your bed. Didn't one of your friends paint it? It's in the garage still – I'm sure it is. And so many books! I'm afraid we donated most of those to charity, dear. I hope you don't mind. It's just that we didn't know how to get hold of you.'

'That's OK. There was nothing I needed.'

'And your record player, of course, and all your records – oh, here's something that's stayed the same.

Look at this, Wendy. We didn't paint over this.' She was standing by the closet door, tapping the wall with one brightly polished orange fingernail. Up and down the woodwork, a series of notches were drawn in blue ink with the date and my name below each line. The lowest notch was dated 4 August 1966 and had my full name next to it with a little heart after it. I leaned over and stared at this.

'That's my mother's handwriting.' I looked at Wanda. 'I was two and a half – almost three. Strange to think of it, huh? In this same room?'

Wanda nodded and I refused to include Janine.

'Janine?' my dad called from the front of the house.

'Oh, there's your father, ready to eat.' She swept us out of the room, like two little piles of dust, and closed the door behind.

Later on, during lunch, there was a time when Wanda went to the bathroom and Janine was in the kitchen getting dessert ready, so my dad and I were alone together. He suddenly turned his whole body towards me, like he'd been gearing himself up for this moment, and asked in a sort of gush: 'So how long are you going to work for the circus?'

'What do you mean?'

I expected him to say something sarcastic about what a drop-out life I was leading, no roots, no home, no man, no children, living in a white-trash trailer. Instead he said that he'd always thought I was such an amazing kid.

'You were always studying, and reading – half of the time books I couldn't even understand. And you did so well in school. Sometimes I used to lie in bed at night thinking about things you'd said, things you'd just said in passing, you know, at the dinner table.

Things that seemed more – I don't know – complicated than should be coming from a kid. This is when you were in high school, I mean. When you were older.'

After Mom left. Just say it. After Mom left and there was no-one else to talk to, so we occasionally had to talk to each other. I stared at my place mat, played with a fork, tracing parallel lines in the white tablecloth.

'I mean, I don't care what you do,' he continued, 'as long as you're happy, and you manage to make a living for yourself. I'm just surprised. I thought you might end up doing something different, you know, like writing a book, or teaching in a college. Or something for the government, maybe.'

All at once I felt like crying, which totally surprised me. Why should I feel sad? It was pretty hysterical what he was saying: 'something for the government'? I tried to laugh but my throat was tight, so it came out as a strange little cough.

'Oh, believe me, Dad, there's a lot of high-level diplomacy involved in working on a big top crew. It's a touring United Nations.'

I could tell he didn't really understand what I meant, but I guess he could hear the sarcasm.

'No, really,' I added, sticking in the knife just a little deeper, 'I'm storing it all up for an exposé. Why else would I be hanging around with all these low-lifes?'

Dad frowned. 'Wanda seems very nice. Do you ever see that friend of yours? Does she know you're in town?'

'Barbara? No.'

'Oh. That's too bad. You two used to crack each other up. I remember sitting in here some evenings, and I'd hear the two of you in your room, laughing up a storm.'

Stoned out of our minds, probably.

'James was never like that. He never had those kinds of friends. Always sort of a loner.'

Dad finished off his beer just as Janine brought in a bright yellow angel food cake from the kitchen, which matched what she was wearing, incidentally, and Wanda came back from the bathroom.

I decided to stay on a while after Dad and my little tête-à-tête, but this turned out to be a big mistake. After Wanda left, Dad went out to get something from the hardware store for half an hour, and I was stuck making very tiny talk with Janine. Then I sat around for a while reading back copies of *Reader's Digest* until Dad came back and we watched the television news together, and then all three of us ate dinner on little tray tables in front of their favourite TV detective show.

'So, Dad,' I asked, during a commercial break, 'how's James these days? What's he doing? Is he still in seminary?'

'Oh, he writes us all the time,' said Janine. 'He's in Seattle.'

'Uh-huh?' I didn't want them to know we'd been in touch. They didn't deserve to know about James and me.

'They've given him a job there, in a sort of hospital, as part of his ministry training. We have some photos,' she said, jumping up from the sofa. 'Your father and I went out and visited him this winter, for his birthday.' She went over to a sideboard where they kept their fancy glasses, and from the bottom half of this attractive piece of Americana furniture she brought out a cardboard box with 'James' written in blue magic marker on the top. Before she closed the cabinet door,

208

I caught a glimpse of some other boxes and manila envelopes, a photo album. Were there photos of me in there? Did they have a box with my name on it? The whole time I was there I kept looking for one thing, one single household object, that had belonged to my mother. Anything I remembered her using, a can opener, a beer glass, a place mat. But there was nothing.

'Here's a nice one,' said Janine, handing me a photograph. There was James standing with my father in front of a door in a white building. James was dressed in black trousers, black shirt, but no dog collar. Guess he wasn't a priest yet. He was wearing a short red denim jacket, and it seemed that his hair was thinning or else he'd shaved it off. He looked pretty good – the red jacket was sort of retro.

'That's in front of the Space Needle,' said Janine. 'James invited us to come. We had a great time, didn't we?'

Dad stopped watching the TV for a second, and looked over at Janine, smiled. 'Yup, we did.'

Whoa. Whose family was this? I was feeling very left out in the cold. I found myself wishing I lived in Pennsylvania or something, with a husband and two kids, and a nice little house that Dad and Janine could come and visit at Thanksgiving. I shook my head a few times, trying to snap out of it, and Janine asked me if I was all right.

'I'm fine. Does he have a girlfriend? James, I mean.'

Janice smiled a little smile. 'No. I think they keep him too busy in the hospital for that kind of thing. He always asks about you though, how you are, where you are . . .'

So maybe he hadn't told them either, that we were in touch.

'It's a little hard to keep in touch on the road.' I turned to my dad. 'But I can leave you a touring schedule, and you can always write to me care of the circus's central office, and they forward it on, to whatever town we're at. Or write to General Delivery, a few days ahead of us being in a town.'

'We'll give you James's address,' said Janine.

Right before I left, Janine beckoned me into the kitchen and handed me some leftovers wrapped up in aluminium foil.

'I don't know how much home cooking you can do in that trailer,' she whispered, as if she was giving me some sort of contraband.

'I can cook all right.'

But she kept holding it out at me, so finally I took it just so I could get out of there, and then she held onto it.

'Now,' she said, holding tight to her end of the foil package. 'Please stay in touch. We were so happy to get your phone call. I know your life is a bit topsy-turvy, but maybe we could take a holiday and meet you on the road somewhere. Your dad's going to retire one of these days, after all, and you're his only daughter.'

When she said that very last bit about me being his only daughter, Janine stopped agitating for the first time all day and looked straight at me, like a crazy person who's been jabbering away for months and suddenly comes out with something completely sane and true. I made a quick getaway.

On the way home, I cried a little – some stupid song came on the radio. The one thing I had planned on, after Wanda had forced me to call, was that I'd at least get a chance to ask about my mother, if she'd called, trying to find out where James and I were. But I couldn't do it. I'd kept almost saying something, then didn't. I guessed they would have said though, if they had heard anything. That's what I had to count on.

And what was with my dad? Had he taken some 'how to be a supportive dad' course since I'd last seen him? At the local community college?

I couldn't handle it. Migrating. Just migrating.

In Cedar Rapids, Iowa – mid-June – we shared the lot with a carnival and Wanda and I ended up getting drunk one night after the show, then going to a fortune teller. Just for kicks. Wanda's reading was pretty predictable, lots of hearts and roses. Big romance coming, from every direction. I was expecting mine to be pretty similar.

First the lady told me I'd be hearing from an old friend. A postcard? I hadn't had one of those since the end of last season – never got one at all in New Orleans. Maybe this reading meant I'd be getting another one soon.

The fortune teller also told me she saw some 'difficult aspects' in the cards.

'What do you mean, "difficult aspects"?'

'You see that card there? The Tower?'

The Tower card had a picture on it of a tall stone tower being struck by lightning and beginning to crumble to the ground. This lady had designed and drawn her own Tarot deck – she was obviously really into it, which was good, I guess, because at least she wasn't cynical. She was like a hippie fortune teller; there were lots of dirty naked hippie children crawling around inside her tent. She stroked her long hair away from her face as she spoke, so gently sometimes I couldn't hear her, especially with the noise the kids were making.

'Doesn't look so good,' I said.

'Well, every card has positive and negative aspects, but this one usually means a lot's going to have to be swept away. You know, before it can be rebuilt. And probably in a sudden way, like a bolt of lightning.'

'OK.'

'Probably means the big top's going to fall on you,' said Wanda. 'Or an elephant.'

The towns kept coming: Iowa City, Des Moines, Sioux City.

One of the many things I regretted about my visit home was now every time we got to a new place I half expected or wondered if there would be a letter from Dad. Something, anyway. And I never even used to think about him before. Always a mixed bag getting in touch with people again, I said to Chicken, then realized what I'd just said. Still no more postcards.

Hoxie tried to add a few new fairgrounds each year, but really the only thing that distinguished one week from another was the weather, and the ground surface we were dealing with. Which affected the amount of damage the top sustained when it was rolled out, as well as the amount of aggro Terry would get from the horse trainer for expecting her palominos to damage their knees galloping around on top of hard rocks. There were all the usual day-to-day circus dramas. The new tightrope walker fell off his rope and hurt his back – it wasn't too serious, because his brother rushed under and sort of broke his fall, but he was going to be in hospital for a few weeks. Terry was worried the guy might sue, because he blamed the fall on the wrong tension in his ropes, so Terry fired Scary Gid for being legless once too often, but really as a scapegoat because everyone knew not to let Gid within a hundred miles of any artist's ropes. Matthew split up with the hand-balancer – she sat around outside her trailer, looking depressed – and now he was screwing his way round the *corps de ballet* like there was no tomorrow. He didn't seem that funny any more. Little Danny McClain got a girlfriend: a towner who hung around the whole week in Tulsa, and then followed us to Wichita. His mother Allison was sure a psychotic father was going to turn up any moment. The girl looked about twelve.

After Wichita it was a long haul to the next site in Little Rock, where we were doing a two-week stand including the Fourth of July weekend. Unusually for him, Terry had allowed us two days' travelling time instead of the usual one, and Wanda decided to take a train with some of the other performers. She'd mostly been going with me, and actually it was kinda nice to get some thinking-driving time on my own. I'd see her in Little Rock.

If only Love were more like driving. It often surprises me that people, when they're driving, for the most part follow the rules. With obvious exceptions, of course. Whenever I'm driving around and I catch the eye of other drivers waiting at an intersection, their feet hovering between the brake and the accelerator, eager, so eager for me to pass, so they can jump back into the current that will rush them along to wherever they need to go next, I marvel at the way it all works so smoothly. At the self-control inherent in the system. These people are dying to get going – to be gone already – yet they wait. Why? It's not exactly a characteristic trait of our culture, to be patient. How is it that more people aren't losing it every second? How is it that there aren't a million more crashes every day? The answer is obvious, of course – no-one wants to die. And they don't want their shiny new sportscar to get smashed up, or their kids getting hurt, or anybody else's kids, if they're that sort of empathetic type. Fatal car crashes are not a superior way to go, unless you want to be like James Dean. For one, they're undependable – who's to say you won't just be maimed or left comatose? And there's no time to say goodbye – you may have left the house in a bad mood, you may have been late for work. They're out of control – you may end up killing everyone in the whole family but your two-year-old girl, whose life is now a mess because you felt lucky and tried to make that light. So be a good driver, says Smokey the Bear. Be a responsible citizen of the roads and cheat the Grim Reaper for that little while longer.

But Love doesn't work this way, and this is a problem I ponder a lot. Because dead hearts don't make dead bodies, and I include my own. So how do you know with whom you're dealing? And does that mean that people can do what the fuck they want, and get away with it? Hearts that got injured along the way get better again, sort of, partially, and it's really difficult to tell that they were ever in a crash. The people that did the damage get right back on the road; they don't get their love licences taken away or anything. The victims start back on the road too, thinking, well, I was being good last time and I got hit anyway, but I didn't die, so maybe this time I'll just drive the way I want to, and even if I crash into someone, so what? Fuck 'em – they'll survive. I did.

I pulled up to the field in Little Rock about five in the afternoon and there was good old Sid to welcome me.

'Hey, Sid. Where do you want me? Are the guys from the train here yet?'

'Who? How the fuck should I know?'

'Oh, give it up, Sid. You're such a dick.' I ended up parked bang-slap against the big generator all week, the noisy one.

After hooking up, I took a little walk around. Allison McClain was sitting on the fold-out veranda of their King of the Road, smoking a cigarette.

'Hey, Allison.'

She waved. 'Hi there yourself.'

I leaned against their little picket fence. 'How's Danny? Still got his girlfriend living with you?'

She rolled her eyes, exhaled a big cloud of smoke. 'Don't.'

Allison was in a wheelchair. Two years ago, when he was about fifteen, her son Danny had been playing around with some fireworks he'd bought for the Fourth of July, and he'd had an accident. Danny was a nice kid. He always kept an eye out for the smaller kids during the show. Like last season, the Russian husband-and-wife bicycle act had come with a one-year-old daughter, and Danny used to take care of her when her parents were performing, wheel her up in her pram to the tent flap so she could see them performing, and he hardly ever forgot. Anyway, two years ago, I guess he'd been messing around with these fireworks and one of them just blew up in his face. Allison and Danny senior were up in the air at the time – on the trapeze – but someone managed to get word to them and they cut the act short. Allison raced off to the hospital with Danny, while big Dan changed clothes for the web-spinning he did after the interval. Danny was fine, it turned out – only superficial burns, but they wanted to keep him overnight to check on his eyes – and on the way home, Allison ran a red light and got ploughed into by a mail truck. She smashed up her spine and that was it: grounded for life. Now she just sat around all day, smoking, doing bits of sewing for anybody who asked and would pay her. The McClain family were third-generation circus people.

'Seen Wanda around?' I asked.

'Nope. Can't say I have.'

The next morning, Wanda still hadn't arrived. I woke up really early while everything was still quiet, and I could hear the birds twittering, and the far-off rushing of traffic on the Interstate. I pulled back the curtains on the little window beside my bed and it was a beautiful morning, the sky still pale, but warm-looking. I could smell wood smoke and, knowing what that meant, traced it to a plume rising in a far corner of the site. Frank Olliquorcio.

One of my favourite things about the circus was some of the old characters you met come-to-life, kind of like that oldie time exhibit at the city museum Barbara and I used to frequent. Hard apples like Chicken, for example, and Antony, the trumpet player in the circus band, who came from Russia and from time to time referred darkly to his relationship with Stalin. I never believed it until once he got a week-long visit from a bunch of black-suited bruisers straight out of a KGB casting session.

Frank Olliquorcio was a blacksmith. Chicken thought he was weird, because he never socialized; he

216

drank, of course, but you never saw him drunk. He had this inner focus to him, like a samurai blacksmith. Even Chicken didn't give him shit, to his face. He was about a hundred and two years old, but he must have been of some use to the circus, because sure as shit they would have fired him if he wasn't. Maybe he was someone's father-in-law, or parole officer, or something. He didn't do much, really. Shoes for the horses, reshaping the strongman's little iron bars, lots of pickety jobs. But at least he never caused any trouble. He worked bare-handed, squinting against the heat, over a big stone grate full of red-hot coals. Christ knows how he lifted this thing into his pick-up truck when we moved. A unit like this does have a few real welders on the crew, unionized and all that, with giant blowtorches and Darth Vader face masks, so that's how come it must have been somebody owed Frank a favour. On the other hand, they probably paid him about five bucks a week.

He looked up when I approached and nodded – there were some nails sticking out of his mouth. 'All right?' I said and crossed my arms, rubbing the skin where it was breaking out in goosebumps. Frank was used to me watching him work. In the height of the summer he usually worked bare-chested under his leather apron, so you could see the muscles in his old arms and the white scars from various burns he'd suffered over the years, but this morning he was wearing some sort of fleecy body-warmer, covered with charcoal rubs. He bent over his iron like a father over a cradle, the glow of the coals making his brow shine. Behind him, the sky was getting brighter, streaks of pink and orange bleeding up the page, almost like they were reflecting off the flames of Frank's fire, and when the sun appeared on the horizon it was easy to imagine it was a red-hot coal that Frank was lifting into the sky between the grip of his tongs.

I figured I'd walk over to the office, see if Terry knew what was up with Wanda.

'Wanda? She went home,' said Terry. 'Some sort of family crisis.'

'Family crisis?'

'Her sister, or her mother. Can't remember.'

'What about the show?'

'Petra's going to do the Shetland pony act, with Matt. Until she comes back.'

'So she's coming back?'

'She better. She owes me about a hundred more shows.'

Wanda turned up early Saturday morning and I caught up with her later, in her hamster cage of a room. She was throwing stuff around in a panic, because Terry had pretty much demanded she do both of the Saturday shows, and the matinée was starting in half an hour.

'Are you OK? How's your mother?'

'My mother? She's fine – why? Did she call?'

'No. I thought you were with her.'

'Oh, that's right. That's what I told them.' She grinned at me as she struggled into her white leotard. 'I wasn't with my mother, Paulie. You won't believe it. I'm in love – fucking zip, can you do it?'

'You've got plenty of time. There.'

'Thanks.'

'So there was no family crisis?'

'Nope. Yuck, got my period on the plane. Remind me to change my tampon. How was *your* week?'

'Nothing special.' I sat down on the box she used

for a chair. 'I was sort of worried about you, actually.'

'You were? Sorry. Well, I'm back now – even though I wish to fuck I wasn't.' She was scrabbling around in the suitcase under her bed, and she pulled out her show shoes, the little ballet slippers she used for walking around backstage. 'Just wait till you meet him. You'll love him, Paulie.' She lay down on the tiny bit of floor space. 'Gotta warm up.'

'So when did all this happen? In Wichita?'

She laughed but it came out as more like a grunt because she had her legs over her head, with her thighs pressed against each ear. 'No, no – I worked with Marc last year, in a circus in Montreal.' She uncurled herself. 'He started fucking around on me, though, with some bimbo, so I left and that's why I ended up working for this raggedy outfit. I didn't think I'd ever hear from him again, the jerk, then last Saturday, in Wichita, just a couple hours before the train, I got this phone call and he practically begged me to come to Montreal for the week. Even paid for the plane tickets.'

'So you just took off, then and there.'

'Sure. I had to.' She stood up, began stretching her arms over her head and to the side. I picked up a makeup stick on her table.

'What's he do?'

'Marc? He's a ringmaster. Youngest ringmaster there's ever been.'

'How young's that?' Got this image of a little eight-year-old lying on top of Wanda.

'Twenty-nine.'

'Oh. Right. Not so young.'

'It is for a ringmaster. You have to have done a little of everything to become a ringmaster.'

Wanda crashed into the end of her bed. For a dancer type, she was clumsy; she was always crashing into things. Shooing me off the box, she started rubbing on foundation, propping up her square of mirror so she could see better.

'I guess I'd better go,' I said.

'OK. Is my rope good? I haven't had time to check it.'

'I'll do it.'

'Thanks. Let's get something to eat between shows. I'll fill you in on everything.'

From then on, nothing was the same. The usual things happened: Chicken got a bad summer cold so he was even meaner than usual, one of the Mongolian acrobatic troupe – this tiny woman called Ionen – got pregnant and the rumour was it was Tex's so now all the men in the Mongolian troupe were threatening to kill him, Terry broke a few fingers when his hand got caught between a rope and one of the lighting towers. All more of the same, except now, everything that happened around Wanda and me was filtered through ever-present, Marc-coloured spectacles.

Marc would feel this way about that act. Marc would be so much better at the improvised dialogue in the gaps between acts. Marc pronounced his name 'Mahrc', because it's French, the French spelling, and he hated it when people Americanized it. The more I heard about this guy, the more I hated him. But what I hated most was that she'd never told me about him.

'Have you got that book still?' she asked me one day.

'What book?'

'The one with all the saints.'

'It's somewhere around. Why?'

'I want to look up Marc's name—'

220

'Patron saint of lawyers. Invoked against sudden and unexpected death.'

'That's Marc? No shit? Thanks.'

'No problem.'

'What was it you said – inwhat against what?'

'Invoked against sudden and unexpected death.'

'Well, I guess I chose well. Sounds like a good guy to have around in our business.'

'If you believe in these sort of things.'

'And you don't?'

'No.'

'Then why'd you bother to look up Marc's name? Why do you carry the book around with you? Why do you hide it in your trailer?'

'I don't hide it in my trailer.'

'Sure you do. The first time I picked it up off the floor, it was like I was picking up your pet rattlesnake or something. You went about as stiff as a board.'

'What are you talking about?'

'Oh, come on.'

'I don't know what you're talking about.'

I was working the cotton-candy stand that afternoon and I knew I should be going to turn on the machine now, before people started arriving. It was a good excuse to walk away, but Wanda followed me.

'Look, Paulie – it's fine you not wanting to like Marc, and being all weird about him for whatever reason even though you've never laid eyes on him in your life. I mean you don't have to like him – I don't care – just don't get all funny with *me* because you're jealous.'

I stopped walking. 'Jealous?!'

Two guys from the ring crew looked up at the sound of my voice. The one named Jack whistled softly. 'Cat

221

fight,' he said and the other guy chuckled as they walked on.

I lowered my voice. 'Jealous? That's good. Jealous of who exactly? I mean it would have been nice if maybe you had told me about this guy earlier, if maybe you could have *shared* this little bit of information, that you had this, you know, great love in your life you were holding a torch for, but then, who am I? I'm nobody. I thought we were friends, that's all, and then you suddenly disappear without warning and come back practically wearing a wedding ring. It would have been nice to have had a little warning.'

Wanda was standing there with her hands on her hips. When I stopped talking she let her mouth drop open in mock amazement.

'*Excuse* me? You're pissed I didn't tell you? I cannot even believe you are saying that to me. Look – I didn't tell you about Marc because I never expected to hear from him again and I just wanted to forget about it. But who are *you* to talk, girl? I mean at least when I'm with Marc, I don't feel like I'm standing next to a fucking shadow half the time, like I'm best friends with someone whose life started the day before I met her, and for God's sake don't try and lift the lid up on anything, or you'll get your fingers snapped off, it comes down so fast and hard. Talk about not telling, well now you know what it feels like, I guess.'

'I've told you lots of things. I have to start making the cotton candy.'

'Bullshit. Tell me one thing you've told me.'

'I took you home with me, for Chrissakes. That's my family – big deal. There's nothing to tell.'

'Oh yeah, then what about your brother? I guess you have one since your dad mentioned him at the dinner

222

table. And it's bullshit that Chicken met you in your home town – he told me you were living with a bunch of hippies in North Carolina. What about the postcards in your old book? And what about the million-dollar question? What about that one, huh – I mean, what *is* the deal with your mom? Is she dead, or in prison, or what?'

I flung my hand up to stop her and walked away. This time she knew not to follow.

Chattanooga, Huntsville, Tuscaloosa. Petra swore she was going to fucking kill Newcastle Nick who, during a Wednesday matinée, started hammering away on an old exhaust pipe just as Petra was passing with Goldenrod. Goldenrod freaked and pulled so hard that Petra's arm almost came out of the socket and she strained a muscle in her shoulder. 'You fucking son-of-a-bitch!' she yelled at Nick, 'you fucking loser!', so loudly I wondered what percentage of the audience was hearing it. Later on she complained to Terry: 'The jerk's been told a thousand times. He does it on purpose.' A whole lot of the elephants got sick because the new trainer, who wasn't very experienced – like, not at all – fed them some hay he'd got cheap, which turned out to be rancid, so the elephants went down with gastroenteritis and had to miss three shows. If you've never experienced elephant diarrhoea, you don't want to. The only time I saw Wanda was in the ring, under the spotlight. I knew she was hanging out in the canteen after shows, because sometimes when I was walking by, I heard her laughing.

And then, just when I thought things couldn't get any worse, Chicken died.

We were appearing that week in Winona,

Mississippi — a nice site, grassy, even, no rocks. Chicken didn't turn up when the spool truck started doing its thing, but this was no biggie. He'd probably tied one on the night before and slept in, missed the 5 a.m. drive-out call, out of Jackson. I hadn't noticed his red van around, though Sid could have tucked it behind a telephone pole or something. So I walked the top myself, laid out flat on the grass, repaired a repair we'd done a few weeks ago which must have caught on something, and did a little fortifying on a corner which Chicken would probably have left until it really needed it, but I figured preventive sewing was no bad thing. After lunch, when the top was up and people were getting ready for the show, I was helping un-box a new batch of programmes by the side of the front door and Hoxie came up, looking sombre.

'Pauline. Got some bad news.'

I straightened up to face it. Whatever was coming. All my life I'd been expecting this kind of thing. I smiled at Hoxie. 'Oh yeah?'

'It's Chicken. He's dead. The police just called me — they were driving by the lot in Jackson, and they saw the van still parked there, so they swung by just to check everything was OK. Anyway, they couldn't get in — you know how Chicken always kept it locked — but when one of them went around and looked through the window they could see him lying on the floor. Heart attack. Probably didn't even know what hit him.'

Tex Hamilton was standing around nearby, supposedly checking over today's show order, which always changed a little depending on people's injuries and the animals, and he'd been listening in.

'You know I *saw* his van this morning,' he said, 'and I was one of the last out. That's terrible. I thought maybe it had broken down and someone was coming back to get it.'

'Is there anyone you want me to call?' asked Hoxie. I realized he was talking to me.

'Hoxie. You know we weren't really related.'

'Oh,' he said. 'Yeah, I guess I knew that.'

'He's got a daughter in Oklahoma.' The nice lady in her seersucker dress. 'You should call her.'

At the end of the week Hoxie gave me Chicken's hat, the one with its hatband of waxed cord. And his block of wax, and the knife he'd always carried in his belt, for cutting cord.

'Look, I had to go back and clear out the van,' he said, 'get it towed. His daughter doesn't want any of this stuff. I thought maybe you could still use them.'

No more Chicken. The last time we'd gone out drinking together, only about a week ago, because we'd been hanging out more since Wanda and I weren't, he'd told me some cockamamie story about how he had been there when Ronald Reagan was shot, and that John Hinckley had just been standing there in the crowd, how he wasn't responsible at all. Chicken implied he could have told me a thing or two about the truth of the matter if only he'd been at liberty to speak. When I'd asked him what he'd been doing there anyway, in Washington that day, he said, 'Wouldn't you like to know, missy? Same kind of things *you* were doing before I met you, I guess.' Meaning we'd take our own secrets to the grave, wouldn't we? And we had.

I felt really bad on the drive to the next lot in Texarkana – it was like the Tripping Society had taken over the radio airwaves, so many goddamn awful songs. But in Texarkana, Wanda and I made up.

She walked up to me backstage during the matinée,

when I was standing holding one of the palominos waiting for its entrance.

'I'm really sorry about Chicken,' she said.

'Uh-huh.'

'Are you going to the funeral?'

'What funeral?'

'Isn't there going to be a funeral? I mean, his family must be doing something, aren't they?'

'How would I know?'

I wanted to be acting differently; I wanted to say something softer, but I couldn't do it. And I was afraid she was just going to walk away again now, and that would be it.

'So,' she said. 'I guess you're head canvas girl now.'

'Guess so.'

Head canvas girl. Made me feel like shit. Wanda took a few steps forward and peeked through the gap in the flap.

'How's Marc?' I asked.

She turned around and looked at me, waited a second before she answered. 'He's fine. He's meeting me in Dallas, end of the month.'

'You must be excited.'

'I am.'

My cue came and I walked the horse forward to the edge of the ring. When I came back through the flap, Wanda was still there.

'How about a beer?' she said. 'Afterwards? You got time?'

We went back to the female sleeper and sat on the steps outside her front door. It was a quiet evening, just the sound of the band from inside the top, sun low in the sky behind the line of trees at the edge of the city park.

'I've been missing my TV!' she said.

'You should have come and got it.'

'Yeah, well . . .'

We finished our beers pretty much in silence, and I knew I'd have to be getting back for the second-show prep. It was now or never fix it.

'My mom just left. It's no big deal. She ran off with this guy when I was fifteen, and that's the last we ever heard of her. I mean, there's no big trauma, compared to what some people go through. She's just never got in touch. Maybe that's why I didn't tell you – because there's nothing to tell.' I almost said about the postcards, but it had been hard enough getting all this out. Wanda was listening, being really quiet, for her. 'And since then, since I left home I mean, I've just been wandering around. Pretty aimlessly. Chicken and I did meet in a supermarket – I told you the truth there – but it was in North Carolina. My brother lives in Seattle and he's training to be a priest.'

I waited for her to say something. She put down her beer bottle and stood up, stretched her back.

'Here,' she said, reaching out an arm to help me up. 'We don't want to miss the show.'

Texas: Galveston, Houston, then Dallas. The third head cook in seven weeks threatened to blow the show because Hoxie wouldn't give him a raise. Danny's little girlfriend went home again, with her daddy who had come to get her. In Galveston, as if it was a reward for my truth session with Wanda, an anonymous letter came for me, my name typed on the envelope. Inside was a postcard, with a picture of a motel on it. Just an ordinary one-storey motel, made out of different coloured bricks laid next to each other, red and beige.

227

A few red and blue cars were parked in the spaces out front, looking like toy cars. The Traveller's Inn, it said. Prophetstown, Illinois. Someone had drawn a circle in blue Biro around one of the doors, but I couldn't tell what the numbers were – too small.

'I'm sorry,' written on the back.

I showed this postcard to Wanda. Somehow it was more upsetting than any of the others. The others I'd been able to brush off, like prank phone calls – who cares who makes prank phone calls? But this one left me with a bad feeling in my stomach, and I kept getting the postcard out, over and over. I didn't like it.

'And you've no idea who it's from?'

I shook my head.

'Weird.' She handed me the chocolate shake she had just whipped up for me in her brand-new blender. I don't know if this is a common symptom of someone happy in love, but she kept buying household appliances, and they all ended up in my trailer. We had a sandwich toaster, a foot spa, a new La-Z-Boy recliner, and an ice-cream maker.

'Could it be from your mom?'

'I doubt it.'

'Couldn't she have found out where you are? From your dad?'

'It's possible, I guess.'

'What are you gonna do?'

She handed the postcard back to me and I put it message-down on the table. I shrugged. 'Nothing.'

'Why don't you call the hotel? Find out if there's someone staying with that name.'

'Whoever wrote this is probably long gone.'

'Well, what's the date on it?'

I picked the thing up again. 'June something,

228

looks like. It was forwarded, from the main office.'

'Shit. That took a while to get here. Maybe she's hired a detective to find you. Maybe she's been looking for you for a while.'

'Don't get carried away – I'm not that hard to find.'

'Would you want to see her? If it was her?'

Long yellow plait pulled over one shoulder. My mom looking right at me, listening.

'I guess.'

'Then call the hotel – nothing to lose.'

Except my innocence. 'What, and just ask for her?'

'Sure. What's her name?'

'Lydia. Lydia McCall. But she could be using some other name – who knows? She might have gone back to her maiden name. Maybe she's married again, I dunno. Nothing would surprise me.'

'What's her other name, before she was married?'

'Harding.'

'Lydia Harding. That sounds familiar – where have I heard that name?'

I went over to the bed and pulled *Saint Days* from under the mattress. 'The book,' I said, throwing it across to where she was sitting. 'Inside the front cover.'

She opened the book. 'I knew I'd seen it before.'

'Check out all the other postcards.'

Now that I'd started telling her things, I couldn't stop. And it felt OK; it was a relief.

I did call the hotel in Prophetstown, but they said there was no-one staying there with that name, and when I asked if there had been someone of that name in June, the lady on the phone said they weren't allowed to give out that sort of information unless I was the police. The card went back in the book and

229

I tried not to think about it, even though it felt like something rotting under my mattress.

So Marc didn't turn up in Dallas. He sent Wanda a dozen red roses but he didn't come himself, and if I'm totally honest, I was hoping this was a bad omen. On the other hand, I'd been gearing myself up for the big meeting. I'd been practising the right kind of smiles, and thinking about the funny, cute things I was going to say, the easy balance I would find between relaxed familiarity and sensitive detachment. So, in that way, if it was never going to happen, if all that rehearsing was going to go to waste, I'd be disappointed, but I'd get over it. I knew that Wanda didn't take shit from anyone, so she wouldn't put up with no-shows for long.

'What did he say?' I asked.

We'd gone into the suburbs on Tuesday morning, to a mall, and now we were sitting in a sports bar, a baseball game playing above our heads on the big-screen TV.

'Oh, well, you know, he was really cut up about it, of course. But considering the situation' – in a freak storm, a few hundred miles east of Quebec city, their big top had collapsed mid-evacuation and two audience members had been killed in the panic – 'he felt like he had to stay. He is the ringmaster.'

I couldn't imagine our ringmaster blowing off a romantic liaison. Tex would have been the first off the lot, after he'd made sure there was no blood from the audience spattered onto his costume.

'And he can't come any other weekend?'

'No – they all fly out on Saturday.'

'Fly out? Where are they going?'

'France.'

'France?' Hallelujah. 'Shit. How long are they over there? You didn't tell me.'

'For a few months. Not that long, I guess, unless the tour gets extended.'

'And is there a chance of that?'

'I guess so. It sucks.' She tipped back the bottle of beer she was drinking and signalled to the bartender. 'Do you want another one? I shouldn't be doing this, but frankly, I need some fun. I'll sleep it off before the show tonight.'

The last place I went with Sherman Brothers Circus was one of the sweetest places we'd been to. Second week of September, and the weather was ideal. We were parked on this faultless green meadow, ringed around with wildflowers except for the bit in the middle that they kept mowed for travelling shows like us. Smack on the border of Oklahoma – it was like circus life out of a children's book. I wondered what even Chicken would have found to bitch about. We were only about thirty-five miles south of Lawton, where his daughter lived. Would his grandkids have come to the circus this week, if he'd lived? I missed him.

Wanda and I bought some stripy deckchairs, took to lying out in them at noontime, sipping iced tea, eating ham sandwiches without any crusts, and reading. Her, a *People* magazine; me, a collection of Mark Twain stories Kate had given me. Whenever Wanda went in to get a snack, I grabbed her *People*.

She seemed to have bounced back from Marc's no-show. On Friday night, as she was climbing out of her box backstage, she waved me over. I was standing

231

around waiting for the interval, shooting the breeze with one of the other cotton-candy vendors, Darlene. Darlene did the payroll accounts for Terry and typed up his paperwork.

'What's up?' I had to talk a little loudly because we were standing right behind the band platform. 'Did something go wrong?'

'No. But I have to talk to you. In the intermission.'

'Sure.' She was looking weird, sort of buzzed-out. 'Is it Marc? Have you talked to him today?' Maybe she'd copped off with someone else last night. We'd been playing poker in the tent after the show, and I'd gone to bed early. I knew she thought the new groom working for Petra was kinda hot, and I'd seen them talking earlier.

'I called him just before the show.'

'They're still flying out tomorrow, right? To France?'

'Yeah. Look, we can't talk now – I'll talk to you later.'

'Sure. I'll come to your room after I'm done.'

Her room was a complete dump, worse than I'd ever seen it.

'Jesus. I can see why we hang out at my place.'

'Shut up and listen.' Wanda took both my hands and pulled me over to the bed. There was about an inch and a half of free space on it, but we just sat down on the junk. I took my hands away – it made me nervous holding hands, like we were sisters in some eighteenth-century novel.

'So what is it? What's the big news?'

'I'm packing.'

'Why? Did Terry finally give you a better room? Or – don't tell me – you bought that RV we saw, the one with that woman painted on the side who looks like

Dolly Parton. Maybe it *was* Dolly Parton—' I was babbling because I didn't want her to say what she said next. 'Maybe it was her RV and she was inside—'

'No, no, shut up, let me tell you. I'm blowing.' She was speaking quietly, in this intense, excited whisper. 'Marc got me a job with his circus. Somebody dropped out last minute, because their kid's sick or something and they don't want to go to Europe, and Marc talked to the owners about me, and they went for it! He's booked a connecting flight for me, out of Dallas, at 7.30 tomorrow morning, to New York, and I have to pick up the tickets at the airport. So I'm just going. Can you believe it? I'm actually going.'

'How are you going to get to Dallas by 7.30?'

'That new groom of Petra's? He said he'd drive me. Do you want to come along for the ride?'

'Did you sleep with him?'

She laughed, and her laugh was a sudden gust of wind going through her. I could tell she was really happy; I could tell nothing was going to make her unhappy.

I stood up, knocking a lot of stuff off the bed. 'Wow. That's great. I can't believe it. That's fantastic. God, Marc must be so happy. And *you*. You'll have to tell me all about Europe. You know, because I've read lots of books set over there, in London, and Paris, and Russia . . .'

She frowned. 'I don't think we're going to Russia.'

'Really? Too bad.' I picked up a dirty mug from the floor by her bed. It was mine. 'Do you want me to wash this? You'll be great – they'll love your act over there.'

'Well, who knows? Who cares? Are you OK, though? I was worried you'd feel weird. What with Chicken dying and—'

'What is it with Chicken? Everybody acts like he was my long-lost dad or something.' I laughed and tripped over a pile of cassette tapes. 'I'm a big girl, I think I can take it. No, I mean, of course I'm bummed that you're going, but you know, we'll see each other soon. Won't we? You know what the circus is like – small world and all.'

'Totally. I mean I'll make it happen, if it doesn't happen by chance.'

'You'll make it happen? Wow. OK. I look forward to hearing from you on that one.'

'Marc can talk to the—'

'Look, you get packing. Feel like a hot-dog or something? Some coffee? I'll get us some food or something, yeah?'

'Great. Thanks a million, Paulie. You are the best.'

I walked without hesitation in a direct line to the generator nearest to my trailer, lifted the little metal cap and yanked out the cables which connected one to the other. Neatly rolling the cables around my arm, I strolled back to my only home, ripped them out of their sockets at that end, opened the aluminium door and threw them inside. Folded up one of the stripy deckchairs, took it inside too. A minute later, I came out again with one blender, one sandwich toaster, one television and one foot spa. It took two trips. Then I took all the stuff over to where the welders and the mechanics had their *ad hoc* shop. I could hear the band banging away at the music which got everyone back into the tent for the second act. After laying everything out on the flat-bed at the back of the truck, like it was a garage sale, I picked up a sledgehammer and smashed them all to shit, one by one. So many pieces. I noticed a welder's mask and a blowtorch nearby and I was just about to pick them up and do some more basket-weaving, so to speak, when I saw some of the guys from the crew coming over to investigate the noise. I dropped the sledgehammer like it was a murder weapon and skipped around the other side of the truck, took the outskirts route back to my trailer, went in the driver's door, locked it, started the engine and drove away from the one stripy deckchair, sitting all forlorn on the grass.

Drove away from the circus for ever.

Nowhere

For about six hours, I just drove, hardly seeing the road signs. Then about midnight, this picture of Kate came into my mind, Kate's spinsterish hairstyle and her denim shirts, Kate doing the bookstore accounts behind the counter, Kate standing in the doorway of her sister Amy's room, lost in her own thoughts. Kate. I'd go home to Kate's house – I knew she'd be happy to see me, and I didn't have the strength to go someplace new.

To amuse myself, on the long drive back to New Orleans, and so I wouldn't think about Wanda, I played one of my favourite driving games: Where's Mom? This consisted of imagining my mother installed in various outstanding lives, various fabulous occupations. Maybe she was living in Hawaii, being a massage therapist. But not just any kind of ordinary massage therapist. She was one of those really esoteric ones, who take you back to your birth experience and completely re-align your body, who make you weep and moan because all the painful memories caught up in those tight muscles get released. And the reason she had never got in touch with me was because this place in Hawaii was like a sort of spiritual community, an ashram, and to join it you had to give up your old name, your old life entirely, to purify yourself, to make a new life, to be born again. Father Bill had gone there with her, but he hadn't been able to stay the course. My mom, however, had become like the Queen Bee. She was getting closer to enlightenment every day, and in the odd moments she thought about me and James, she knew she was helping us in a much more global, spiritually enlightened way than she ever could have at home.

That was just one of my fantasies.

Sometimes I'd imagine she'd done something, something highly illegal but for a good reason, while she was still living with us. She'd got involved with some seditious political group, and when she left, she'd been on the run from the CIA. She'd gone to Father Bill for sanctuary and confessed everything, and he'd devised this cover-up plan to sneak her away. Did he tell his wife Diana about it, or did he not, to protect her from police questioning? Anyway, ever since, my mom had been forced to adopt a whole new identity, and she knew she'd be endangering my life – and her own – if she ever got in contact, so she'd left me alone. But she knew where I was, because she got people to find out for her. That's why I got that feeling sometimes, that I was being shadowed. It was Mom's spies checking on me so they could tell her I was OK.

This was a game. It passed the time.

The first thing I saw when I pulled up to Kate's house on 23 September, around three in the afternoon, was a Sold sign. It was driven into the ground, out front, like a nail into a crucifix. I got out of the car and my body felt like it was still moving, as if the vibrations of the last twenty-eight hours of driving had replaced the rhythms of my heartbeat with this, a steady buzzing, the constant hum of coin-operated Magic Fingers under a mattress. If I walked across solid ground, would the world stop quaking? I went on up to the front door, skirting the Sold sign like it was a sleeping Dobermann. Knocked, then rang. Unsurprisingly, no-one answered – she was bound to be at the Bluebird. I pushed my way between some bushes and looked in the living-room window, cupping my hand against the glass. Kate's furniture looked back at me; everything seemed the same. At least there weren't any packing boxes.

I couldn't face getting back behind the driver's seat, so I walked the four miles to the bookstore. I don't know if they were having a heatwave for this time of the year, but everything Kate had told me about the heat had not been exaggerated. I was swimming in it after a half-mile, baking in my own juices. Halfway there, it got so bad I had to dive into a Quickie Mart, though the blast of cold air upon entrance made me feel a little queasy. I hung out in the aisles for a while, then I bought a Hershey bar for Kate, because she likes them, and an ice-cold Sprite for me, and plunged outside again. It was as if the plant life had gone mad as well – lilac bushes spewing out their scent, magnolias like fat ladies waving white handkerchiefs at the end of limp wrists, great swathes of greenery erupting over ironwork balconies, and everywhere the smell of rot. I could smell the river, even though it was miles away, and it didn't smell too good. I felt like I was tripping. All the way over, I kept seeing people I thought I recognized. Occasionally I was so convinced they were going to stop and talk when they saw me, I even got my smile ready. Just about everyone looked familiar. By the time I reached the Bluebird, the Hershey bar was liquid.

And Kate wasn't around. There were about five customers milling about – not bad for a Thursday afternoon. I walked through to the café, expecting to find her behind the counter, but there was a woman there I didn't know.

'Hello,' she said, looking up from whatever she was doing. She was pretty, wearing a red bandanna which presumably prevented the sweat from pouring down her forehead and onto the food. There was an air conditioner on the wall behind her, which from the sound of it was making a valiant effort, but by no stretch of the imagination could you have called it cool. 'Can I help you?'

'Is Kate around?'

'Should be. Wasn't she there when you walked in?'

I went back around front. Kate was there now, frowning at some receipts hanging off the cash register. When she saw me, she started and her elbow knocked a little tower of cashier books off the counter.

'My Lord! Where'd you come from?'

'Sorry. I didn't mean to scare you.'

She leaned over to pick up the books. 'Thought I was seeing a ghost.'

'No.'

She took the rubber band out of her ponytail, re-did it so it was tighter. 'Have you been driving a long time? Would you like something to drink?'

'Sure.'

We got two sodas out of the fridge in the café and sat down.

'Maddy, this is Frances – she worked here for a while last winter.'

239

The woman behind the counter smiled a lazy smile at me. 'Hey,' she said.

'So did your brother reach you?'

'My brother?'

'He rang here a few weeks ago. I told him I didn't know, but I thought you were back with the circus. Did he manage to find you?'

'No.'

'That's too bad. It seemed like he really needed to talk to you.'

'Doesn't matter.'

'You should call him.'

'Sure. So you sold the house?'

'Oh. Yes. You went by, huh? I sold it last week. I'm going to live at my sister's for a while, until we figure out the money.'

She looked around the store, then back at me.

'But it won't go through for at least a couple of months. You're welcome to park up in the meantime.'

Kate insisted I stay in Amy's room again, this time because it would be too hot inside the trailer. About two in the morning, I gave up on sleeping and got up to go to the bathroom. Maybe it was the lighting in Kate's bathroom – there were these two old-fashioned globular lamps either side of the mirror over the sink – but the area all around my mouth looked deathly white, up to the nose and across my chin, as if the blood had withdrawn from just that section. I checked out my tongue, but that looked normal. While I was sitting on the toilet, I thought about families.

Kate's sisters. Jonas's parents, even the trapeze-flying McClains.

If those families managed to hang together, in all kinds of different circumstances, then why hadn't mine? What was the failure we had allowed to happen? What was the lack in me that my family didn't really seem to care much about me, or me about them? Or I didn't try to, or they didn't try to, or we all just weren't capable of it. What was wrong with us? There was this sadness in me rising up, which I didn't want to face. In the lining of every internal organ, so wholly and deeply embedded that I did not know if it were possible to take it out without losing the patient.

On the way back to the bedroom, I stopped outside Kate's bedroom and listened at the door. She was snoring, gently. I finally managed to get to sleep about three but then I woke at dawn with a start. Wanda had been speaking in the room. I could swear I'd heard her. I lay there, my heart banging, wondering if Kate, who had got up for some reason, had been talking on the phone in the hallway. But no, it was Wanda's voice I'd heard, Wanda's Midwestern nasal, not Kate's Southern lilt. I even wrestled with the desire to search through the house, as if Wanda had followed me here and was hiding out somewhere.

It took me about two weeks of not sleeping, not working at the Bluebird, not doing anything, before I rang James. Kate just left me alone; she was doing her usual non-intrusive thing but this time it made me mad. Didn't she realize I was having problems? Maybe she didn't want to get it, was the conclusion I came to. Maybe she only wanted me independent and seemingly trouble-free.

At first I couldn't find James's number in the letter he'd written last winter, and when I did find it, the person who answered told me he'd moved to a different room, and then went away for a while and came back with another number for me to call.

241

A man answered.

'James?'

'No. This is Lawrence. Can I help you?' This was a priest's voice if I'd ever heard one. A deep voice, a deep cardinal voice. I felt like, if he asked me to, I'd confess every one of my sins.

'I was wondering if I could speak to James.'

'Sure, I'll just get him – may I ask who's calling?'

'Yes. This is (*queeniemegpauliefrances*) Gert. His sister Gert.'

The phone went very quiet and I wondered if this Lawrence guy had put his hand over the phone so I couldn't hear what he was saying.

Then suddenly it was James talking. Unmistakable.

'Gert?'

'Hi there.'

'Wow. It's you. You called – that's great. Where are you?'

'I'm in New Orleans. My boss said you needed to talk to me?'

'Yes. I've been trying to get hold of you.'

'Uh-huh.'

'So how are you? Happy Birthday, last week.'

'I'm fine – it's kind of ridiculously hot here for October, but never mind.' I hadn't talked to James since he was fourteen. 'How are you?'

'I'm OK,' he said.

'That's good.'

'Listen, Gert – I was wondering if you'd be able to come out and visit me some time. Is that possible? I know you're probably working, but I really need to see you.' He stopped talking and I had this weird feeling he was covering the phone again, like Lawrence had, to say something private they didn't want me to hear.

'Sure. I guess I could come out some time. I don't have much money though.'

'You could stay here with me – Lawrence wouldn't mind. Are you still with the circus? Does it ever come out our way?'

'I quit the circus.'

'You did? Why'd you do that?'

'I dunno – just my way, I guess.'

He didn't respond to that. 'So you're back at the bookstore now.'

'I don't know. I'm not sure what I'm going to do.'

There was a long pause.

'Well, look,' said James, 'why don't you think it over?'

We talked for another minute or so. Then I spent the whole rest of the day watching TV. I still couldn't get the circus schedule out of my head: three o'clock, afternoon show, five o'clock, clean up the ring, sweep the horse shit from the sawdust, pick up all the empty popcorn boxes and ticket stubs, six o'clock, another show. When Kate came back, I was in a pretty bad mood. She cooked some food, and afterwards we took instant coffee up to the balcony off her bedroom because it was too hot in the house.

'So what did you do today?' she asked.

'Nothing much.'

'I've been looking at the money. You know, if you want to come back and work at the Bluebird—'

'That's OK. I should probably get going pretty soon, shouldn't I?' If she wanted to help me – if anyone wanted to help me – they'd have to work for it. And what did James need to see me for anyway?

'OK.' She took a sip of her coffee and sat there. 'I didn't realize you were planning on leaving.'

'Well, you're selling the house, aren't you? I can't stay here for ever.'

'I guess not. Where will you go?'

I leaned forward and swatted a bug off my foot.

'Where will you go?' Kate asked again. It wasn't like her at all, to ask a question twice. I looked up at the stars and wondered what Wanda was doing over in France.

'Frances?'

'Yes?'

'Can I ask you something?'

'Fire away.'

She looked tense, but I wasn't going to make it any easier. 'Why'd you come back here? You seem sort of shell-shocked. Is anything wrong? Did something happen over the summer?'

'Happen?' I laughed. 'Nothing *happened*. This is just how I normally am. I guess you got a shinier version last winter, huh? Sorry about that.'

Kate looked down at her lap. She probably wasn't used to people bullshitting her. 'Don't apologize.' She waited another few seconds. 'I guess I just wondered if anything had happened. Because of your brother calling.'

'Uh-huh.'

She started rubbing two fingers up and down the balcony wall behind her and the green paint on it was coming off, marking her skin.

'I didn't mean to pry—'

'Doesn't matter. There's nothing to tell, anyway. I could make something up, if you like. If that would make me more interesting.'

Kate stood up then, crashing into the wall of the balcony as she tried to get around the back of my chair.

She'd gone all white and she was stammering something about hearing the phone ringing—

'I'm sorry,' I said.

She stopped, her back still half turned away.

'If you really want to know, I might go and see my brother. That's probably what I'll do.'

Once I was on the road again, I felt better right away, of course. So what if I liked moving? Was that not OK? There were a lot of people out there who felt just the same. I liked eating junk food from roadstop places, and I liked listening to the people in these places, watching them, which I could never have done in the same way if I hadn't been alone. I loved listening to the radio and changing the channels constantly. I loved not worrying that I was annoying anyone by doing this, or not wondering if they liked this song so maybe I should have left it on, or not being embarrassed to admit I really liked this corny Carpenters song.

I thought up lots of brilliant things I could have said. To Barbara before I left home. To Jonas, to Michael, to Wanda, in her room that night, when she'd told me she was blowing. I guess it was inevitable to have those sorts of thoughts. I guess I couldn't just put it all behind me, not right away. Funny thing was, on this trip, even though I was going somewhere brand new, all the roads looked the same and I didn't feel my customary optimism about the place I was heading to. From New Orleans I drove North, on I-55, all the way to Chicago, where I veered off West, brakes screeching, onto I-90/94, the same interstate now all the way to Seattle. I drove right by the exit signs for my home town, and it was only the ghost of me, sitting in the passenger seat, who turned her head as we passed. I also passed pretty darn close to Prophetstown, Illinois and the Traveller's Inn – I looked it up in my road atlas.

At night, I watched the headlights coming at me on the other side of the freeway. Were there any girls like I had been in those cars? Running blind into their future? Would they stop at a rest stop and pick up a Louie, who'd lead them to a Michael, who'd send them to a Jonas, and so on, and so on? I remembered how once, when I was about seventeen, I thought I'd seen my mother at the wheel of a white Volkswagen Rabbit. I couldn't have been younger than seventeen, 'cause I had my licence. I was driving back from Barbara's house, about six in the evening, and I just glanced at the profile of this woman as she surged forward for a green light. Her hair was the right colour – she was even wearing a flowery blouse like one my mom had owned. But more than that, there was something about the tilt of her head, the way she moved it around as she drove, those little angles and rhythms that make you recognize someone you love from behind, even when they may be standing next to a thousand silhouettes similar to their own, with identical hairstyles. Right away, I ditched my plans to stop for groceries and started trailing the Volkswagen. The more I watched this woman, the more convinced I became, so convinced that I even pulled down on my indicator before she did, when we got close to the right turn leading to home, because I just knew she was going to turn there, too. She didn't turn, but this was even more arresting proof of her identity. She didn't turn because she couldn't turn. It was too much for her. I kept following, never passing. Six miles later she got on the freeway ramp and started heading North, to

Minneapolis for all I knew. I got on the freeway too, kept right on following for about another five miles, and then I lost my nerve. I didn't want to acknowledge that my right foot was beginning to lift imperceptibly but steadily off the accelerator but it did, and the Volkswagen was getting further and further ahead, and I let it go. She hadn't been ready, and neither had I.

In a similar kind of way, I started slowing my pace the closer I got to Seattle. Sort of ignoring I was doing it, but driving shorter days, taking longer lunches, reading every section of the left-behind newspapers. I parked in freeway lay-bys and truck stops, once overnight in the car park of a Kohl's grocery store. Every night I dreamed about my mother. Once or twice in the past, I've dreamed of people I was about to meet – Jonas, Wanda – before I laid eyes on them in real life, before I recognized their faces in the dream. But even as I've dreamed, some part of me has known that they were coming, that these were real people, waiting by the side of the road ahead. My mother dreams were like this. I woke up each morning expecting to pull back the curtains and see a thundercloud the size of Texas looming above the trailer.

One evening I stopped at a Howard Johnson's just over the border of Montana, a place called Glendive. It was 9.30, later than most Americans eat. This was the evening of the fourth day driving, and I was beginning to lose heart. It was ridiculous – what was I looking for? What was I expecting out of James? What was all the fuss about Wanda? I should go back – the circus was the perfect life for me. I had found my niche, sewing holes, stacking poles, dismantling cages, walking horses, handing props, making the ropes tight so somebody else could walk them. Plus, there were lots

247

of other circuses. What had happened to my spirit of adventure? Pick another city, any place, another country. Start again in Glendive, Montana, translate myself, choose a new name. Inside my bag, right next to me on the orange plastic-covered bench, *Saint Days* beckoned, with all its characters to choose from. I ordered a grilled cheese sandwich, but couldn't eat any more than a few bites, so I asked them to doggy-bag it and walked back to the trailer, not sure where I was going to park for the night.

A young girl was sitting in the passenger seat, hunched over as if by making herself small she was hoping I wouldn't notice her.

'Uh . . . hello?' I said, opening the driver door.

She waved without looking at me. I sat down behind the steering wheel and closed the door. The radio was playing, and a grey backpack with graffiti scribbled all over it was by her feet.

'How did you get in?'

'You left the doors open.'

I knew I hadn't, and I hoped she hadn't broken the locks. 'So what are you doing in my trailer?'

'I thought you were staying in the hotel. I saw you eating inside, and I thought you were going to check in tonight.'

I hadn't even noticed there was a hotel attached to this place, but she was right – there was. 'No. I'm not going to stay.'

I was about to ask her name, and how old she was – she looked about eleven – but decided against it. Something was so strange about this encounter, I wanted to see what would happen next if I didn't force it. Also, I was thinking about the legend of Saint Christopher, who while being instructed in his new

Christian faith was told to take up a 'humbling occupation'. So he went to live in this little hut near a river that was difficult to ford, and he dedicated himself to helping travellers across. One day this small child appeared, who needed to cross the river, and when Christopher picked the child up, thinking it would be no problem, he could barely handle the kid's weight. When they got to the far shore, of course the kid revealed himself to be actually Jesus and he told Christopher he had just carried 'the whole weight of the world' upon his shoulders. Maybe this was my Jesus.

'Do you want something to eat?' I asked her, showing her the grilled cheese. 'I couldn't finish this.'

'No thanks.' She pushed the search button on the radio and waited for it to find another station. 'Do you like this song?'

'It's OK.'

'Where are you driving to?'

'I'm going to Seattle.'

'Why?'

'I'm going to visit my brother.'

'Your little brother or your big brother?'

'Little brother.' I figured if I was patient she would eventually come out with her own info. 'I'm going to turn on the engine,' I said, 'so the battery doesn't run down.'

She nodded. The song finished, followed by the ten o'clock news. I waited. I imagined if this were the end of the world. What if a nuclear bomb was at that very moment dropping down from the sky right above us, and this was where I was going to be at the end, in this car, in this parking lot, with this young girl I didn't know, when the air turned orange and my melted skin draped itself across my bones. Would I grab the little girl's hand, when the flash came?

'I live just down the road,' she said. Bingo.

'Oh yeah?'

'In the blue house, after you pass the police station.'

'I guess I don't really remember it.'

'It sort of stands out, because it's blue. My brother painted it last summer. He chose the wrong colour, the wrong number at the paint store, and they wouldn't give us our money back. My mother didn't care – she said it didn't matter, but my brother's girlfriend says it's awful, and she's embarrassed to live there now. They're getting married next month, and I have no idea why – it's not like she's pregnant. Do you have a boyfriend? I saw you walking into the restaurant.'

She was a beautiful kid, wide face, big cheekbones, with olive skin and brown eyes. Her hair was dark brown and cut in a sort of asymmetrical bob along the line of her jaw. I really wanted to ask her name.

'No. I don't have a boyfriend. How about you?'

She frowned as if she suspected me of patronizing her, which I was. Maybe this wasn't anything – her turning up in my car. Maybe it was just a mistake.

'You know, I should probably get going now.'

The girl didn't do anything. She didn't make a move, like she knew I didn't mean it when I said things like that. She just sat in her seat, staring ahead out the window, as if we were already driving.

'Look, do you need me to do something for you?' She shook her head again. 'Can I drive you home? It's late, and it's only a few miles back, isn't it? Won't your mother be wondering where you are?'

She sighed and picked up her backpack, opened the

250

car door. 'My mother knows exactly where I am,' she said and started to climb out.

'Wait a minute. I'll drive you home. It's late. I'd feel funny about you walking.'

'OK,' she said, shutting the door again and putting her backpack on her lap. It was such a quick movement that I felt like I'd been duped, as if she'd known all along I would offer her a lift.

We pulled out of the Howard Johnson's and I turned left, back the way I'd come. When we had driven about a half-mile we passed a mini-mall on the right side of the road, and she turned around to look.

'Would you drop me at the mall?' she asked.

'Don't you think you should get home? I don't want to get you into trouble. Or me, for that matter.'

'You won't get into trouble. Look, there's my house, it's right there, see.'

You couldn't really tell it was blue at ten o'clock in the evening. We stopped for a traffic light and she turned around again, looked back at the mall.

'I'll buy you an ice-cream if you drop me.'

'OK, OK. I get that you don't want to go home. You have to tell me how old you are though.'

'I'm fourteen.'

I wasn't sure if I believed her but I put on my blinker and turned back to the mall. It was a stupid thing to do maybe, but I had this crazy fantasy going, that I could help this girl in some way. Maybe I could affect her life in one evening. Maybe I wasn't the centre of this story, maybe she was. Maybe it was her birthday. Maybe I wanted to procrastinate on getting to Seattle. When we walked into a Baskin Robbins, there was a line of people in front of the counter. The girl headed straight to the counter first and then made an abrupt swerve in the opposite direction so I followed her over to stare at the ice-cream birthday cakes in the refrigerator case. After a minute or two, eyeing the clowns and elephants in strawberry and pistachio, I asked her if she maybe wanted a cone.

'Wait a minute,' she hissed at me.

'Anna!' somebody called from across the room. 'Anna!' I turned. A girl with long blond hair pulled back from her face in a row of sparkly bobby pins was walking towards us, licking a dark brown ice-cream cone. 'Anna. Your brother's looking for you.'

Anna spun round. 'I know. I just saw him.'

'You did? 'Cause I saw him out in the car park about a half-hour ago, and he had no idea where you were. I told him I thought you had gone home.'

It was my turn to be stared at by the girl with the cone. I turned my back on her and fixed my gaze upon a display panel offering a free trip to Disneyland if I could only eat enough ice-cream in a month.

'Well, OK then, Anna,' the girl said. 'Hope you don't get in trouble again.' She shrugged and joined a few other girls who were hanging around by the door, waiting to leave. As soon as they did, Anna relaxed.

'Would you like a cone?' she asked me. 'My treat.'

'Sure. But – Anna – I can't really ignore what I just heard. Shouldn't I take you home if your brother's looking for you?'

She was walking towards the counter as I said this. Suddenly she stopped and threw her hands over her head, held them frozen for a few seconds, fingers flexed in the air, then let her arms drop with a heavy sigh. A man and a woman, probably out on a date or having a night away from their kids, looked up and smiled.

'Look! It's really OK,' said Anna. 'I know you're OK, I can tell. You're not going to hurt me, are you?'

'No.'

'You're a grown-up, are you not?'

'I guess so.'

'So OK. What flavour do you want?'

I didn't know why I was having this conversation, why I was eating ice-cream with a kid I didn't know. I wanted to look up Saint Anna in my mother's book. I wanted this Anna to give me a reason for my next move, so I wouldn't have to decide myself. We sat down at one of the plastic tables.

'Do you get along with your brother?' I asked.

She shrugged.

'What about your mom?'

She took such a long time to answer I thought she wasn't going to. A familiar device.

'I get along with my mother fine, but she's dead. My brother's a pain in the butt.'

I took five or six licks of my cone in a row.

'I'm sorry about your mother. When did she die?'

'Last week.'

'Last week?'

'She'd been sick a while.'

She kicked off one sneaker and picked it up, looked inside, poked around in it with a finger. I really didn't want whatever comment I made next to be about me, but I thought it would inevitably be that, and stupid as well. Maybe I just wouldn't say anything, like I usually didn't. But this was a child – come on.

'Do you have any other brothers and sisters?'

God. Loser question. Anna shook her head. Try again.

'I haven't seen *my* mother since I was fourteen.'

Anna nodded, as if she wasn't surprised. She crumpled up the napkin that had been around her cone and wiped her mouth with it. 'Well, you should probably get going now, huh? Back on the road?'

It was like both me and the cone were finished. I could tell I hadn't succeeded at whatever I had been supposed to do. But she didn't seem upset, or even surprised. I pulled at the skin on my neck, which is something I do when I'm nervous. Then a guy in a green plaid shirt and jeans, with scruffy hair, walked into the Baskins Robbins and looked around. For a split second I fantasized about him pulling out a rifle and spraying us with bullets. When he caught sight of Anna, he headed straight to our table.

'Anna. What the *fuck* are you doing?'

The two servers behind the counter froze in their bent-over positions, scoops in hand.

'I was just coming.'

'You were just *coming*? What's that about? You *know* your curfew is ten o'clock, it's always been—' He stopped and looked at me, sitting there at the table with his sister, listening. 'Excuse me. Who's this? Who are you? Anna?'

'I don't know who she is,' she said. She looked at me, and I knew what she wanted me to do.

'I'm nobody,' I said. 'I was just sitting here, having a cone, and your – I guess she's your sister – sat down too.'

'Oh. I'm really sorry to have bothered you, ma'am. Anna's always picking up people.'

'That's OK. No problem. Really.'

Anna got up from her chair and walked out of the place with her brother. Through the glass walls, as they passed out of sight, I saw him clamp a hand on her shoulder and direct her towards the exit. Now the servers behind the counter were looking at me, as well as a couple of other people who'd seen me and Anna talking. I threw the rest of my cone into the trash and headed out. Back behind the wheel, without hesitating, I turned west, towards Seattle.

When I dreamed of my mother, I wondered if it was because she was dreaming of me.

Seattle

The Brotherhood of Saint Benedict was a 1930s apartment building, built in a U-shape around a central
grassy section. Nice, peaceful-looking place, up in the
hills overlooking the water, a neighbourhood called
Queen Anne. Across the street where I parked the
trailer there was a stretch of grass with a clear view
over the city skyline and the Puget Sound. It was a
beautiful spot, something clean and pure about it. I
could imagine drug addicts, or whoever came looking
for help, getting better here. I sat on the bench for a
while, feeling slightly wired from driving all night,
watching the ferry boats dividing the water, and the
snow-capped peaks of a far-off mountain range turning
red as the sun rose behind me. It was 7.30 in the morning, 15 October.

James had told me on the phone the previous day
that the residential section of the building was to the
right. As I walked up the central steps, two or three
from the street leading to a sidewalk skirting a grassy
courtyard, a man passed me, heading for what looked
like a drop-in clinic on the left. He was wearing a
brown corduroy jacket that had seen much better days.
Through the glass doors of the clinic I could see a few

people milling around the reception area, in bathrobes; in another room with a large picture window a television was on, and a lady in white was laying cups on a table. Instead of turning right, I walked straight on to the main entrance. SAINT BENEDICT'S HOSPITAL was printed on a large white sign on the original brickwork over the double doors, with a smaller brass plaque to one side of the door on the left; this one was engraved in elegant script: *Welcome to the Brotherhood of St Benedict*, it read, with the opening times underneath. Next to a white phone welded into the side of the building, a third sign: 'In an emergency outside of normal hours, please use white phone to contact night-time staff'. Saint Benedict was the patron saint of victims of poisoning – they should have had that on the plaque.

'So is this like a seminary with hospital attached?' I had asked James on the phone the day before.

'No. I actually dropped out of seminary. Last year.'

'You did? So what are you doing there?'

'I'm working. And I live here, with the priests.'

He was basically a hospital orderly, as far as I could tell, with an eye on eventual monkhood.

As I stood on the lawn, I thought of all the days and months my brother had walked across it, all the mornings going to work, from his rooms to the hospital, to the clinic and back again. Wearing what? Not priest clothes, like I'd imagined. Hospital whites, I guess. Up and down the waxed hallways. While I'd been doing my life, day to day to day. Once upon a time, I couldn't have imagined us apart. I remembered all the mornings of our childhood, James and I staring out our respective car windows, schoolbags on our laps, fighting over the middle space in the back seat of the white second-hand Saab my mom used, to drive us to school. The slippery seatbelts and the bumpy texture of the plastic upholstery under my hands. All those days, years and years of them. Mom used to bring us apples when she picked us up, and we really wanted Ding-dongs or Cheetos, like our friends got.

I walked back to the entrance door of the right-hand wing. This part still looked like an apartment building. I found James's name – my name – on the list and rang the bell. Almost immediately, as if he'd been sitting on a chair right next to the intercom, James's voice came back at me.

'Hello? Gert? Hi. Come on up. Take the elevator to the third floor and turn left – it's the second door on the right.'

I hadn't brought anything with me, flowers, or a present, or anything. No photographs – I never took photographs. Wanda used to take photographs all the time, and it made me uncomfortable to think she still had all those images of me, like she had a Voodoo doll or something. And I suppose Jonas had some too, if he hadn't burned them after I'd disappeared. As I was going up in the elevator, I got this vision of Mom sitting in the apartment with James, sitting right now at the kitchen table, sipping tea, with a nervous grin on her face. James and she were going to surprise me – that's why he'd needed to see me. They'd been afraid that if they'd told me, I wouldn't have come. She was feeling sick to her stomach because she hadn't seen me in so long, and she didn't know whether I'd hug her or spit in her face. She'd have a lot of explaining to do, she wouldn't know what to say at first, she'd—

James opened the door. He was wearing jeans and a long-sleeved T-shirt advertising what I presumed was a local eatery. Bare feet. Hair cut so short it might as well have been shaved, but it was the same colour as my mum's, dark blond. He was really skinny.

There was a small crucifix attached to the door frame and as I passed underneath it I felt like I was being watched.

'You don't look like a priest.'

He smiled.

'Well, I'm not. Like I said. But most of them try to blend in a little more these days, anyway.'

'Who?'

'The priests.'

'Oh.' I nodded.

Then he hugged me, which caught me off guard. Hugging wasn't big in our family. Maybe it was a priest thing. 'Are you hungry? You must have driven through the night. I could make you some eggs.'

'Sure. Maybe just some toast.'

'I can definitely do toast.'

We walked down the hall into a small kitchen with one window and no view, unless you counted the wall of the apartment building next door. A round table was neatly laid for two, with plaid-patterned seersucker napkins under two spoons. A small glass vase with a few yellow daisies in it.

'Sit down, you look tired. Did you come in the trailer?'

'Yup.'

'Cool. Janine told me all about it. Can we camp out in it one night?'

'If you want.'

'I guess you're probably over the thrill of trailer living, right?'

'It's OK.'

I was trying to match up this young man, his thin back turned to me as he found some bread and put two slices in the toaster, with the hesitant, over-serious boy I'd known. He was obviously more confident now, more in the world, but it would have been pretty strange if he hadn't been. He knew how to welcome someone, all the words to say, what to offer. Somehow I missed the old James.

'This is nice.'

James looked around the kitchen. 'You mean the apartment? It's Lawrence's place, really. I only moved in a few months ago.' He opened the fridge, and got out some butter. 'What would you like on your toast?'

'Got any cinnamon?'

Mom had always made us cinnamon toast in the fall.

'Cinnamon?' He didn't remember. 'I don't think we have any.'

It struck me then that maybe James wouldn't remember some of the things I remembered, and vice versa. Of course this was obvious, but I'd never had a particular reason to think it until now.

'Just butter then.'

'You sure?'

'Yeah. Or some honey maybe.'

He fetched a jar from the cupboard and brought over my toast on a blue ceramic plate. 'You look exactly the same.'

'God, don't say that. What did I look like before?'

'I don't know, you look great, anyway – I suppose circus life keeps you toned, lots of fresh air and exercise.'

Chicken's dead body, sprawled out as I imagined it across the dirty floor of his red van. Hoxie's paunch, filled up with beer, then cinched in and up over his

260

snakeskin belt. The pasty complexions of the Mongolian troupe surviving on sloppy joe mixes and vodka. Wanda's long runner's limbs, skin stretched as tight against her muscles as canvas across a frame. 'It depends.'

'I probably look older than you do, now.'

I didn't like to say, but I knew what he meant. There was a sort of creakiness to James's movements. It wasn't his looks exactly, though his face was a lot more weather-worn than you'd expect. Mostly it was the way he carried himself; he moved cautiously, like an old man who needed not to fall down again. He seemed pretty used-up.

'Is it hard work, working here?' I asked. 'It must be intense. You wrote me once about talking someone off a ledge or something.'

James smiled, shook his head, didn't say anything right away. He poured himself coffee from a glass pot on the stove.

'It's not so bad as you'd think, really. Well, it's tiring, I guess, but they're OK, the people who come in. They're just people, they're not . . .' His voice trailed off, and he stood there, leaning against the kitchen counter, staring at the floor. For about a minute. I thought his coffee mug was going to tip, spilling all the hot coffee to the ground in a steady stream. I was just about to ask if he was OK when he lifted the mug of coffee to his mouth. It was as if someone had jiggled the wires and reconnected his battery, like one of those drones in *Star Wars* waking up.

'Sorry. Spaced,' he said. 'Would you like some coffee?'

'That's OK.'

'Tea?'

'Sure, but I can make it.'

'It's OK – no problem.'

'Actually, I will have coffee.'

'Fine.'

The coffee poured, James sat down opposite me, and we tried to make conversation. 'So how did you meet Lawrence?' I figured we couldn't just launch into the big stuff – that would be like turning up at somebody's house because you happened to be passing by and then asking them five minutes later if, by the way, you could borrow a hundred dollars.

'Lawrence? He's one of the priests.'

'A real priest? Not in training?'

'No. Full-fledged.'

As if on cue, a sound of a key in the lock. James got up from his chair.

'Speak of the devil.'

'He knew I was coming, right?'

'Sure.'

A tall man walked into the kitchen, holding two bags of groceries. He switched one bag over to his other arm and stretched out his free hand. 'Hi, I'm Lawrence. You must be James's sister. Nice to meet you.'

I stood up. 'Same here.'

He was wearing a white shirt with the dog-collar effect, and chinos. He had really deep-set brown eyes, and I couldn't believe it but I was wondering why such a handsome black guy had ended up Episcopalian when he could have been preaching soul music as a Southern Baptist. What a thought. I had to look down in case he was a mind-reader.

'How was your drive?'

'OK, thanks.'

'You must do a lot of driving. James told me you work for a circus?'

'Sometimes.'

Lawrence began to unpack the groceries.

'Has James been taking care of you?' he asked.

'I made her some toast,' said James.

'I'm fine.' I felt like I couldn't sit down. No-one said anything for a few minutes, and I finished my coffee standing up.

'So, James. Do you have to work today?' I asked, when the silence got too much.

'Did you buy some pasta?' James asked Lawrence, opening a cupboard over the sink. 'No. I don't have to work.'

'Should we go somewhere? I might crash for a while now, I guess, but maybe later.'

James pulled a newspaper out of one of the shopping bags and scanned the headlines.

'Lawrence?' he asked, still scanning.

At first, I thought he was asking about the pasta again.

'OK by me,' said Lawrence, that deep voice I'd heard on the phone. 'What about that new coffee place near the opera house? Isn't there some sort of circus thing going on? I saw the tents just now – or maybe that would be too much like work for you, Gert.'

He smiled at me, and I shrugged. It was weird hearing a stranger using my real name.

'Well, just so long as you don't let them recruit James. We don't want to lose him.'

'Do you want to put your stuff in your room?' said James.

I was sleeping in Lawrence's bedroom, on the kind of narrow single bed you'd imagine a priest would have. Lawrence said it was no problem – he was on night duty a lot in the hospital, and when he wasn't, he'd sleep on the sofa in the kitchen. The decoration was sparse in Lawrence's room, but pleasant. Pale green curtains with a thin-lined pattern, like circles traced on by ice skates. A small desk made out of pale wood, chipped and scratched, that looked like it had been salvaged from a school. On the window-ledge was a black-and-white picture of a dark-haired woman, in a lead frame. She was back-lit, Lawrence's mother probably. Or grandmother, hard to tell. A bendy lamp next to it, and on the bedside table a bible, along with some other spiritual-looking titles, except I noticed a Le Carré spy novel at the bottom of the pile. The mattress was hard, but any place free of mildew, warm and relatively soundproofed seemed extra-plus comfortable to me. On the desk were thin piles of paperwork and a large glass paperweight with a white flower inside.

'Come and see my room,' said James.

James's room was slightly larger and had the nicer view, out onto the central courtyard. I sat down in a junk-shop armchair, across from the window.

'So does Lawrence own this place?'

'No. It's all church housing, part of the pay. I used to be in a little studio on the ground floor.'

'How come you've got the nicer bedroom?'

'Lawrence offered it – said it was too noisy for him. You do get woken up if people are brought in during the night. You know, freaking out.'

'Does that happen a lot?'

James shrugged. 'Occasionally.'

The room was messy. I spotted a small gold chain with a crucifix on it hanging around one of the posts of the bed. His closet door was open, and inside was hardly anything, only a few shirts and a winter coat hanging on wire hangers. A chest of drawers stood next to the armchair, its top drawer half open with a T-shirt poking out, making a break for freedom. Against the wall behind the open door was a rickety bookshelf, its top two shelves filled with rows of paperbacks: Kurt Vonnegut, Walt Whitman, Douglas Adams, some home doctor do-it-yourself pharmaceutical manuals along with a few other medical reference books. Also *Drawing from the Left Side of the Brain*, a few titles in what looked like German, and a copy of *Anna Karenina*.

'Hey,' I said, reaching over and pulling it out.

'Yeah. I remembered it was one of your favourites, so I went out and bought it last year.'

'Did you like it?'

'I haven't read it yet.'

I replaced it.

On the bottom shelf was a stack of photo albums – five or six of them. They looked faintly familiar.

'I picked those up in June, when I was home. Go ahead and take a look if you like. I didn't even know Dad had them.'

'What, are they—'

'Photos of us, yeah. And Mom. You'll love all the seventies outfits. Your hair has some particularly fine moments.'

James walked over and pulled one out. Its cover was turquoise with white plastic flowers. 'Take a look.'

'Not right now, thanks. A little later. I think I need to take a nap.'

'OK.' James put the album back on top of the pile.

'When did you move in here?'

'Early July, a few weeks after I got back from seeing Dad. Have you talked to him? Oh, I know what else I wanted to show you. Besides the albums.' He crouched down on the floor and pulled something out from underneath his bed. 'Ta-da. Recognize it?'

Of course I did. It was James's strongbox – the one we had buried in the field behind our house the day Dad and Janine got married.

'I dug it up and brought it with me, when I left home. Just like you said to do.' He suddenly looked so hungry for approval – naked for it – like he'd just won a spelling bee or something. 'I noticed yours was gone too. I used to want to go and check on them after you left, to see if yours was gone, but I always felt sort of superstitious about it, like I might jinx something if I did, you know? It was a lucky thing they never put any houses in that field – kids still ice-skate on it, you know – it's an official recreation ground now. Did you take it with you right away, or did you come back later for it?'

'I took it with me when I left.' It was sitting in the trailer outside, inside a closet. I hardly ever looked in it; the only thing that still felt like it had any relevance was my *Saint Days* book and that lived under the mattress. James's box still looked brand new – what was in it? I remembered buying them all those years ago, at the Treasure Island. At the checkout, I'd run into this boy from school, and I hadn't wanted him to see what I was buying, so I pretended I'd forgotten something and went back into the aisles to get some shampoo. 'I can hardly remember what's in it.'

'Really?' He looked very surprised. 'I know exactly what's in here. Of course, I've been adding to it lately.' He lifted the box onto his lap and rubbed it as if it were a magic genie lamp. 'Wouldn't you like to know?'

I felt a little weirded-out, because just for a millisecond there was something a little cruel in James's eyes. Nothing obvious – very, very subtle, like the reflection of something across the room, in the curve of his pupils. But it was definitely there. I felt like, ever since Lawrence had got back actually, James was sort of shifting shape in front of me, sort of revving and idling, and the first impression I'd had of him was being overlaid with another, and then another, but I couldn't pin any one of them down. Maybe I was just over-tired. I had driving eyes, driving brain.

'I really need to take a nap, James.'

And the glint was gone. 'Of course,' he said. 'I'm such a wiener, making you look at my room and all my things! It's hard to break out of old family patterns, you know? Seeing you again after all this time. Just kick me if I get too needy.'

Later that afternoon, James and I went down to the Seattle Center, where there was a huge municipal fountain shaped like a giant copper bowl, with a dome in the middle that shot out flumes of water in all different directions, some twenty feet high or more. Twice, while we were sitting there, the jets of water performed a choreographic display to the sound of music coming through giant loudspeakers, first to the pounding of gamelan drums, then to a medley of Sousa-like band tunes. It was a cold day and we kept having to move when the wind changed direction and the spray from the fountain spattered against our faces and clothing. Somehow because it was the West Coast, I'd expected sunshine.

'In the summer, this place is full of kids. Playing in the water, running through the spray.'

'Does it get pretty warm here?'

'Sure. Not like Southern California, but it's beautiful. The winters are what bum people out – all the rain – but I don't mind it. I wouldn't want to live anywhere where it was nice all the time.'

'Do you remember the winters back home?'

'God, all that snow. And Dad always out there shovelling.'

'I don't remember that.'

'Sure. He got a snow-blower after you left.'

'What was it like? After I left. Pretty rough with Janine, huh?'

I was building up to a sort of apology for bailing out on him, but I didn't know how to say it.

'It was OK. It was better actually, in a lot of ways.'

'Better than what? Better than when I was there? Thanks a lot.'

'No, not that. I meant with Dad and Janine. Dad was a lot happier.'

'Didn't she drive you crazy?'

'Who? Janine? No. She was nice to me.'

'I bet the house was really clean.'

James smiled. 'I guess.' He looked so sad all of a sudden, sitting there in the light drizzle which had started to come down. Deep-down sad, like I was.

'I'm sorry I just took off there. Without warning you.'

He looked up through the steam coming off the fountain. 'Where did you go?'

Louie and his broken-down car, Michael, that woman in the alley lifting her skirt, the bunkhouse at the orchard, cups of tea sitting on a wooden kitchen table in North Carolina, the first big top I ever saw going up, Chicken's van, the blue stripe on my trailer, the Bluebird, Kate's sisters, Wanda's wet hair, the neighbourhood of trucks and trailers, the trapeze bars glinting under the ceiling of white stars against a dark blue top, little sister Amy's bedroom with its toy horses, Wanda packing to blow, the line of smashed-up appliances.

'I just wandered around for a while.'

After two more days, we still hadn't really talked about anything big, and I hadn't mustered the courage to look at the photo albums either. I kept thinking I would, but I wanted to do it on my own, and James never seemed to go to work. When I asked him how long he had off, figuring maybe he'd cleared the books for my visit and this big talk we were going to have, he said he was on a kind of retreat from work at the moment. All the staff have to take them, he told me, otherwise the emotional burnout factor is too strong. James slept in a lot, which suited me fine. I was waking up early, still on Central time, but I usually just made myself some toast and coffee and went back to bed. There were lots of books around the place. I even tried reading some of Lawrence's theological books – they were a little hard going, but if I alternated between them and a copy of *The Hobbit* I'd found on James's bookshelf, then I was OK. Some mornings, I got dressed and went out for a walk. Ended up sitting in the trailer, thinking about everyone back at Sherman Brothers. It was the last week of the tour, this week – they'd all be going off to their winter places. I wondered who Hoxie had put in to replace Wanda's act.

One beautiful day when the morning rain had cleared, James and I took a ferry across to Bainbridge

Island, to the oldest town on the Western seaboard. Or maybe just in Washington State. Of course, it wasn't very old at all by East Coast standards, only about a hundred years; you forget how recent all of American history is. I didn't know if James was doing the same thing, but I kept studying his behaviour during all these outings, studying his personality to see if I recognized anything. Not stuff from the past, not anything I should have remembered, but more like elements of his grown-up personality which coincided with mine. The whole genetics versus environment thing was looming large in my mind. I mean, we'd been through a lot of the same experiences, James and I, good and bad. I just wondered if they had affected him as well, similarly, or not at all. He didn't seem like a runner.

On the ferry ride back, I finally asked him about it.

'Is it weird being with me?'

He was watching a kid playing with a little plastic airplane that you could launch by stretching an elastic band back from the tail and letting it go. The boy was kneeling down in the gangway between the seats, trying to make it work.

'Weird? Why?'

'I dunno, because I'm related. I keep looking at you and wondering if you're thinking what I'm thinking.'

He turned and looked at me.

'I doubt it. Why would I be thinking what you are? You see that couple back there?'

He nodded towards a middle-aged twosome sitting by themselves near the central food station. She was dressed in a turquoise polyester dress that ended just below her knees, and the white slip she had on underneath was showing, where she'd crossed her legs. Her fingernails and hair were frosted. On her feet, cream-coloured pumps with a black line around the edges.

'Who are they, do you think?'

'I dunno.'

'Just make it up.'

'What do you mean?'

'She's Russian, or Polish or something. I heard them talking while I was getting our food. He's just asked her to marry him, and they were talking about how her family back home will react, and whether they can get her mother to come over for the wedding.'

'Her mother must be pretty ancient. Is the man Russian too?'

'No, he's American, or he sounds like it. He met her on the assembly line at the Boeing factory.'

'They said all this while you were in line?'

'No. I just made up the bit about how they met.'

'And the point is?'

'Well, my point is, in reference to your question about us thinking the same things, those two can hardly understand two words they say to each other – I'm not sure she even gets that she's agreed to marry him – but they seem very happy, anyway. Look, they're holding hands, and she's cuddling up to him. So it obviously doesn't matter how similar they are – or whether they're even on the same wavelength. I guess I'm saying I wouldn't worry about what I'm thinking. We have a lot more in common than those two, so our ratio of mutual understanding is probably a little better. And it doesn't matter anyway. It's all fine. It's all going to be fine.'

'Are you on drugs?'

James laughed and laughed at this, like it was the best joke he'd ever heard, which maybe it was, considering where he worked. But I had to get across what I was trying to say. Because it wasn't all fine.

'Do you feel like you're smarter than most people?' I asked.

'Don't get mad.'

'I'm not mad. I'm asking. Seriously.'

'If I think I'm smarter than everyone?'

'Yes.' I started picking at the aluminium foil corner of a ham and cheese sandwich I'd finished earlier. 'Because *I* do. I have this secret, snobby feeling going that I'm better than most people. More clued-up. And I go around judging people all the time, almost unconsciously, putting them in little hierarchies, based on their intelligence, except occasionally when I meet someone obviously smarter than me, and then I'm filled with self-loathing.'

'Wow.'

'I know. It's fucked up. And there's other times — lots of times — I feel like I'm the biggest loser in the world. I swing back and forth between the two, like I can't decide. I just wondered if you were maybe like that too, if it was a family thing. Not from Dad, but from Mom, maybe.'

'Why not from Dad?'

I shrugged. 'He doesn't seem much of a deep thinker.'

James laughed again and shook his head. 'You and Dad, you really don't get each other, do you? You just have to translate with Dad — he thinks about things a lot.' He frowned. 'Not that he always makes the right decisions.'

I waited for him to say more about this, because it seemed like he might, but he didn't. I turned away to

272

look out the window as another ferry passed, going the opposite way. It had started to rain again, but there were still a dozen passengers or so out on the deck of this boat, their rain hoods pulled over their heads, eyes squinting into the wind.

'I don't think I'm smarter than other people,' said James. He scratched his forearm. 'I used to think I was sadder.' He coughed. 'But I don't any more.'

We sat in silence for a while after that. A rainbow appeared over the city skyline and people started walking around to the other side of the ship to get a better view of it, but we stayed where we were.

'What is it? What are they all looking at?' asked James.

The Russian lady and her fiancé walked past our seats, heading for the deck. They were arm in arm.

'What about staying in one place?' I asked.

'What about it?'

'You don't seem to have a problem with it.'

'I've had some problems, but not with staying put, no.'

'So have you fixed your problems?'

He looked away. 'Not all of them.'

'Well, that's comforting at least. All this "it's going to be fine" stuff was starting me thinking I'd been adopted.' Or he had. 'I just move on, whenever things get too intense.'

'Why do things get too intense?'

'They just always do. Don't they?'

'At least you get to see lots of places. I envy you for that.'

'I guess. But then I start to worry that I'm just following some sort of genetic destiny, that I'm actually incapable of sticking the course.'

James looked at me. 'You're worried you're like Mom, huh?'

'Maybe. Sometimes. I don't know – who knows? – it's not like she's around to compare stories.'

James scratched the side of his face and then he sort of patted my hand where it was lying on my knee. I couldn't tell if he was being ironic. And I didn't want his sympathy, anyway. I just wanted more information.

The next day – almost the end of the week – we were sitting around the apartment after dinner, and I was thinking I couldn't stay much longer in Lawrence's place without feeling awkward. Maybe I could find a job in Seattle. Why not? Get a space for the trailer. Stick around, just for a few months. Tonight it was James who seemed restless. Talk about not staying in one place – he couldn't stay in one place in the kitchen.

'Do you want some coffee?' he asked for the second time.

I was sitting on the sofa paging through a large book of photographs.

'I really like those,' James told me. 'I got it from the library.'

They were shiny black-and-white photographs of freakish-looking people. Some of them reminded me of folks I'd seen at the circus – not people in the ring, people sitting in the audience. That was where the real weirdos turned up, men in their fifties, their fatty bodies sort of squashed down by life, wearing a circus T-shirt over a grimy white shirt, loitering around the box office, bugging Terry about posters for next year's season and mumbling about how they'd seen the best aerial act ever in 1927, in Wichita, Kansas, on the hottest day of the century. Sometimes they'd turn up wearing white-face, and it was smeared above their hair-lines and clotted around the bristles of their stubbly beards.

'Hey. Sis,' James said, again. 'Did you hear me? Do you want some coffee?'

'No, I'm OK.'

'I think I need some.'

I doubted that. The way he was jumping around, what he needed was a Buddhist monk to appear and lead him in some meditation. What he needed was a CD of Benedictine monks intoning quietly into head-phones wrapped around his head. He put the kettle on the gas.

'Or some ice-cream!' he almost shouted. 'That's what I want! That would hit the spot, exactly. Couldn't you go for some? Gert?'

I looked up from the photos. 'Sure. If you want.'

'I know this great place, not very far away. Feel like stepping out?'

'Whatever you say.'

'Of course you want to – you circus girl!' He'd been calling me 'circus girl' all day and it was really start-ing to bug me. 'You're up for anything! I'll just get my coat. It will be my treat – if I have enough money, that is.' He sprinted down the hall to his room.

'What about the coffee?' I called after him.

'Can you turn it off? I'm just changing.'

Out on the street, James seemed really happy.

'When I first got here – a year ago? – I never went out. I was so nervous about what people would think, how people would see me. Being a priest – even want-ing to be one – is like wearing a badge that says "Challenge me". You crash right into people's histories with religion – the Sunday schools they hated, the hours of boring sermons they were forced to sit through – or there are nutters who want you to cure their three-year-old's leukaemia.'

'How did anyone know you wanted to be a priest?'

He looked down at his clothes. 'I used to dress the part a little more, I guess. And then after I dropped out of seminary I felt guilty, so I wore this big wooden crucifix for a while, as penance. But people just know, somehow. They have a nose for it, the ones who are looking. Anyway, for six weeks, after I got this job, I think I left the grounds of Saint Benedict's twice. There's really no necessity to leave. You can get what you need on campus, so to speak, and if you can't, there's always someone you can ask, to pick you up some milk, or razors or whatever. I just stayed in after my shifts, reading, praying. I was being a good pilgrim. But really I was just so afraid of going out into the world. I think seminary training messes you up that way – it's partly why I dropped out. You'd get so used to just being with other priests, other priests-in-training, and you'd all read the same books and talk about the same issues, and the world would become this tiny place, where everyone must surely be concerned with the same problems, except then when you got out you'd realize that 99.9 per cent of the world have never given these things one second's thought, at least, not consciously, though everyone dies at some point, and then they put themselves on a sort of crash course.'

In the circus, the more dangerous the act, the more God-aware the artists had tended to be, kissing the crucifixes round their neck, crossing themselves, last thing before leaping on the wire.

'That's why I like working at the hospital – things are more real. Last year, last winter, only about a month after I started work, I saw this lady on top of an apartment building threatening to jump – didn't I write you about it? Her ten-year-old kid had rung the police and the police were already there, but the thing was, she was asking for a priest. I was working at the clinic that night, and the paramedic guys, and the doctor in charge, they came around asking for a priest. Neil ended up going and at the last minute he asked me if I wanted to go along, to get some experience. The paramedics said they didn't mind so I jumped in the ambulance. As soon as we left, though, I was panicking, because I really didn't have any idea what I was getting into – I started feeling really uncomfortable. But maybe God was sending me on this trip for a reason, even though I didn't even know what I believed any more, as far as God went.' James stopped walking. 'I've got a better idea. Than the ice-cream, I mean.'

'What?'

'A club! Do you feel like a club? I haven't been dancing in months.'

'Dancing? You go dancing? I don't know. Aren't I a little old?'

'You look about fifteen. Come on, it'll be fun.'

He turned down a side street and within a few blocks we were in an emptier part of town, deserted used-car lots, strings of lights illuminating the fluorescent signs taped to the cars' windshields. A twenty-four-hour convenience store, a Greek shish-kebab take-out place, the hulking shadow of a Russian Orthodox church.

'So what happened?' I asked. 'How did they talk her down?'

277

'Well, when we got out onto the roof, there she was, this woman, standing on the edge of the little concrete lip. The cops were standing a few yards away, with her son – apparently, they'd been trying to get him to go downstairs but he refused to leave, kept saying if he left she'd jump, but that she wouldn't do it in front of him. Maybe he was right: she kept glancing over at him, and then her eyes would roll back in her head, like a horse spooked by a ghost. When they told her there was a priest there, she stretched out her arms to Neil, a real melodramatic gesture, like a 1930s movie star, and she said "Father! Father! Do it. Say it. Do them for me, Father!" At first, I didn't know what she meant, but then I figured out she wanted him to perform the Last Rites, so she could jump with God's blessing.'

He suddenly stopped at a door in a wall, a door with no identification of any kind and no handle. It looked like the kind of door you find at the back end of stores, facing the parking lot, where you pick up your new stereo equipment to load into your waiting car. James knocked.

'Where are we?'

'This is the place.'

'I thought we were going to a club.'

'I changed my mind again.'

The door opened, and a small man with grey hair shaved close to his head, stood in the doorway. 'Hey, Karl,' said James.

'Brother Jim! It's been a while. And who've you brought with you? A nun friend?'

'Actually, she *is* my sister – ha ha.'

'Ha ha,' I said.

Karl grinned at me, and his teeth seemed unnaturally

white. He stuck out his hand and I shook it, partly because it was trembling and I wanted to stop it. 'Welcome, sister. Come on in.'

We went into a sort of bar. The place was very dark, with low ceilings and no windows, except at the front, where the whole wall was glass, like a shop front. It was a long, rectangular-shaped room, and as my eyes adjusted to the darkness I could make out a bar to one side, and a few tables in the distance. James led me to a couch and some armchairs along one wall. All the furniture was pretty ratty – the upholstery had tears in it and the wood was scuffed. *Über*-scruffy. We sat down on a sofa that might have been green some time, but was now sort of olive-coloured, as far as I could tell in the dim light. It smelt of spilled beer, but one thing the place wasn't, was smoky.

'It's not smoky,' I said to James, having to speak loudly over the noise of the music that was playing. Experimental jazz, not my kind of thing.

'What?'

'No smoke!'

'Karl's got a thing about cigarettes. He hates them. There's no smoking allowed.'

'Do you come here a lot?'

'Used to.'

'I thought you never used to go out.'

'I got over that eventually.'

Karl approached our chairs. 'Can I bring you two a drink?' he asked.

'Wow. Service!' said James. 'Is this what happens when you stay away too long?'

Karl extended his arms, palms up, towards James. 'What can I say? The prodigal son returns.'

'Or maybe it's what happens when you bring your

cute sister along. I'll just have a mineral water –
actually, no, could you bring me a coffee? Have you got
any coffee?'

'Are you kidding? This is Seattle. And for your
sister? I'm sorry, I don't know your name.'

I really really really wanted to lie. 'Gertrude. Gert.'

'Gert then. What can I get for you, Gert?'

'I kinda feel like some tequila.' Chicken and I used
to drink tequila.

'Circus girl!' said James.

'Some tequila! Wonderful. I've got a bottle of
fantastic tequila someone brought me back from
Mexico a few months ago. I've been waiting for the
right occasion to open it.' He smiled a lugubrious
smile and went back to the bar.

'Makes it sound like he's not going to charge us for
it,' said James.

'What's his story?' I asked. 'What's with the accent?'

'Karl's? I don't know. He used to be a teacher.'

'What did he teach?'

'I'm not sure. Mathematics, I think.' James seemed
distracted. He was looking around a lot.

'How'd you meet him?'

'I can't remember – here and there. I'm just gonna go
to the john.'

He walked over to a door by the bar with Rest Rooms
spelled out on it in jagged metal scraps, and Karl
looked up as he passed. Smiled, nodded. There were
only three other people in the whole place: a man in a
forest-green duffle coat, who looked like he was
asleep, and, at a table for two, a man and woman – she
was seriously under-fed – huddled over a book as if
it was a log fire, each of them holding one side of the
book down. On the wall above my head, shelves jutted

280

out from the wall, each about a foot long, like a wall built for rock-climbing practice sessions. There was a speaker on one of the shelves and the music was coming out of it.

'Did this place used to be something else?' I said to James when he came back.

'A sports shop. Athletic supplies. This is where the shoes were displayed, I guess, above our heads.'

'I get it.'

Karl brought back our drinks on a fake antique Coca-Cola tray. I resolutely avoided eye contact with him when he set the shot before me, and after waiting for a nod of approval once I had tasted it, he wandered away again. I felt a little guilty, like I'd passed by a homeless person, begging for some change.

'I want to hear the end of the story.'

'What story?'

'You know – the lady about to jump.'

He drained his cup of espresso in one go, followed straight by the accompanying glass of water. 'So she was standing there on the ledge, looking at us all, waiting for some kind of answer. I could feel that she was save-able, maybe. I looked down at my hands trying to remember the first lines of a psalm, any psalm, but my mind was a blank, even though I know every one of them off by heart – you could ask me for any of them right now and I could recite it, no problem. But that night I couldn't remember a single word. I kept looking at her son; I didn't know what to do; the cops were holding him.'

'I can understand why someone would want to kill themselves.'

'Don't say that.'

'I can, though – can't you?'

281

'No.' He sounded really pissed off all of a sudden. 'No. It's a stupid thing to do. And it's cruel.'

'I'm not saying I'm going to do it, OK?' He shot me this wounded look, as if I'd been making fun of him or something.

'Anyway, eventually Neil went into a huddle with her and they brought her back to Saint Benedict's.' He leaned back against the sofa, like he was exhausted from telling the story. 'That's why I wanted to become a priest, to help people, like Neil did that night.'

I kicked back the rest of my tequila. 'So why aren't you working at the moment?'

He didn't answer. He was lying there with his eyes closed.

'Did the woman get better? That priest saved her, right?'

'Neil? No, he didn't save her. She saved herself. People only ever save themselves.'

I stared at him, his crew-cut hair, the long-sleeved T-shirt he'd changed into, his brown corduroy trousers, worn at the knees.

'I'm going to get myself another drink.'

A while later, somebody changed the music, just as Karl let in two men through the door where we'd come in. They checked us out as they walked by and one of them nodded at James, who half raised his hand in greeting. They fell into two armchairs, facing each other, further up the wall from us.

'Doesn't anyone come in the front door?' I asked. Every so often, people walked by the front window of the place and peered in, cupping their hands around their eyes. Some of them even tried the front door but it was locked, and nobody gestured to them that they should go round back.

282

'How did you find this place?'

James shrugged. 'I don't remember. I wanted to bring you here because I used to spend a lot of time here, for a while, six months ago. So I wanted you to see it.'

The music coming out of the speakers above our heads was quieter now, a woman's voice which occasionally went to a raucous and tortured place, but mostly hovered at monotone depressive.

'I can see the attraction.'

'Excuse me for a second,' said James, getting up from the sofa, which seemed lower to the ground than it had been fifteen minutes ago. 'I just want to go say hello to someone I haven't seen in a while. OK?'

'Sure. I'm going to the bathroom.'

There was only one toilet, and I sat on it longer than I needed to, my head a heavy weight on an inevitable downward journey through my splayed legs and towards the sticky floor. Like one of those tippy birds, with the liquid inside their glass necks. I was an easy drunk – didn't take much. Finally willing myself to stand again, because I wasn't sure if I'd been sitting there for a few minutes or twenty, I slid out of the stall. I didn't feel sick, just disconnected, as if my body was made up of wooden vertebrae that had become misaligned and were sticking out from my spine in all directions. I smiled at myself in the broken mirror over the sink. I played with the light pull, switching it off and on a few times.

'Hey, sis,' I said. 'Hey, circus girl.' I looked pretty awful, actually. My hair was frizzy and needed cutting. My face looked pale and draggy and fat.

When I came back into the bar, James was leaning over the man who had been sleeping it off ever since we came in. Karl was standing next to James, and

James was yelling right into the sleeping guy's ears.

'GEOFF! Wake up, Geoff. Ge-off. How long's he been here?'

Karl shrugged. 'He came in about six. Early. He was fine.'

'What would he have taken? What'd you give him?'

Karl glanced at me and shrugged. 'Nothing you wouldn't. He must have come in under.'

'Is he OK?' I asked James.

'No.'

'Is he a friend of yours?'

'I know him.'

Karl looked at his watch, as if he had somewhere to go. He wiped two fingers down either side of his mouth, as if he was waxing down a moustache. Then he laughed.

'Look, Brother Jim, it'll be fine. He'll wake up in the morning with a hell of a headache, that's all.'

'Where's your phone?' asked James.

'What are you going to do?'

'Call the clinic, get somebody to come pick him up.'

'What – an ambulance?'

James lifted up one of the guy's eyelids. 'He needs to be checked out. Yeah, an ambulance – is there a problem?'

Karl started walking up and down. I could tell he didn't want to talk in front of me. He kept giving James these hard stares then glancing at me, the same pattern about three times.

'I don't know – is there? A problem?' he said finally. 'It seems to me it's none of our business, this man's problems.'

James straightened up. He just stood there, looking at Karl with a blank expression. This lasted for what seemed like a half-hour, but must have been about fifteen seconds. Then he sort of sagged; the front of his T-shirt bunched up where it had been smooth.

'You know, I couldn't care less,' he said quietly. 'Really. Gert, would you help me? You're strong, right? We'll get a taxi.'

I expected Karl to protest, or to be grateful or something, but it was like he stepped out of shot. He walked over to the two guys who had come in a few minutes ago, and asked if they needed anything. Started shooting the breeze, as if nothing else was going on. Meanwhile, James and I tried to figure out a way to get Geoff vertical between us; I was picturing the red diagrams of bodies on the Health and Safety posters we had backstage. No-one took any notice. James had to prop him up against the wall, leaning against him with his own body, while I opened the back door.

Outside, it had got cooler, but after a few yards lumping this guy along, I'd broken out in a sweat. He was a big guy, tall, two heads above me, and in this condition a dead weight.

'What are we going to do?' There were no taxis around, no cars passing.

'Let's just get him to that bench, if we can. I'll find a pay phone and call the hospital.'

We laid him out on the bench, his legs hanging over one end, and I sat down on the other while James crossed the road to use a phone he'd spotted, by the traffic lights. The moon was out, half full. Half empty, whatever. I still felt drunk, but hazy-drunk; the buzz was wearing off, and I kept wiping my eyes so that I could see better. I imagined Kate tucked up at home, in a warm bed, the early hours of dawn. And Wanda, wherever she was, sleeping next to Marc. And

Chicken, under the ground, up in heaven. Jonas, Michael, all asleep; maybe not Michael. I looked down at this guy's face next to my right thigh. He had heavy eyebrows, not really dark, sort of dark blond, with hairs growing every which way, corkscrew. There were two vertical lines cut deep into the space between, like cuts made in the flesh of an apple with a short knife. Once he had been a baby.

'It's OK,' said James, a little out of breath. 'They're sending someone. We can hitch a ride back in the ambulance.'

It was about 1.30 by the time we got back in the apartment, and Lawrence was waiting up. He didn't say anything when we walked in – he was just sitting there at the kitchen table, in a spotlight cast by the hanging overhead light, open book in his hands.

'Hi,' said James.

'Hi, Lawrence,' I said.

'Hello, Gert.'

We stood there for a second, at the edges of what felt like this invisible force field of disapproval coming off Lawrence, then James asked if I wanted some tea or something. 'Something to warm us up,' he said.

'I'll do it,' said Lawrence, standing up and cutting James off on his way to the stove.

'*Fuck!*' James spun away from Lawrence, as if he'd stuck him with a knife. 'I can boil water on my own, OK?'

I looked down at my hands, which is what I usually do when people lose their temper. I didn't know what was going on – it had come out of nowhere. Lawrence didn't say anything, just stood there, his hands raised in a sort of priestly calming gesture.

'You know, I don't think I want anything after all,' said James. He put the kettle on the stove, though, and lit the gas. 'But I'll turn it on for you, Gert. I'm gonna go to bed. OK, sis? Thanks for all your help tonight. You were great, a real saint. Ever think about applying for the priesthood? There's a space going. And oh, Lawrence, is my sample cup in the bathroom?'

After a moment's pause, Lawrence nodded.

'Great. Thought so. Thanks a lot. No problem. Just give me a second and the bathroom's all yours.' James left the room, catching his hip against the corner of the kitchen counter and swearing. I stood there, in the doorway of the kitchen, listening to the sound of the water heating up.

'Would you like some tea?' Lawrence asked.

'Sure. I'll make it. So you didn't have to work tonight after all?'

'It was quiet. They didn't need me, so I came home early.'

'We went out for ice-cream. Too bad – you could have come along.'

The kettle started whistling and Lawrence lifted it off the heat. In the hallway, the bathroom door opened, followed by the sound of James's bedroom door closing.

'Where did you go for ice-cream?'

'Well, we ended up not getting any.'

He put down my mug of tea on the counter next to where I was standing.

'Can I ask you some questions, Gert?' he asked.

'Some questions?'

'Yes.'

'Sure. I guess.'

'Thank you. Were you with James the whole time tonight?'

'Yes.'

'Did he get up and go anywhere, at any point? To talk to somebody by the bar, perhaps, or to the bathroom?'

I could see James going through that door again, marked Rest Rooms.

Lawrence took a sip of his own tea. He was wearing a gold signet ring on the third finger of his right hand. I wondered how old he was. It was hard to tell, early fifties maybe, but that could have been because he was acting so fatherly. He could have been much younger.

'You must find these questions strange.'

'Strange?'

'Well, you must wonder why I'm sitting up waiting for a young man who's not my son.'

I was cupping my hands around the warm mug, and I studied its contents as if there was something really interesting in there. I felt like I was in the principal's office. I coughed.

'I thought maybe it was a priest thing – are there curfews or something?'

Lawrence shook his head. 'No, no curfews. Not usually. I'm asking questions because it's my job. I didn't ask James to come and live with me – he was assigned to me.'

I looked straight at Lawrence for the first time since coming into the room.

'Assigned to you?'

'Yes.'

'James tried to commit suicide four months ago.'

'What?'

As soon as he said it, I had *déjà vu*. Hadn't I dreamed this moment? The pool of light on the table, this revelation, the mug of tea in Lawrence's hand, white enamel shining? I had been at this moment before. And in this moment, James was standing in the quiet, dark hallway, listening. I was sure of it, because he had been there before. But I was afraid to glance that way, in case Lawrence wondered why. So that's why he'd gotten so pissed off at the bar, when I'd said I understood why people would want to commit suicide.

'Are you all right?' asked Lawrence.

I nodded.

'Did you hear what I said?'

'Yes.'

'Does it surprise you?'

I shrugged. Was he implying I should have seen it coming? That I should have been there for James?

'You should know he wasn't himself at the time. He'd gotten into drugs – it can happen here, James certainly isn't the first. Nobody had realized, which is a credit to James's ability to cover up; the staff are pretty used to the symptoms. Anyway, last summer he went home to visit your folks and—'

'My dad.'

'That's right, your dad. And a few weeks after he got back, instead of turning up for work one night, he went down to one of the late-night ferries, swallowed a whole lot of pills, waited until the boat was halfway to Bainbridge Island, and then jumped overboard. It would have had the desired effect, except that someone saw him and raised the alarm. They fished him out, half-conscious, and brought him back here.'

'What did my dad say? When he heard.'

'I don't think James has told him.'

'You mean no-one's told Dad his son tried to commit suicide?'

'James is an adult.'

'Don't you think he should know?'

'We have strict confidentiality agreements with any-one who comes to us, especially people who have attempted suicide. I shouldn't really be speaking to *you* about it.'

I wanted Lawrence to shut up now. He'd told me, even though he'd had no right to. Now he could stop talking. Now we could all go to bed.

'I was hoping James would speak to you about it himself – I presumed that's why he had asked you to visit. You mean a lot to him. But I think that after tonight, it's too dangerous for you not to be let in on the situation. It's very important he doesn't get involved with drugs again, Gert.'

Why was he telling me that? Did he think I was a druggie, just because I lived in a trailer and worked for a circus? I knew he expected me to say something. To have the appropriate emotional reaction. To sympathize with his position? To thank him for watching over my brother?

'Right,' I said.

Déjà vu of me saying 'right'. *Déjà vu* of me having *déjà vu*. It went on and on, this *déjà vu*, like the mirror in a bridal shop. I guessed there was no saint for suicides.

'What's going on?'

I'd woken to the buzz of what sounded like twenty helicopters circling the neighbourhood, and when I came into the apartment, the television was on and James was watching the news.

'Hey,' he said. 'How are you feeling?'

'I'm fine. Why?'

'Well, not everybody is unaffected by a whole lot of tequila. I don't know your parameters.'

On the television, a reporter was standing in the parking lot of a Target store, with the words, Breaking News, across the bottom of the frame, in a dynamic white font. There were a lot of police cars parked at crazy angles behind him. It looked like a 70s TV cop show – sometimes it seems like they just park that way for the effect.

'What's going on?' I asked again.

'Some guy with a nifty collection of rifles, holding the store hostage.'

'Is that why all the helicopter noise outside?'

'Yeah. It's only a few blocks from here.'

'Really?'

'Just down the street.'

'How many people inside?'

'About twenty, they say – they'd only just opened up. One guy's been shot – the shop manager. There are a couple of kids in there. Their mother was waiting out in the car, while they went in to get some school supplies.'

'What's he want?'

James shrugged. 'Who knows?'

I walked to the fridge, took out the milk and poured myself some cereal. The television had the same effect as always: James and I just sat there like dummies, spooning our Wheaties and zoning out. Nothing was going on at the Target, you could tell; the journalist was straining to think of more stuff to say. Cops standing around in the background, shifting their weight, kids lined up on the other side of the parking lot fence, their fingers poking through.

'So. I guess Lawrence spilled the beans last night,'

said James. I suddenly noticed James's strongbox, on the floor next to his chair, the lid open.

'What did you say?'

'He told you. About me.' James nodded, still staring at the screen. 'You don't need to worry. It's all right now. I'm much better.'

Jesus. What could I say?

'That's good.'

'It's been a confusing time and, you know, the drugs didn't help.'

'Is that why you knew all those people last night? Is that why you knew that place?'

'That's why I took you there. I didn't go there to score. I was trying to build myself up to telling you, and I thought it would sort of ease me into the subject. It's a hard thing to just bring up, you know?'

I nodded, biting my thumbnail. I'd pulled up one knee to my chest, and was resting my chin on it. We kept on watching the television. James sniffed.

They were interviewing the mother now, the one who'd been waiting in the car. She was standing next to a policewoman, talking to the camera, appealing for her kids to be released, because I guess the gunman had turned on a TV inside the shop and was watching it while simultaneously talking to the cops on a store phone.

'This is fucked up,' I said.

'Do you want a bagel?' asked James. 'Lawrence went and got them. Still hot.'

When I sneaked a look at James, at the counter slicing my bagel, with his back turned, I got a flash of his body floating in the cold water, if no-one had seen him jump. Had he been wearing a coat? With stones in the pocket? Pills and jumping overboard – this hadn't been a warning shot. He'd obviously really meant to do it. In my head, he'd succeeded, and I went into this morbid fantasy about how, if he'd died, they would have found me on the road, and maybe I would have heard about it on the phone from Dad, or even worse, Janine. Of course, I'd been up half the night already following these little mole trails, and also wondering – God help me and forgive me – if this was it. If this had been what James needed to tell me. And I hated myself for being a self-centred, selfish little shit, because, if it was, I was disappointed. So why had he got his strongbox out and opened it up?

'Here you go.' He put the bagel down in front of me, on a little white plate.

'Thanks. Has Lawrence gone to work?'

'No. He's gone to visit his sister or something. I think he just wanted to leave us alone.'

The TV cameras kept zooming in on the windows of the store, and occasionally you felt like you could see some movement, but mostly it was just glare and reflection. They didn't know what to film.

'So, was it the drugs that made you do it?' I asked, still watching the screen. 'Sort of like an overdose?'

James sat down on the chair opposite me, facing away from the TV. He seemed ready to talk. 'There were other reasons, too.'

'If you don't want to tell me, it's OK.'

'No. I want to tell you. I have to tell you.' He coughed into his hand. 'I don't really know how to begin.'

All this time I was still staring at the television screen, and even though I was listening to every syllable that came out of James's mouth, even listening to the breaths in between, at the same time I kept on

293

thinking about the people inside the Target store at that moment, the hostages, what they must be feeling, who they were thinking of and praying they'd see again, and all that. I got very focused on this. I knew this was the moment; I felt like I was walking down a hallway and in the room at the end of the hallway whoever I was coming to visit would be laid-out, still, dead. But I think that in times like that you sometimes look at anything, the pictures on the wall, a stain on a tablecloth, the rim of a trash bin, rather than at where you're going.

'You know that postcard you got from Prophets-town? From the Traveller's Inn?'

'How do you know about that?'

'I wrote it.'

Greg Cazan: that was the name of the TV reporter guy they had on, interviewing people – his name was flashed across the screen, across his chest area. 'What were you doing at the Traveller's Inn?'

'It was on my trip home last June. Dad and I had to go there.'

'You had to?'

'Yeah – do you mind if I turn this off?'

'Sure, sorry. I'll just make myself some tea.' Anything to get away. I stood up and filled the kettle, put it on the gas, stood over it with my back to James as it began to hiss. This was stupid. I could face this, whatever it was. I turned around and smiled at him. 'Does Dad know that you tried to kill yourself?'

'No. You're the only one.'

'Why haven't you told him? I mean, it sounds like you guys are pretty close, if you're going on little road trips together.'

'It wasn't a little road trip.'

'What was it then? Were you meeting Mom?'

'Why do you say that?'

'I don't know. I thought the postcard was from her, when I got it.'

'Had you heard from her before?'

'I don't know. No.'

'Me neither.'

He picked up the bagel I'd left lying untouched and lifted it as if he was going to take a bite. Then he placed it back on the plate.

'She shot herself, Gert. Mom. I've got the police report in my box, if you want to see it. She killed herself, in Prophetstown, in that hotel, nine years ago, only a couple of weeks after she left us. She was all by herself – there was never a question of somebody else being involved. The police contacted Dad, and he—'

I turned around and shut off the gas. Like I've said, I'd been waiting for this moment for years. I'd known it was coming, known it was out there, but what I hadn't understood until now was that I'd also been expecting, been waiting faithfully for the happy ending too, the photo-negative, the reversal of all my beliefs, like Scrooge at the end of *A Christmas Carol*, somehow as sure that it might come as well. I thought about how there was never going to be a reunion, an awkward, tense reunion, a speechless, longed-for, necessary reunion. The first fifteen years of living with Mom had planted this tiny, fucking pathetic seed of optimism in me and eight years of desert life since hadn't quite done the killing job.

'I found this news clipping when I was home – I broke into the locked drawer of Dad's desk, because I was looking for money to score – and I found an envelope with the clipping inside and her death certificate.'

'So he knew?'

'He says he didn't tell us because he wanted to protect us from it – he said he was going to tell us when we were old enough. He said he couldn't bear to tell us.'

I realized I was kneeling on the floor, my head against the door of the oven. I stood up.

'It's awful about those people.'

'What?' said James.

'Those kids on the TV. Stuck inside that store. What's going to happen to them?'

'What are you talking about, Gert?'

'I'm gonna go now.'

'What?'

'I have to go now.'

'Go? Where?'

'Nowhere special. I'm sorry. I know it's not very kind, but like I said, it's what I do.'

'You shouldn't leave.'

'Maybe not but—'

'You really shouldn't leave.'

'Maybe not, but I'm not— You have to understand it's not really possible for me to stay. Me and Mom, you know, not really the ones to rely on to stick around.'

'Don't say that, Gert. You're not like her.'

'How would you know?'

I went to Lawrence's bedroom, grabbed my suitcase, which of course I'd never unpacked, and left James there in the kitchen, looking at the bagel.

Prophetstown

If this had happened, what else could?

If I was like my mother, which I'd always known I was, if I was her, then I was dead. Then I had to disappear too; I was gone, like an unfortunate swimmer who has misjudged the tide, like a Polaroid print in reverse, I faded away. Whatever it was had led her to Prophetstown, and that decision, it would get me too in the end. I could feel it – why try and fight it? I slid onto the B roads.

Gertrude is not afraid. She is afraid. She is not afraid. She is afraid to stand at the edge of this rock and lower one foot over, dipping it into a frigid swimming pool of air, lower and lower it until her balance is gone and she can't help but topple over, 10,000 feet down into the canyon below. She doesn't know where she is – is this a dream or is she awake? She has found a boulder to stand on. It looks like her mother's face – there's the nose, there are the hollows for eyes, there are her lips. She is standing, balancing on the lower lip, and her mother's chin curves away underneath her. What will it feel like to fall? Like flying? How long will she fall? How long will she know it? Will she regret it the moment she's gone? Will she claw at the air, trying to take it back? Will it hurt when she finally hits? Will she die instantly? How long before someone finds her? Before they know? Maybe they'll never find her.

She drives out of Yosemite.

In Nevada, there's a girl kneeling by the side of the road, holding a piece of paper in her hands. She's looking down at the piece of paper, maybe she's reading it. She's kneeling on the grass in front of a pile of bouquets, bouquets wrapped up in plastic and tied with pastel ribbons, baby blue, pink, yellow. Some of them have little cards attached to the plastic. There's a ribbon tied around the pole of a traffic sign in front of the girl, and what looks like a photograph stuck to it as well. The young woman is kneeling in front of all these things, with her piece of paper in her hands, and she is swaying, a little bit.

Gertrude sees her out of the corner of her eye as she drives by. She turns the car around and drives by again. Then she turns around and drives by, once more. Is there a Grief and Loss Society? Providing examples? Showing her things to provoke a reaction? Because she doesn't feel much of anything. Are they trying to show her people who are worse off, people who are going through the same things, to make her feel better? Fuck that.

She leaves Nevada.

In Nebraska, Gertrude's standing outside a bar – she's not sure where. It's the middle of the night, though, and she's standing just inside the strip of light cast by the illuminated sign over the door. She can't remember whether she's been inside – she doesn't feel drunk.

298

She feels like she's tripping – she feels very alive. She wonders where her car is parked. Three people come out of the bar, and Gertrude slides along the wall until she's out of the light. Two of the people, a man and a woman, are being followed by the third, another man, hair the colour of wet hay. He's wearing a yellow button-down shirt and blue jeans.

'Don't go, Julie,' he says, like he's reading a script, 'don't do it. Don't walk away from me.' His voice is slurred. The woman slows down, and stops, but she doesn't turn around. 'What? You wanna fuck me up? You wanna fuck up my life? Do you? This is the rest of my life we're talking here. Don't fuck me up. Don't keep walking, Julie. Don't fuck me up.'

'Just go home, Kurt.'

'Go home? Fine, OK. Fine. Home. That's great. Do you wanna fuck up my life, more than it's fucked up already? Do you want to add to that? Do you want to make me do something? Julie. This is it, if you walk away. This is it.'

'Shut up, Kurt. You're drunk.'

'No, don't – don't do this, Julie. Don't fuck me up. Do you wanna fuck up my head for ever?'

After Julie's gone, Kurt wheels around and notices Gert standing there in the shadows. He stares at her blankly for a few seconds, as if he's wondering whether he knows her, whether she's with him, then he smiles, sloppily.

'What the hell. You gotta try, don't you?' he says, and flounders back into the establishment.

In Prophetstown, she spits at the mirror, two times. The spit runs down her left cheek, then off her face and across the glass. She goes to a drugstore and buys a double pack of chewing gum, comes back to her room and chews all twenty sticks of gum, one by one, taking them out of her mouth and sticking them onto the face in the mirror, in stringy clumps, like flecks of old porridge. It's a small mirror, just enough room for the face, with no frame. A face covered with Quasimodo gum scars.

She experiments with other substances. Lipstick's a cliché and too colourful. She wants to scratch the glass, scratch the face, but there's nothing sharp enough around. She thinks about lighting. The overhead light is brighter, but the little fluorescent shaving light makes the face look washed-out, and she prefers this. Her eyes are in shadow.

She talks to the face.

'What are you doing?' she asks.

'What are you doing?' she repeats.

'What are you waiting for?'

She goes to the hardware store and buys some wallpaper paste and the Sunday *New York Times*. She mixes it all up in the sink. It takes a little persistence, because at first the strips of wet paper keep slipping off and falling onto the floor, but as the paste begins to dry it gets easier, and she covers the mirror in sixteen layers of newsprint. Then, with her fingers, and a knife she's kept back from Room Service, she gouges out some eye holes and a mouth hole for breathing.

Then there is nothing left to do, or nothing she can think of. Her sneakers stick to the bathroom floor where the papier mâché strips have left paste. Now she has to get real. Now she has to really do it. Has anyone ever asphyxiated themselves with papier mâché?

And there's something else bothering her. She

300

noticed it the first night, lying on the floor, watching television and eating the bacon cheeseburger and ice-cream sundae she'd ordered. That's when she saw it, because she was on the floor. About two inches above the fuzz of the green and yellow shaggy carpet, and a foot in from the edge of the wall where it turns the corner to the bathroom, there's a tiny rust-coloured spot. Only the size of a penny, maybe even smaller.

Of course it would have depended on where the body had fallen, and the angle of the gun. She knows this is the right room, because she's gone and looked it up in the local newspapers, on micro-file in the Prophetstown Public Library, and then she even went and asked the police about it. They were really nice and sympathetic – they remembered her brother. She told them he was fine. She told them she just wanted to see the place: she was sure they 'understood'. She wonders if they've tipped off the hotel owner – but you can't refuse somebody a room, can you?

She doesn't know exactly where in the room her mother did it. She gets down on her knees to stare at the little spot again. Blood must be hard to get off wallpaper. But then again, they've probably changed the wallpaper since. This is probably just a ketchup stain, maybe tomato juice. Maybe someone was having a Bloody Mary one night, a salesman, after a hard day trying to get rid of his insurance policies, and he kicked the glass across the room by accident, on his way to the bathroom. On the other hand, it was such a tiny spot; you could only see it if you were looking from exactly the right angle. It would have been easy for the cleaning staff to miss. What a job that must be, cleaning up after a shoot-out. Who did that – who

301

mopped it all up when some lunatic went mad in a post office? Or a McDonald's? The usual cleaners? She guesses it would have to be someone connected with the forensics team. Christ, what about when it was kids' brains they were scrubbing off the carpets? Who was going to clean up after her?

The next day, pissed off with her hesitation, she goes into the motel office and gives them the last of her money. This is her attempt at burning bridges. The lady behind the counter has faded blond hair and a pleasant face. Her fingers are very tanned.

'Are you enjoying your stay?' she asks. She looks a little worried. She probably knows all about why Gert is there, so Gert gives her a big smile.

'Very much, thank you. It's just what I needed.'

She looks relieved. 'Oh good. Do you want the maid to come clean your room? You had the Do Not Disturb sign on all day yesterday, so we weren't . . . we weren't sure.'

'Sorry. I was up all night, working. So I slept in.'

'What do you do, if you don't mind me asking?'

'Not at all. I'm a real estate agent.'

'Really? So young. My sister-in-law's a realtor. I've always thought that would be a fun job, getting to see inside all those people's houses. So should I tell the maid to come this morning? Is the heating working OK? Supposed to be a cold snap coming.' She hands Gert a bill. 'So. That's ninety-six dollars for another two nights, mid-week deal.'

'What a bargain. Could I have a few of those mints?'

'Help yourself.' They're the chocolate-covered kind, in silver crinkly paper. Gert remembers them from restaurants they used to stop at on family vacations.

She considers saying this out loud, but doesn't, in case it gets quoted in a newspaper later.

As soon as she gets back in the room she starts running a bath, so that when the maid comes in, she can shout from behind the closed bathroom door. She doesn't want the maid to see the mirror.

It's actually kind of nice sitting on the edge of the bath, in the steam. She takes her shoes and socks off and rolls up her pants, sticks her feet in the water. She still has about seven dollars left, so she can order something from Room Service tonight, and then it will all be gone, her money. Two days ago, she'd driven the trailer to the empty parking lot of a boarded-up plastics factory and left it there unlocked, walked back to the motel. It had never been registered in her name, anyway.

She hears the maid coming in. 'I'm in the bath,' Gert calls out through the door. 'Don't worry about in here. I can do it myself. I'm a pretty tidy person – there's not much to do.'

'OK,' says the maid.

'If you could just leave some cleaner for me, maybe.'

'OK.'

It doesn't sound like the maid's first language is English.

'How long have you been working here?' Gert yells.

'Excuse me?'

'I said, how long have you been working in this hotel?'

'Two years.' The maid's voice is close to the bathroom door now – she must be dusting the TV or something.

'Have they redecorated recently?'

'Excuse me?'

'Have they changed the wallpaper or anything, since you've been working here?'

'The wallpaper? No. I don't think so. I'm going to vacuum, ma'am. Sorry.'

'That's OK, it won't bother me.'

She leans over and dangles her hands in the water, making currents back and forth. Can she force her own face under the water and keep it there? She tries to think of all the movie deaths she can remember, while the maid vacuums up against the crack of the door. If there was a hairdryer under the sink, she could electrocute herself, but this place is too cheap. She should have bought one before she spent all her money. Get it going high-speed and drop it in the bath – that would be quick, wouldn't it? But then again, the cord probably wouldn't reach from that little outlet all the way to the bath. Did it work the same if you stuck it in a sink and then put your hand in the water? Probably not. Where had her mother got hold of a gun?

Shit. She's so tired of thinking about it. Why does she have to do anything? Why can't people just fade away when they want to? It had seemed the perfect thing to do, the only thing to do, coming here, but she hasn't really thought it through. She's just a fucking pseudo-suicide, her and her papier mâché mirror.

In the night she wakes up, her heart pounding. The room's dark. She looks across at the door; she can just make out its outline by the parking lot light coming through the cracks. She has that feeling again, like she had at Kate's, that someone has just been in the room with her, talking to her. She wraps the sheet around herself and pads over to the door. There's no-one outside, of course. The parking lot is totally still. She closes the door. In the morning, she rolls over, gropes for the television remote and watches re-runs and game shows until four. When it begins to get dark again, she decides she needs help.

She walks back to the abandoned trailer, early evening, and from the little clothes-hanging space in the cupboard where she stored her tools she fishes out the only dress she still owns, one that she bought in New York for going to shows with Louie's customers, and a pair of black shoes she used to wear in the ring. The dress is not in great shape, so back at the hotel she rings up reception and asks if she could use an iron.

'Sure, I think we can find you one.' They're probably happy to hear Gert's voice.

She irons the dress, takes a shower, washes her hair with the crap hotel shampoo and generally tries to beautify herself. The whole ensemble doesn't really work without makeup, so on the way down the strip she steals a lipstick from Walgreens and puts some on in the bathroom at the bar. Now she really looks the part. If she can only find a particularly nasty travelling salesman, with a gun in his car and a mixed-up conscience about his sexual urges, she'll be home free. It would be so much easier if somebody else did it, pushed her life along and off the track. At least she knows her own limitations.

'Buy a girl a drink?' she says to the man who seems most likely, sitting at a table by himself in the centre of the room.

But maybe she's misjudged him — he's looking alarmed, like she's a talking bar stool or something.

'Sorry.' She smiles. 'Are you expecting someone?'

The man looks around. There's nobody nearby. The whole bar's pretty empty; she has no idea what night of the week it is. He's wearing a brown suit with a white pinstriped shirt and a tan tie. He looks like a loner – that's why she's chosen him. He has on a wedding ring.

'I'm bothering you. Sorry.'

He still doesn't say a word, so she walks back to the bar. Guess she chose wrong. A few minutes later though, he's hovering at her shoulder.

'Excuse me, miss? Were you wanting a drink?'

Driving back to the Traveller's Inn, in the man's car, she thinks about her mom. She's glad she doesn't believe in an after-life because she doesn't figure her mom would have liked seeing her little girl in this scenario. The man's started touching her breasts now, with the hand not holding the steering wheel. Even so, she's beginning to worry he's not the kind of man she'd been hoping for. For one, she thinks he's probably never done this before. When she told him the price, out in the parking lot, he agreed so quickly she figures she could have told him any price. He makes a stop at a cash machine on the way back and while he's out of the car, Gert checks the dash compartment. No gun. Just a scraper for iced-up windows, a few road maps and a packet of Kleenex.

She's doing this for a reason; she has to keep that in sight. If this isn't the guy, there'll be another one, more desperate. Or if they're all sad losers, she can use the money she earns to buy a gun herself, right?

It isn't so bad. His body's a little flabby, sure, the kind of soft bagginess you get with guys in their fifties, like they've lost weight recently and their skin doesn't quite fit any more. But he's dry and cool, and he doesn't smell bad. As per usual, it doesn't take more than fifteen minutes and afterwards he obviously wants to talk. She reaches for the remote, still lying underneath him, and switches it on, hoping he'll get the hint. The man stays where he is, just turns his head so he can see the screen.

There's an MTV video on, some heavy metal band she doesn't recognize.

'This is the kind of stuff my kids like to watch.'

'How many kids do you have?' she asks. She wishes he'd get off her; she feels like she can't breathe.

'Four. Two girls, two boys.'

'That's nice.'

He lets his body roll off her to one side, which is good except now he's actually talking *to* her and she doesn't want to make eye contact.

'They're pretty good kids. Very different types. One of my daughter's into sports, running around with her gang of friends – she's a real daddy's girl, always glad to see me when I get home from these trips, gives me a great welcome. The other one's sort of a stay-at-home – doesn't like to go out so much. She's a bit stockier, you know, than her sister, doesn't burn it off with all that nervous energy, I guess. And my youngest son, he's eleven, there's the real genius of the family. He's got one of those brains – I don't know who he got it from, because it sure as hell wasn't me. We'll be standing at the checkout in the supermarket and he watches the numbers as they come up on the display, and he can always get the total, every time, before the machine does.'

'Wow. That's amazing.' There's an old Cyndi Lauper video on now and she wishes she could turn it up, drown out what this man is saying.

'I know. His teachers figure he'll be in college by the time he's a teenager.' The man runs a hand up and down Gert's thigh. 'I don't like to talk about my other son.'

This sounds more promising. Aren't men supposed to sleep it off after sex? She shivers.

'Are you cold?' He sits up and reaches down to the foot of the bed, giving her a flash of his butt. The coverlet he hands her is one of those nasty, thin kinds, feels like it's got some sort of waxy covering. He plumps up the pillows and lies back against the headboard.

'Do you mind if I turn off this light?' she asks.

When he says no, she switches off the light, and the room is dark except for the flickering blue light from the TV, on their faces.

'Last time he turned up – my oldest – he told everyone in the neighbourhood he had this great new job, in the army. When the truth was he came home to borrow six thousand dollars from me, and I know I'll never see that money again.'

'So he doesn't live with you.'

'No way. Kicked him out when he was sixteen – eight years ago. Called Social Services to come and get him.'

'Why'd you do that?'

'I got home from a trip to find his mother sitting in the kitchen with a black eye and her shoulder in a sling.'

'He beat her up?'

'You bet he did. Wouldn't believe it, huh? This is when the girls were still little, nine and ten. I had to call somebody to come get him right then, because I knew if I didn't, I was going to do something I'd regret later. Of course, his mother didn't want him to leave – pleaded with me to give him another chance – but for

308

me, he'd crossed a line. Anything but hurting her, I could have taken. Drugs, sex, whatever, I could have handled it, maybe. But not hurting his mother – she's it for me, she's the line you don't cross.'

This seems a pretty funny thing to say, considering Gert's lying in the guy's wet patch.

'His mother's the one person I'd do anything for, you know? And I know she feels that way about me. I mean, she's the person I drive carefully for; Christ, she's the person I stay *alive* for, even when I don't want to, you know?' Gert's not looking at him while he's saying all this, but she hears the tone of his voice change now. 'So what am I doing here?'

She listens to him getting dressed, putting on his underwear, his pants with the keys jingling inside, then his shirt. Then there's a silence.

'I'm leaving the money on the table,' he says. 'OK?'

Gert lies there in the blue light for about fifteen minutes after he's gone. Then she rolls over and opens the bedside drawer and takes out a book. Inside the book, tucked between the pages, there is a series of postcards. On every postcard, the handwriting is the same.

'James. It's Gert.'

'Gert! Where are you?'

'I'm in a motel.'

'What have you been doing? I've been really worried about you.'

'Uh-huh. How are you doing?'

'I'm OK. A woman rang for you.'

'Oh yeah?' Wasn't Mom this time.

'Your friend Kate. Just to see if you were OK.'

'What did you tell her?'

'I said I didn't know.'

From where I was lying, in the morning light, I could see the pile of bills that had been left on the table by the door. Two hundred – he'd added fifty more than I'd asked for.

'Can I ask you something, James?'

'Of course.'

'Whatever happened to Father Bill? Didn't Mom run away with Father Bill? How do we know he didn't shoot her?'

'The police were pretty sure there was no-one else involved. All the people at the motel said she'd checked in alone, and they'd never noticed anyone coming to visit her or anything.'

'She could have picked someone up though, in a bar or something.'

'Mom?'

'Well, we don't know, do we? Someone could have followed her back to her room.'

'There were no fingerprints on the gun except hers. There wasn't any sign of a struggle.'

'Do you think she was in love with him?'

'With who?'

'Father Bill.'

'Who knows?'

I lay back on the wrinkled pillows and pulled the covers up to my chin. It felt so cold in this room – the weather must have turned.

'Are you there?' he asked.

'I'm gonna hang up now, James.'

'Don't you want to ask me some more questions?' He sounded so desperate.

'I can only take so much information at a time. You know?'

He was silent.

'There is one thing, actually. Why did you write me all those postcards?'

Another silence.

'James?'

'I don't know. I missed you.'

'Did you want me to think they were from her?'

Another long pause.

'I guess so. Partly. I thought maybe you'd feel better, like you were protected or something, on the road. Like somebody cared where you were.'

'How did you find me?'

'It was hard sometimes. But then you started writing to me. Are you going to be all right, Gert? What are you planning to do?'

'I don't know.'

'Would you promise to call me? If you're feeling—?'

'If I'm feeling like Mom?'

'I guess. How did Mom feel?'

'Brave.'

'Brave?'

'Yeah. She had to be brave to do what she did.'

'I don't think it's brave. I don't think it's brave at all. I think what I'm doing now is braver.'

'What's that?'

'Staying alive.'

There was such a long silence then, I wondered if he'd hung up without saying goodbye.

'James?'

'Yeah?'

'I'll call you again. In a day or two.'

'You promise?'

'I promise.'

* * *

311

I didn't take a bath. I lay there for a while, holding the phone in my hands, listening to the dial tone. Then I called information and asked for a number in my home town. It was a long shot, but you never know.

'Hello?'

'Hi. I was wondering if I could speak to Barbara.'

'This is Barbara.'

'Barbara. This is Gert.'

She didn't say anything for a moment. 'Gert McCall?'

'Yeah.'

'Wow.'

'I know. Pretty weird, huh?'

'Where are you? Are you home?'

'No. Not far.'

'Don't you work for a circus? I heard that, I guess.'

A clock started chiming in the background where she was, and I remembered how there had been an old-fashioned clock on the half-moon table in the entrance hall of her house, right next to the phone. Their house had been full of old stuff like that, stuff her grandparents had brought over from Europe.

'Hello?' she said.

'Hi. I'm still here. So, how are you?'

'I'm fine.' She sounded a little wary of me, a little suspicious, which wasn't surprising. Had I even said goodbye to her?

'Are your parents OK?'

'Well, my dad died.'

'Oh yeah? I'm sorry. So did my mom.'

'Really?'

'Yeah. She killed herself.'

'God, Gert. Were you – were you with her?'

'No.'

'That's terrible.'

312

'Yeah. It's OK. Thanks.' I turned over in the bed so the phone was between my ear and the pillow. 'So I might be coming home for a visit soon, maybe in a couple of days. I just wondered if you'd like to get together for a drink, or something.'

'Sure. If you want. I'm in a band, right now, so my nights are pretty tied up.'

'You're still playing.'

'If you can call it that.'

'Shut up, I bet you're great. Maybe I could come see you play. We could meet afterwards?'

'Sure. Why don't you give me a call when you get into town?'

'I will.'

When I rolled over to replace the receiver in the handset, I ended up on top of *Saint Days*. The postcards were still strewn across the bed from the night before. I opened up the book and looked at my mother's handwriting: Lydia Harding, December 1968. A year before I was born. Two years after she'd married Dad. She'd probably never imagined her life would end the way it did. Or maybe she had.

There was a knock on the door.

'Who is it?' I called.

'Would you like your room cleaned?'

'Sure. Come on in.'

The maid turned her key in the lock, pushed the door open and rolled her trolley into the room. It was a different maid this time – an older lady, near retirement age probably.

'Hi,' I said.

'Hi.'

I started flipping through the pages of *Saint Days*. Even though I'd done this hundreds of times, I still thought, every time I did it, maybe I'd find some little clue I'd missed before, something she had underlined, a word or two scribbled in the margin, one of her Sunday school smiley faces near a relevant passage. Before I realized the consequences, the maid entered the bathroom.

'Shit.' I jumped off the bed and stood there frozen, halfway to the door, not sure what to do. It was totally silent in there.

'Sorry about the mess,' I called out. 'I'll clean it up myself.' Silence. 'I'll get some extra-duty stuff from the hardware store.'

She came out of the bathroom and went straight to her trolley without looking at me, her face like stone. 'It's OK,' she said. 'I can probably get it off.'

'You shouldn't have to do that.' I followed her back into the bathroom. She was spraying something at the layers of papier mâché. Then she picked up a plastic brush and started scrubbing. It wasn't having much effect.

'Here, let me do that. I can't let you do that.'

She stepped back, sort of obsequiously as if I'd wrenched the brush out of her hands or something, and watched me set to it. 'You're probably going to need a knife or something,' she said. Then she sat down on the edge of the bath. I started picking at the crud with my fingernails.

'Are you the one whose mother killed herself?'

I flicked some crud off the end of my fingers into the plastic-lined waste basket. 'Uh-huh.'

'I thought so.'

Maybe that was why she was being so nice about the mirror.

'Here – try this.' She handed me her room key.

314

'Maybe you can work it underneath that piece there and pull it all off.'

'Thanks.'

'She was a nice lady,' she said.

'Who?'

'Your mom. She was a nice lady.'

'You remember her?'

'Sure. You would. You know, after something like that. The police even interviewed me, because I was the last one to see her. Anyway, she was very polite. Some people can be real assholes, you know, but she wasn't like that. She told me about her kids. About you – I guess.'

All this time, I hadn't stopped chipping away at the mirror. Digging and scrubbing, trying to get the fucking stuff off. Now I let my hands drop.

I turned away so the maid wouldn't see my face. I was bent over, not able to speak. I couldn't hold everything in; I couldn't own it, it was going to split me open. I felt like an animal.

The maid stood up. 'I'll go get a knife or something from housekeeping, should I? How about that? I'm sorry, I didn't mean to upset you. Tell you what – it's almost time for my break. Why don't I come back after lunch this afternoon some time? Before I clock off? Would that be good? I'll come back later.'

She took her keys out of my hand gently, and left.

When I'd pulled myself together, I went back to *Saint Days* again. What struck me this time was all the violence in these guys' lives. Saint Sebastian, tied to a post, pierced by arrows shot into him with the crossbows of a firing squad. Saint Blaise, shredded alive by wool combs. Saint Catherine strung up on her wheel, Saint Joan on her burning stake. Saint Elmo, rolled in pitch and set afire by the emperor Diocletian. Saint Apollonia, her teeth pulled out one by one. Saint Barbara, locked up in a remote stone tower by her father, and then he beheaded her. Saint Lawrence, tied to a gridiron and roasted slowly over a hot fire. Saint Agatha locked in a brothel and repeatedly raped. Saint Agatha stretched out on the rack and then they sliced her breasts off, one after the other. Saint Agatha, as she lay dying, thanking God for giving her the patience to suffer.

God give me the patience to suffer.

Jesus Christ. What had I suffered? What were my problems, compared to these, and the countless people probably going through similarly torturous things right now, in the twentieth century, on this day?

The book fell open at my own name.

Saint Gertrude, the patron saint of souls journeying to the next world. Did she know when she named me? Was she trying to will me strength, just in case? Did she think about it later? When she was here, contemplating the barrel of a gun? Did she think about me?

I'd never, ever know why she'd done it. That was the hardest thing. What had that word been in Michael's home-made dictionary? I went and fished the book out my suitcase, got back into bed.

Acatalepsy – that was it. The unknowableness to a certainty of all things.

That's what I would have to live with.

I sat on the bed for a few more hours, until the light began to change behind the mustard-coloured curtains. I didn't turn on the TV; I didn't read. I just sat there, staring at the floor in front of me. Finally, I began to think about Saint Kevin.

Saint Kevin, the B-cast Saint Francis, the nature lover, the one who let that egg sit in his hand for weeks, until it hatched and the little birdie flew away to find its mother. It seemed like the point of that story was that Kevin knew, after the egg was laid in his hand, that if he'd gone rushing around collecting firewood, or cooking a stew for his supper, or for a walk in the woods at twilight, or even if he'd just gone to fetch his Bible so he could read it by the fire, the egg would have been disturbed, and it might never have hatched, and that single life would have been lost. All the effort put into creating that life, wasted. And I guess Saint Kevin loved life so much that he was able to sit still for as long as it took.

I'm no saint. I know I can never be, and I don't really want to be anyway. But there was something to be learned from Kevin, something about staying still, Kevin style, which I had never done. There was something about just sitting on the bed, in this room with the rusty spot low down and the gunged-up mirror in the bathroom, in this room where someone I loved so much was, and then wasn't. Just sitting here, holding all that in my open hands, waiting for it to hatch.

Because the problem is I love life too, just like Saint Kevin. Maybe not as much, definitely not as much, but just a little, just enough. I wish I didn't – I really do. I wish I could hate it. But I don't.

So what if I just sit here for a while? Sit and wait for my life to catch up.

And now I can begin.

THE END

THINGS TO DO INDOORS
Sheena Joughin

'AN EXCITING NEW TALENT'
Sunday Telegraph

Sisterly sharing is taken beyond the pale when twenty-six-year old Chrissie finds a postcard from her boyfriend to her sister signed, 'Kisses, Nick'. Within moments she severs her two central relationships and looks boldly forward to the haphazard pleasures of an independent life.

Her lyrical journey, from lovelorn waitress to self-contained mother, takes us through the pubs, parks, parties, patisseries, peeling houseboats and rackety flats of west London to the shores of Lisbon, Ireland and Brighton. But Chrissie's attempts to escape the emotional convolutions of London only ever seem to lead to encounters that intensify rather than dispel her growing sense of how knotty life can be.

'SHEENA JOUGHIN HAS AN UNUSUAL CLARITY OF VOICE AND A CRAFTY DUALITY, SOMETHING BOTH BROODING AND LIGHT, IN HER WRITING. THE HURTS AND NASTINESSES BETWEEN HER CHARACTERS ARE PARALLELED WITH A CASUAL PERSISTENCE OF GOOD NATURE AND GOOD HUMOUR IN THIS FUNNY, PIERCING BOOK ABOUT LOSTNESS, CHILDISHNESS AND GROWING UP'
Ali Smith *Times Literary Supplement*

'SHE WRITES LIKE AN ANGEL AND THINKS LIKE THE DEVIL. JOUGHIN IS A MAJOR DISCOVERY'
Fay Weldon

'[JOUGHIN] IS ALREADY A MISTRESS OF MORDANT COMEDY . . . A TALENT TO WATCH'
Daily Mail

'VERY FUNNY, VERY EDGY, VERY ACUTE. I LOVE THIS BOOK'
Julie Burchill

'JOUGHIN HAS A MERCILESS EYE FOR UNFLATTERING DETAIL AND FOR THE INSECURITIES OF BOTH SEXES . . . EXTREMELY FUNNY'
Daily Telegraph

0 552 77153 8

BLACK SWAN

PAINTING RUBY TUESDAY
Jane Yardley

'BRIGHT, ENGAGING AND VERY FUNNY'
Guardian

It is the summer of 1965. Annie Cradock, the only child of
exacting parents who run the village school, is an imaginative girl
with a head full of the Beatles and the Rolling Stones. Annie
whiles away the school holiday with her friends: Ollie the rag-
and-bone man (and more importantly his dog); the beautiful
piano-playing Mrs Clitheroe who turns Beethoven into boogie-
woogie and Annie's best friend Babette – streetwise, loyal, and
Annie's one solid link with common sense. But everything
changes when the village is rocked by a series of murders and the
girls know something they've no intention of telling the police.

In the present day, the adult Annie is a successful musician
and teacher in a stifling marriage. Her American husband is an
ambitious man uncomfortable with emotion and impatient
with his quirky wife. He's taking a job in New York – but is she
going with him? In a Greenwich Village shop Annie discovers a
photograph album from her past – only then can she begin to lay
her ghosts and come to terms with the bizarre events of 1965.

'HIGHLY ORIGINAL . . . TOLD WITH HUMOUR AND
POIGNANCY BY A HUGELY LIKEABLE HEROINE . . .
AN ENTERTAINING AND COMPELLING READ FILLED
WITH ROUNDED, MEMORABLE CHARACTERS, AND BOTH
DARKLY FUNNY AND MOVING'
Time Out

'*PAINTING RUBY TUESDAY* IS INDEED A COMIC NOVEL,
BUT ONE WHICH IS ELEVATED BY THE MUSIC WHICH
FLOWS THROUGH IT, AND THE UNUSUAL AND ORIGINAL
DESCRIPTIONS'
The Scotsman

'I LOVED IT . . . I THOUGHT IT WAS WONDERFULLY BLACKLY
COMIC IN THAT UNIQUELY ENGLISH WAY . . . INTERLACED
WITH AN UNDERSTANDING OF HOW FRAGILE MODERN
RELATIONSHIPS CAN BE'
Isla Dewar, author of *Giving Up on Ordinary*

0 552 77101 5

BLACK SWAN

A SELECTED LIST OF FINE NOVELS
AVAILABLE FROM BLACK SWAN

THE PRICES SHOWN BELOW WERE CORRECT AT THE TIME OF GOING TO PRESS. HOWEVER TRANSWORLD
PUBLISHERS RESERVE THE RIGHT TO SHOW NEW RETAIL PRICES ON COVERS WHICH MAY DIFFER FROM
THOSE PREVIOUSLY ADVERTISED IN THE TEXT OR ELSEWHERE.

99588 6	THE HOUSE OF THE SPIRITS	Isabel Allende	£7.99
99934 2	EVERY GOOD WOMAN DESERVES A LOVER	Diana Appleyard	£6.99
77105 8	NOT THE END OF THE WORLD	Kate Atkinson	£6.99
99863 X	MARLENE DIETRICH LIVED HERE	Eleanor Bailey	£6.99
77131 7	MAKING LOVE: A CONSPIRACY OF THE HEART	Marius Brill	£6.99
77097 3	I LIKE IT LIKE THAT	Claire Calman	£6.99
99990 3	A CRYING SHAME	Renate Dorrestein	£6.99
99935 0	PEACE LIKE A RIVER	Leif Enger	£6.99
99954 7	SWIFT AS DESIRE	Laura Esquivel	£6.99
77182 1	THE TIGER BY THE RIVER	Ravi Shankar Etteth	£6.99
99910 5	TELLING LIDDY	Anne Fine	£6.99
99978 4	KISSING THE VIRGIN'S MOUTH	Donna Gershten	£6.99
77080 9	FINDING HELEN	Colin Greenland	£6.99
77178 3	SLEEP, PALE SISTER	Joanne Harris	£6.99
77153 8	THINGS TO DO INDOORS	Sheena Joughin	£6.99
77104 X	BY BREAD ALONE	Sarah-Kate Lynch	£6.99
99977 6	PERSONAL VELOCITY	Rebecca Miller	£6.99
99904 0	WIDE EYED	Ruaridh Nicoll	£6.99
77106 6	LITTLE INDISCRETIONS	Carmen Posadas	£6.99
77088 4	NECTAR	Lily Prior	£6.99
77093 0	THE DARK BRIDE	Laura Restrepo	£6.99
77166 X	A TIME OF ANGELS	Patricia Schonstein	£6.99
77087 6	GIRL FROM THE SOUTH	Joanna Trollope	£6.99
77155 4	LIFESAVER	Louise Voss	£6.99
99780 3	KNOWLEDGE OF ANGELS	Jill Paton Walsh	£6.99
77101 5	PAINTING RUBY TUESDAY	Jane Yardley	£6.99

All Transworld titles are available by post from:
Bookpost, PO Box 29, Douglas, Isle of Man, IM99 1BQ
Credit cards accepted. Please telephone 01624 836000,
fax 01624 837033, Internet http://www.bookpost.co.uk
or e-mail: bookshop@enterprise.net for details.
Free postage and packing in the UK. Overseas customers:
allow £2 per book (paperbacks) and £3 per book (hardbacks).